INVASIVE SPECIES

KARLE JOHNSON

A HellBound Books Publishing LLC Book
Houston TX

Karle Johnson

**A HellBound Books LLC
Publication**
Copyright © 2019 by HellBound Books Publishing
LLC
All Rights Reserved

Cover and art design
By Carlos Villas

Additional Editing by Andrew Troth

www.hellboundbookspublishing.com

Acknowledgements

My mother, Judi, used to tell me bedtime stories when I was just a boy. I remember them as vividly as I can now I'm thirty-something years removed from that time. She told me stories of princesses, dragons and evil wicked men, and the hero of the story was a character named "Prince Karle." My mom ignited my love for storytelling and I cannot thank her enough.

While my mom ignited my love for telling those stories, my dad, Randy, was the person who educated me. When I was in third grade, I picked up his copy of *Jurassic Park* and read it cover to cover. Although my eight-year-old mind didn't quite comprehend most of what Michael Crichton had written, and it took several more years to fully appreciate it, my dad didn't scoff at me or get frustrated. Instead, he talked with me about the book. We've had many conversations about other books ever since. It's kind of an activity we share, along with going to Arkansas Travelers' games. He also opened up his library to me, thereby opening up the world. The next book of his I picked up was Stephen King's *Cujo*. Holy Shit.

I brought that book to school one day, and my teacher mentioned to my parents that she had serious misgivings about me reading such a book. She wondered if my parents shared in her misgivings. My mom and dad simply shrugged their shoulders and said, "At least he's reading."

Thanks Mom and Dad. I love you so much, and if this sucker ever hits the *New York Times'* Bestseller List, I swear I will pay off your mortgage.

To my brothers, Chuck and Guy, and to my sister-in-law, Liz, thank you all for your conversations and input. Not for just this story, but for all the stories I have written—or will write.

This book would never have been written if not for my wife and eternal muse, May. I can't thank you enough for sticking with me and putting up with my moods, my mannerisms, and my mistakes. I love you more than you will ever know. This book is all for you.

To Sherry Oldner, one of the strongest heroines in the world, and her sons, and my brothers-in-law, Steven and Jonathan; thank you for being a great "second family." You are truly an inspiration.

I would also like to thank James Longmore at HellBound Books for giving *Invasive Species* a shot. After so many rejection letters, an author can get lost in the dark world of self-doubt, wondering if giving up is the only option. Your email, James, was a bright spot in the dark. Thanks so much.

Thanks go out to Alex Marroquin, who edited *Invasive Species,* and through his hard work, made it all the better, and to Matt Hammock, my "first reader" and a dear friend; he was the first person to say, "You know, you might have something, here."

And I like to think that I do have something here, and if you're reading this, I hope that you do, too.

Karle Johnson
April 30, 2019

Dedication

For Clay Oldner, a master storyteller.

Karle Johnson

INVASIVE SPECIES

Chapter 1

<u>Cole Vaughn Goes Out to Pasture</u>

The air was dry and unseasonably cool for a May evening in the Ozark Mountains. It was an odd sensation, like looking directly into the eyes of someone while they had a conversation with someone else. Memorial Day barbeques had happened, but there were few pool parties, which were staple this time of year. Those who did venture into the water ran the gamut from being slightly uncomfortable to unbearably cold.

It seemed summer (at least in Maldus, Arkansas) had been delayed—delayed as in an airplane with a chipped windshield or wonky hydraulics. Everyone wanted to get on with it, but something just didn't feel right.

One person who wasn't complaining, however, was Cole Vaughn. Thursdays were his night to patrol the grounds of Everly Ranch. Even with the Gator his boss, Ranse Everly, had bought for the crew, Cole would be pouring sweat as soon as he stepped out the door during a normal summer patrol. But this wasn't a normal summer night. Not at all. Normalcy had gone bye-bye around the same time the kids got out of school. The folks of Maldus just hadn't realized it yet.

Everybody who worked for Ranse hated taking the night watch, but it was a necessary evil—and a simple one at that. Even the boss-man himself took shifts.

A lot of folks around town thought Ranse much too young to run such a large, complex organization. Especially Jim Richmond, the head of the Maldus branch of the Arkansas Agriculture Association, and Warren Maxxy, the owner of Maldus's largest ranch. On numerous occasions, Maxxy had offered to buy Everly Ranch outright with cash. Ranse had turned him down every time, and Warren would grumble his distaste and walk away shaking his head. They all thought that it would only be a matter of time before the ranch went belly-up. They thought either Ranse's old habits would catch up to him, or the ranch would just tank on its own from the guy's mismanagement.

But the truth was, Ranse just had a different way of doing things. And folks in small towns don't always take kindly to fresh ideas. Ranse was the first to hire Mexicans and black folk and pay them a decent living wage on par with what white guys were making working the other ranches. He also incorporated the Internet and social media on a daily basis, and he used ranching apps on his phone.

Ranse had inherited the ranch from his father, along with a sizeable chunk of money, which he hadn't spent on himself. He'd used the cash to build a guesthouse for Cole and the other foreman, Mick, and then shipped in two three-bedroom mobile homes for the rest of the ranch hands. They were all able to live free of charge, and the only things they had to pay for were groceries, booze, and entertainment. Cole had quickly found a way around the latter by buying a jailbroken Amazon Fire Stick. He logged into the ranch's Wi-Fi and *voila*, free TV! He couldn't complain at all about the living arrangements or the job. Hell, Cole thought he had made out like a goddamned bandit.

Ranse was a tough boss, but a fair one. After his wife left him (taking their eight-year-old son with her), he cleaned up his act and became a downright delight to be around. Every Friday night, Ranse would throw a little party at his house.

The place was a gorgeous home perched atop a large foothill. It overlooked the whole ranch, as well as part of Maldus; Ranse's father was a frugal man, but he'd spared no expense when he built that home for his family.

Now, however, it sat empty. Sarah had gone back to live with her family in Little Rock, and the boy, Noah, went along for the ride. Cole had an inkling the parties were a way of breathing a little life into that big, empty house, a way of easing some of Ranse's loneliness.

Cole loved the parties as much as everyone else, but he wouldn't be attending the one tomorrow. He had Friday and Saturday off, and by the luck of the draw, Sunday and Monday off the following week. A four-day weekend! And all thanks to dumb luck and perhaps an oversight on Ranse's part when he'd made the schedules.

How Cole had come about such a luxury was not the point. What were the plans that came with such a momentous event? He was heading to Oklahoma to make a run at the Indian casinos. It would be a weekend full of gambling, booze, and easy girls. He might even take in a massage at the day spa, though his hard, macho reputation forbade him from mentioning that to the other fellas. And the ranch's strict drug-free policy (thanks to Ranse's old habits) forbade him from mentioning the bag of white powder that would make his trip extra fun.

But before he could do anything, there was the matter of the patrol.

His route began at the shop—which housed myriad equipment and work vehicles, the daily logs and schedules, work orders, and so on—and he took the Gator out to the west part of the ranch. He followed the fence for a mile or so, then turned off to the bumpy, unpaved grounds leading out to pasture. Every so often, he would stop and walk a few yards to search for bobcats, mountain lions, and coyotes through his night-vision goggles. The older ranchers hated that Everly's men used night-vision goggles, but the boys on Ranse's crew hadn't taken a loss in quite some time. If Cole spotted an unwelcomed guest, he'd grab the .22 and fire into the air. If that didn't scare the intruder away, he'd pop 'em one right between the eyes before going on his way. A simple, necessary evil.

In all, the patrol took about three hours—the equivalent of a round trip from Maldus to the college town of Fayetteville. Tonight, however, Cole took his time. Maybe it was the chilly air, or the sereneness of the night, or the way people suddenly feel most alive just moments before they die, but Cole didn't want to go back to the guesthouse right away. He parked the Gator about three miles from the residence, turned the headlights off, and blanketed himself in full, pure darkness.

He didn't need light to know exactly where he was. Cole had worked for Ranse's dad for years, and in that time had created an internal compass, a sixth-sense of the layout of Everly Ranch and its surroundings. He knew if he got out of the Gator and walked about four miles south, he would hit the neighboring land of Warren Maxxy. A few more miles north, and he would be in the town proper. He glanced in that direction and could barely make out the soft, sodium-arc lighting of the town's few service establishments, which had plain, unassuming names like: "Café," "Diner," or "Bar." They were establishments that served plain, unassuming food from greasy plates, or cold beer in even colder, albeit smudged, pint glasses. Cole's stomach began to rumble.

He reached into the storage box mounted on the back of the cart and pulled out a turkey sandwich and a thermos of Mick's famous "cocaine coffee." There were no substances of any kind in the coffee, not counting caffeine, but after taking one sip, you would think there was. Cole did just that and knew that he would be wired until the sun finally peeked over the mountains. He put his feet up on the Gator's dash, ripped a hunk off the turkey sandwich, and enjoyed the night.

The silence was broken by the lazy, electric hum of confused cicadas in the trees—the only real indication that it was still summer. Voices echoed in the distance, it was some of the hands having a late-night drink at what locals called the "trailer park." Soon, they'd all go inside, pass out, and get a good night's rest before worktime reared its ugly head. It was odd, though. Cole couldn't remember being this far out and hearing noise from the residence before, except of course, for gunshots.

Cole became even more attuned to his surroundings. His senses suddenly heightened, and he was sure it wasn't all the coffee's doing. He could hear the cicadas now—not their hum, but their wings. Thousands of tiny exoskeletons *click-clacking* as the tiresome little bugs took flight. He could see them in the dark sky as they blotted out the moon. They were flying away, perhaps from a bat or some other predator.

Suddenly Cole felt like an animal being watched, an animal being hunted…

Something else broke the cool silence of the night: a grunt so loud it was like a snapping tree limb. A low, guttural growl followed and then came the horrified, plaintive wail of a cow. Another. Then another. Something was killing the livestock.

"Fuck me!" Cole tossed his sandwich aside and clambered out of the Gator. He dashed to the back and grabbed his .22 and the night-vision goggles. In the soft, green glow, he checked to make sure the weapon was loaded. He pushed a round into the breach.

"Probably a coyote," he said to himself.

Somehow, hearing his own words was soothing, as if someone was there with him, and as if he weren't alone with whatever was killing the heifers. He heard another grunt, followed by a violent, wet tearing sound. The cow screamed once more, a wail that rose and fell and ended in a wet, gargling rattle.

Then silence.

Unaware of his knees knocking together like bell clappers, Cole followed in what he thought was the direction of the noise. After a few yards, his feet came down into something wet and sticky. His first thought was coyote or cow shit, but the telltale coppery odor was there—freshly butchered, raw meat. He looked down.

Cow guts steamed in the chilly air; the coyote, or mountain lion, or whatever the hell it was, had been victorious.

"Fuck me," Cole said again. Insurance would cover the heifer, but the payout wouldn't be nearly as much as if they'd taken her to market. Hopefully, the predator had only got this one. Hopefully, there was only one and not a pack. Cole couldn't remember if coyotes ran in packs.

Another meaty rip, and a hungry, evil sounding snarl split the air.

Cole jumped.

He shoved the butt of the .22 under his violently trembling arm. He'd shot coyotes and mountain lions before, but always from far away. Never this close. *Never* this close.

Despite how close the noise was, Cole still couldn't see the thing. Scanning the dark countryside displayed in the goggles in sharp shades of green and white, he looked for the flash of a tail or the glow of a cat's eyes.

Nothing.

He would find it, though, and when he did, he would make sure to kill it. Even if he had to spend the rest of the night out here chasing it, he would kill it. One loss was bad enough, but if they were to lose a few more cows, well that put a huge dent not only Ranse's paycheck but the paychecks of everyone who worked on the ranch. A loss of a penny was enough to turn each of Ranse's employees into a fearless dragon slayer. At that moment, though, Cole felt nothing of the sort. He forced his head to hold steady and scanned the other side of the pasture.

And that's when he saw it.

Glowing eyes burned hot in the field of green. They were filled with rage and fury; wide, menacing, they were looking straight at him. Cole let out a small, horrified puff of air. This was no coyote. This wasn't a mountain lion or a bobcat. The only thing that registered in his mind was it was a wolf. He'd seen wolves before, but always up north. Never in Arkansas, and never this big.

The thing in the pasture stood up on its hind legs. Even with the distance separating them, Cole could tell the beast dwarfed him by at least four feet. The fur on its snout, its chest and head was matted and dripping with gore. It stretched and let out a low, heavy chuff. Then it yawned, and Cole counted hundreds of razor-sharp, jagged teeth.

This wasn't a wolf. No sir, it was a *monster*. Wolves don't stand up on their two hind feet. Wolves aren't ten feet tall. And more importantly, wolves don't wear clothing.

Cole could make out a tattered pair of Levi's 501s; they were so stretched out the back pocket was the side pocket. The monster's feet had burst out through a pair of work boots, the remnants of which still dangled around its ankles. On one side of the wolf-thing's chest was a ripped white t-shirt smeared with blood. *I'm staring at a monster,* Cole thought.

The monster stared right back.

In his experience with large predators, Cole had come to learn there are just some animals too big to take on alone. An overgrown black bear had gotten loose on the ranch a few years back, and it had taken three men and twenty rounds of buckshot to finally take the thing down.

The creature in front of him must have been at least twice the size of that bear. He had to get Mick and Ranse. Maybe *all* the hands. Maybe even some of the fellas from Maxxy's outfit. Cole took a step backward.

The Gator was parked about twenty feet behind him. He could make it if he ran. He'd never run from an animal in his life, and he couldn't remember if the old warning that if you ran, animals would chase you was true or not. He supposed it was, in some cases; he had a dog that would chase him from one end of the house to the other. But this wasn't a game. This was life or death. This was kill or be killed. This was pure nature.

The beast stood outlined in the moonlight, its chest rising and falling with every chuff of breath, and it watched as Cole backed toward the cart. Cole's feet slipped in the guts of the cow. Stumbling, his arms flailed in the air as he tried to keep his balance. The wolf-thing took a step forward, and its legs tensed ready to charge.

Then things snapped.

There wasn't a siren or bell, and there was no gunshot—though perhaps there should have been. Cole dropped the goggles and the .22 and ran for his life as his mind switched from shock and awe to pure, white survival. The thing charged after him. Cole could hear its hot, hungry breath and the pads of its feet hitting the ground like the rumble of a freight train.

Cole hit the Gator shaking and sobbing. He whipped around to shoot at the monster, realizing far too late he'd dropped his rifle somewhere in the distance. He got inside, popped the brake and floored the gas pedal. The Gator zipped down the road for a few feet and Cole felt the small beginnings of a breeze being kicked up just before he and the Gator were sent airborne. He tumbled and spun through the air like a pair of pants in the spin cycle, and was able to see what had sent him flying.

The wolf-thing waited for him on the ground.

Cole came loose of the Gator and the cart crashed to the ground before him. The wolf made quick work of it, searching for the fresh meat inside, looking for Cole.

Cole hit the ground a few yards away, his left ankle connecting at just the wrong angle. He felt something inside of him snap and forced himself not to cry out. He tried to get up, but sharp pain radiated from his ankle all the way up his spine. His feet couldn't carry him, no matter how much they wanted to. The wolf-thing was almost done ripping the cart to shreds—Cole had to find somewhere to hide.

Even in his panic, he knew just a few feet ahead of him was the cows' main watering hole. It was a small, dirty pond that lately had a bit of a snake problem. Cole wondered if werewolves were hydrophobic. Hadn't he read that somewhere? In a comic book, maybe, or perhaps he'd seen it in a movie. Cole hated snakes, but he figured he'd make an exception if it meant not being ripped to shreds.

A few yards from the pond lay a small swath of trees where he and some of the other hands would take breaks in the shade, sneaking beers or passing joints around, while the cows grazed and drank. Just after those trees was a large valley with the mobile homes at the far end. If he had heard the occupants, maybe they would hear him. Especially if he screamed really, really, loud?

But could he make it to safety? Could he scramble up the tree on only one good ankle while he waited for reinforcements to come in force with trucks and guns? Wolves couldn't climb trees, could they? Not even gigantic monster wolves. Panic took over, and Cole didn't wait to find safety.

"Help!" he screamed so hard he thought he'd popped a lung. *"Someone, please help me! Please—"*

The wolf-thing was on him.

Cole opened his mouth to take in a deep breath. One more scream ought to do it. Diego, Ricky Lee, *everybody* would hear him. They'd be there in a flash. Cole would be mangled and mauled, sure, but he'd be alive. The wolf, on the other hand, wouldn't stand a goddamn chance against his friends.

Something flashed in front of Cole's eyes, but before he could see what, his eyes were gone and he was engulfed in a world of total blackness. He tried once more to scream but found his breath had been snatched away along with the lower part of his jaw. Blood spewed in a torrent from his mangled face and now he gurgled instead of screamed. He could sense in his blindness that the ravaging was only just beginning. He gurgled again, this time not for help but to ask the God who only moments ago had made such a beautiful night, "Why?"

If it had been hot, if it had only been just uncomfortable enough to make Cole ache for air conditioning and cold beer, he would have sped things along. He would have been in his truck on the way to Oklahoma and far away from the horror that had found its way to Everly Ranch. To Maldus. If only.

As the monster's claws dug into him, Cole felt the thing rip his body from groin to sternum. His bowels let loose and a warm jelly slid down his abdomen.

The wolf began to eat him, and Cole felt every excruciating bite.

The town of Maldus slept. A howl, angry and victorious, broke the cool summer night's sky.

Soon, others would join it.

Chapter 2

<u>Ranse Everly's Wake-Up Call</u>

The phone was ringing. Stuck somewhere between a dream and a stupor, Ranse Everly knew one thing for certain: the phone was ringing. His eyes opened. He looked at the oversized clock that adorned the bedroom wall. Sarah had picked it up at the Mercantile a few weeks before she had left him. It was 4am He didn't have to start his workday for another hour. Mick might be out counting the herd, but other than that, the ranch slept peacefully around him.

The phone was ringing.

Ranse stretched and let out a long sigh, the kind of sigh that regular people who slept regularly sighed. It was still an odd, alien feeling to him: sleeping normally and well. A year separated from long nights and the bitter almost metallic taste of crystal meth on his lips and tongue was a hard thing to forget. He reached over and snatched the phone off the cradle.

Landlines, though antiquated, still served a purpose in Maldus where cell coverage sometimes shit the bed.

"Mmm…Hello?" he mumbled before the phone's mouthpiece was halfway to him.

"Ranse?" the voice that came through was soft and sweet, accented with resentment and hurt that hit Ranse like a glass of ice-cold water. It was a voice he hadn't heard in a while, though he wished he could hear it every day. Ranse was awake now. "Hey, it's Sarah."

"I know who it is," he said, trying to sound gruff and annoyed. He doubted he did. He was certain that his ex-wife could practically hear his heart melting over the line. He choked back the regret and desire in his voice and tried for a tone he used when one of his workers fucked up. "What are you calling so early for? Is everything all right? Is it Noah?"

"Everything's fine, Ranse," she said, a bit touched by his concern. Why hadn't he been so concerned when they were married, she thought? "I wanted to call last night, but I figured you were asleep, or—"

"I just woke up," he said. He knew where she was going and didn't want to hear it. He didn't want to be reminded of his years-long addiction and the toll it had taken on her and their son. "I have a lot of work to do today. What's up?"

"I'm sorry."

"Don't be," Ranse told her. Sarah never had to be sorry. Not to him. "How's Little Rock? How are your parents?"

"They're good. Noah's driving them up the wall, but they would never admit it. They love having him around and take him while I'm out running errands or looking for a job."

"Sarah," Ranse said, rubbing his temples. "You don't have to look for a job."

"Yes, I do," she said resolutely. Her parents were wealthy, had set her up in their guest house. Her father owned one of the bigger food purveyors in the country and had sold it off to the tune of $300 million when Sarah was still in high school. She didn't tell Ranse until they had been dating for a little over a year. He was a senior in college, she was only a sophomore. She warned him, as they drove to her parents' house, that what he would see would make him think differently about her, but it wasn't true. She never once, in the years they had known each other, asked her parents for money. She got an academic scholarship to the University of Arkansas and worked jobs to support herself. She never stopped either, not until they were married, and Everly Ranch was theirs. By then, she was pregnant with Noah and traded her job at the Mercantile for working as Ranse's secretary.

Ranse wasn't necessarily talking about her parents though. He meant to support her and Noah until the day he died, but something in her voice told him not to go down that road.

"Is Noah awake?" he asked, veering the conversation to more neutral ground. Sarah had been awarded full custody in the divorce. No one, Ranse included, was surprised. It partly had to do with her parents' wealth, partly to do with the last bit of meth still caked to Ranse's lips. The last time he saw his son was Christmas Eve of last year. He brought him an Xbox, something that made both Sarah and her parents cringe, but he'd read somewhere that it was good for kids with Down syndrome. "I'd sure like to talk to him," Ranse said. "I miss him like crazy...I miss both of you like crazy."

Sarah didn't answer. Ranse knew that she blamed him for Noah's condition. Before and during her pregnancy. He had been wanton with his drug and alcohol abuse. He smoked like a chimney indoors, and always right next to her. Every time she brought up her concerns, he assured her that everything would be fine with the same aplomb as a presidential candidate facing a sex scandal.

And to Ranse, Noah was fine. Just fine and dandy as could be, thank you very much. Despite his disorder, Noah was precocious and resilient. He helped Ranse around the ranch with things like mending fences or feeding the livestock. The cows especially liked Noah. He was gentle, kind, loving, everything you would ever want from a child. But there were times that Ranse was sure that Sarah saw Noah as broken. Though she would never admit to it, and she loved the boy with all her heart. There were thoughts in her mind that radiated out with telepathic ferocity despite her best efforts to conceal them. Ranse had picked up on them, and the first little fissure began to appear in their marriage. But it was Ranse's addiction, his lack of consideration that was the hammer that split their rock into a million tiny pieces.

"He's asleep," she finally said, "but that's kind of what I wanted to talk to you about. I have some stuff that I need to take care of. My parents are gonna help me, but I was wondering if maybe you would like to keep Noah for a while."

Ranse was stunned. The notion of getting his boy all to himself, at least for a little while, both delighted and petrified him. He loved Noah unconditionally, but Sarah had always been the parent, the caregiver. Ranse's role as dad was relegated to taking him out on the Gator, showing him the cows, foxes, or other animals that came and went from the ranch. Fun stuff. It struck him then that this imbalance could have been another reason that Sarah left him. "Sure," Ranse said, trying to mask his pleasure. "I'd love that. When were you thinking?"

"As soon as possible," Sarah said with a small chuckle. "I was thinking I'd bring him up there this evening if that's okay."

"That's more than okay." Then after a moment, he added, "What's going on, Sarah?"

"It's nothing," she said, though the cold in her voice said otherwise. "I'll explain tonight when I drop Noah off. It's stupid, really."

"Okay."

"Ranse," she said with the same cold in her voice, an interrogative, almost detective quality. "Y-you're clean, aren't you?"

"Yes," he said. He wanted to be insulted but knew that he didn't deserve to be. "I quit everything the day you left. I swear to Christ." *Though a lot of good it did me,* he thought to himself. If he had known that his efforts wouldn't win his wife and son back, he didn't know whether he would have tried. But after a few weeks of clean, sober living, he did notice a change. He was getting more work done, his body felt healthier. Aside from the occasional cold, he felt amazing, so the soberness stuck. The cravings did as well, but he fought them off. He didn't outright ban drugs. Weed was frowned upon but he looked the other way, but there was an unwritten law that if a substance harder than Advil crossed the threshold of the ranch, it and the person it belonged to would be out on their asses.

Sarah didn't sound too convinced.

"Do you promise?" she asked. "Please, Ranse, don't make me go all the way out there for nothing. If you're lying, you'll be putting me and your son in a really tight spot."

"I promise that I'm not lying," he said, urging himself to not get angry. There was a gorge of venom rising in his throat. Formed from countless days of hurt and loneliness, days of self-pity, self-hatred, and self-doubt. "I promise that I'm clean and sober. I have to get ready for work. We'll talk tonight. I really am excited to see you and Noah."

"I'm sure Noah will be happy to see you, too," Sarah said. She made no mention of how she felt, one way or the other. "Thanks, Ranse. This means a lot. Goodbye."

"I love you." The words came as naturally as breathing would. They escaped his lips before he could even consider them. He winced, but thankfully, Sarah hadn't heard them. The line was dead.

Ranse took a shower and got dressed. He made coffee and was surprised to find that even with the phone call he still had some time to spare before getting to work. He sat near the kitchen's island, on a barstool, looking out onto the foothills of the Ozarks. It was something he used to do before he fell into the world of addiction, but he hadn't done since he'd been given the second chance at sobriety. The coffee was bitter and acrid. He hadn't had a decent cup since Sarah left. He didn't know what had made her coffee so good, and she never told him. Maybe he'd ask her when she came up tonight.

There was a knock on the back door. Ranse didn't need to check and see who it was. "Come on in, Mick," he called, then turned back to the view from his kitchen window.

Mick was a lean, tall man with a heavy goatee and the only one on the ranch who actually wore a Stetson hat. He was every bit the Marlboro Man that he rendered himself to be, and for that, Ranse was thankful. The only reason he still had a ranch was that Mick was there to see that it ran properly during the dark days.

"Mornin'," he said in his deep, gravely southern drawl. "Surprised to see you ready this early. Usually, you're scrambling to get dressed by the time I get here." Waking Ranse up was sometimes part of Mick's job description.

Mick took off his hat and ran his hands through his salt and pepper hair. He poured himself a cup of coffee, took a seat on a nearby barstool, and stared off in the distance.

"Sarah called," Ranse said, taking a sip of coffee.

Mick raised one of his bushy eyebrows. It had been a while since he heard that name mentioned around the ranch. It had taken on a taboo, like saying Beetlejuice or Voldemort. "Oh yeah? What did she have to say?"

"She's bringing Noah up," he said. "She has some stuff to take care of, and he'll be staying here for a while."

Mick, normally a stern man, smiled; it was barely visible through his thick facial hair. His eyes squinted, and the vague crow's feet on either of them became more pronounced. Mick loved Noah as though he were his own son. "That's great, Ranse. Just great."

"Yeah," Ranse sighed. "Pretty exciting. Though, I have no clue how we're gonna keep him entertained, let alone well-fed and warm."

"Don't worry about that," Mick said, dismissing the notion with a wave of his callused hand. "The boy will have plenty to do here. And as far as feeding him goes, have you seen some the boys you got workin' for you lately? Some of 'em are fatter-n-shit. Don't go selling yourself short on your parenting skills, Ranse. I saw you when…well, when Noah was around before. You did all right for yourself."

Ranse smiled. "Thanks, Mick. It'll be good having him around. That's for sure."

"Damn straight," Mick said before falling back into silence. He took a sip of his coffee, let a few more minutes pass, then said, "This tastes like shit."

"Yeah, it does," Ranse said. He got up and took his and Mick's cups to the sink. He dumped the liquid tar and rinsed out the remnants. "How are things looking today?" he asked while he washed the cups. "What's on the docket?"

"Well," Mick said, getting up and stretching. A succession of pops and cracks shot off like firecrackers from his spine. He was hesitating. Ranse could tell there was bad news on the way. He could afford some, he supposed. The ranch was doing well, his son was on the way to stay, but still, bad news sucked. "It looks like we're gonna have a busy day or two ahead of us. After I took stock this morning, seems that we're down a few heifers."

Ranse shook his head. "Shit. Cole was on watch last night. He's usually pretty good about locking the cows away. Guess he wanted to hit the casino quicker than I thought."

Mick pondered this. "Speaking of, Cole's truck is still here. Saw it when I got up this morning." His disdain was clear. Mick liked Cole fine, but he absolutely hated his work ethic or his lack thereof.

"That's odd," Ranse said. "Suppose he caught a ride with someone else? Maybe a friend from out of town came by and picked him up?"

"Or one of the many girlfriends he claims to have," Mick said.

Ranse shrugged the thought off, turning back to the cows. "So, how many?" he asked. Mick held up two fingers. "You think it was a mountain lion?"

"That got Cole?" Mick asked with a chuckle. "We could only be so lucky."

"The cows, smartass," Ranse said, smiling some himself.

"Possibly. Could have been a coyote. Could be we just have a couple of mavericks. I haven't gone to look for them yet. Thought you might wanna join me."

There came a knock on the door. Ranse craned his neck and saw who it was. He shot a sly look back at Mick. "You sure you want me to tag along?" he asked. "Come on in, Molly!"

Mick flushed. It was always funny to witness the stony man turn to mush in front of his neighbor. Molly Hyndman was a spinster goat and sheep rancher on the other side of Everly Ranch. Ranse liked her a great deal, they got on well together, were neighborly. When Ranse was in the gutter, she helped Sarah with Noah, and when Sarah left him, there was never a lack of food around the house. Ranse and Molly looked out for each other. They took a united stance against Jim Richmond and his lackey, Warren Maxxy. They were friends, but Mick liked Molly a whole hell of a lot more. Ranse watched as Mick devolved into a sniveling, shy little boy as soon as his neighbor stepped over the threshold.

Molly waved and greeted them both, "Hey boys. Y'all doing all right?"

"Good as can be, Moll," Ranse said. "Mick was just telling me we lost a couple of cows last night. How are you holding up?"

"About the same, kid," she said. Molly always called Ranse kid despite being only five years older than him. "I lost a few myself last night."

Mick and Ranse shot each other a look. No mavericks after all. "You found the carcasses?" Mick asked, stumbling over his words a little.

Molly took it in stride. She liked the guy too. She found his crush endearing, almost too cute. She wished he'd sack up and ask her on a date before she had to do it herself. "Yeah, we did, though there wasn't much left to find. Whatever it was, ripped the poor animals to bits. All we found was one leg, a head and a shitload of wool."

"Jesus," Ranse said. "You have any idea what it was?"

Molly shook her head. "They were smaller animals that got took," she said. "So, any predator was liable to do that to 'em. Thought I'd check with you first, see if you lost anything and if so, maybe take a look at the damage."

"You're more than welcome to join us," Ranse said. "We were just about to head out. Be good to get a third opinion, wouldn't it, Mickey?" Ranse turned just in time to see his friend give him a pleading look. Ranse understood. "Or maybe there is something else that needs my attention?"

"Actually, there is," Mick said, taking on his more managerial, no bullshit air. "A few more heifers have abscesses the size of grapefruits on their legs and few on their snouts. Though since it's getting pretty close to taking 'em to market, you might want to get your ladies looking their prettiest."

"Abscesses?" Ranse asked. Mick nodded slowly, knowing full well that Ranse understood what that meant. "I'll bet they picked 'em up at that fucking watering hole, didn't they?"

"Sid told me he saw some copperheads and a few cottonmouths scurrying around out there."

Molly shivered. Mick gave her a confused look, still not taking the hint. She laughed at his naiveté. She could handle herself against all types of creepy crawlies, but it didn't mean she didn't want a big brave man every now and again. "That's something you might want to nip in the bud, kid," she said. "Once they nest, it gets a whole lot harder to get rid of 'em."

"Damnit," Ranse said. "I'll call Grant and see if he can come out here and take a look at the cows. I'll grab Ricky Lee and the two of us will ride out to the pond. Will you have one of the guys get the boat ready? We'll have to drag the water and see what we can stir up."

"I'll get on it," Mick said. He turned to Molly. "Would you like to join me?"

"Hell, Mick, I already said that's what I wanted to do!" She and Ranse both laughed as they saw Mick's normally tanned face turn into a burning red mass. She popped him on the shoulder and put her arm through his. "Come on, then. You can be my escort." The two walked out the door.

Ranse picked up the phone and called Grant Riddell, the only veterinarian in Maldus. His office opened early, and his secretary was already there. She informed Ranse that Grant had gone to the Mercantile. He thanked her for the information and decided he'd try to catch him there. He grabbed his keys and opened the door to head out to his truck.

Outside, the summer sun was just beginning its long ascent into the sky. It was warm, but the wind blew hard and chilly that morning. Ranse shivered underneath his Mossy Oak work shirt and doubled back inside for a jacket. This was one of the oddest summers he had ever encountered on the mountain.

Chapter 3

<u>The Wolf in Mister Doe</u>

He couldn't remember anything when he woke up this morning; who he was, how he got here. He supposed, as much as anyone in his state could, that it didn't matter all that much. He had gone feral long ago, and feral things think feral thoughts. All that mattered was the hunger, and what to do to satiate it.

He woke up in an open field, the remnants of the clothes he wore hung from him like a sandwich board, stiff with caked blood of whatever he had killed the night before. There were vague recollections of the hunt. He remembered tasting beef, raw and gamey, but there was something else too. Something more delectable. Then he remembered the man.

What remained of his human brain didn't have to work hard to justify killing the man. There was a gun, and it was kill or be killed. No justification needed. He knew the score. There was no need for silver bullets, herbs, or gypsy's amulets. Plain old trauma could do him in as it could anything else that lived and breathed. It just so happened that when he turned, everything else turned with him. His senses, his strength, all heightened. He wondered if the man had a family or friends, not out of any feeling of guilt, but out of pure survival instinct. If the man was missed, then they would look for him. If they found him or the vehicle he was in, they would come, and they would be on the hunt. *Hopefully*, his instinct told him, *you ditched the remnants in a nice, out-of-the-way spot. Somewhere that no one could find it, save for those damn carrion birds that always show up.*

He could vaguely recall a more logical time. After he was…touched…with this affliction. The threat of human casualties was too great. The reason he came here, up to the mountains of rural Arkansas, was that it was sparsely populated. Out here, he could run, howl and hunt without worrying about coming across a human being for dozens, if not hundreds, of square miles. He could feast on foxes, rabbits, or deer. He might find a black bear or a cougar. Then come fall, there would be elk. He had never, ever thought about humans.

But now he had the taste of them, and God did it taste good.

He thought he might go after another. He was feral after all, and you couldn't blame a wild animal for getting a taste for human meat. There were other animals that were known to willingly, but not maliciously, hunt and kill humans after tasting the smallest microbe of blood. And did people blame them? Of course not. They hunted them down, killed them, but that's only if they could catch them. The animal was only doing what came naturally. It was only following instinct.

Feral things think feral thoughts.

But for now, it was time to hunker down and wait for the night to fall. He had to find a hiding spot, shelter. He had to rest and regain his strength. Changing always took so much out of him, his human form. Perhaps a cozy little notch in the mountain, or maybe the hollow of a tree.

His ears pricked up. Some senses, hearing and smelling especially, were heightened.

Somewhere close by, there came the rumbling of an engine. It was a few hundred yards away, but still too close for comfort. It seemed he had stumbled upon a town. A small one, out of the way, but a town nonetheless. Towns meant people. People meant meat.

His penis dangled between his legs free from the confines of clothing. He urinated on the ground, leaving his mark. This place was worth exploring more. When the moon came out to play, so would he.

***

Sheriff Raymond, "Call me Ray," Logue had nothing more on his mind than to get home and smear some Prep H on what had become one bitch of a hemorrhoid. This was the last stretch of his morning patrol, and part of him, one excruciatingly specific part, pleaded for him to cut the patrol short and get some sweet, creamy relief.

If this was Little Rock, Pine Bluff, or Hot Springs, he supposed he could dip out for a few minutes and no one would bat an eye. There were plenty of police in big cities, but there were only three in Maldus: Teague Childress, Bobby Dukes, and himself. People in town told the time just by spotting their patrols. If one of them missed it by so much as a minute, people would hear about it. "Ray Logue's slacking on the job," they would say or, "Maybe we need to reconsider our law enforcement structure." Some passive-aggressive bullshit that Ray had little to no time to humor. But this was small-town politics, and small-town politics are what ruled in Maldus.

It was Jim Richmond who first proposed the daily cruise patrol, by way of Warren Maxxy, of course. He thought that even if they only caught one speeder every other week, it would create a surplus in their budget come next fiscal year. Plus, it would be comforting to the citizenship of Maldus. People liked to know they were protected. While Ray would concede that since the patrols, he had collated a few of Maldus's more colorful citizens, namely Drake Best and Cristina Marsh, the two local meth-heads, he knew the real reason the patrols were established. Richmond and Maxxy, the two local selectmen, were lining their pockets with the proceeds. Small-town politics. It was nothing special.

Combined, their two ranches were twice the size of Maldus. Maxxy's alone was the biggest ranch in the state, and a huge source of income for Maldus (could've been more, but small-town politics). So, the two of those fellas got what they damn well pleased. The only thing from holding Maxxy back from being big-big-time was Ranse Everly.

Everly's ranch was the third biggest in town behind Maxxy's and Richmond's. Maxxy had made countless offers to buy him out, but Everly turned him down every time. Maxxy absolutely detested Everly, and for a while, when Ranse was under the influence of chemicals, he and Richmond made use of Ray and his men to make Ranse's life…well… uncomfortable to say the least.

Was it harassment? Ray didn't think so. Everly was smoking crystal, getting drunk, and partaking in all sorts of madness. It didn't matter that he had a wife and kid at home, let alone a rather high-production ranch. Every night he could be found in the bars or getting high in some rickety truck with Drake Best and Cristina Marsh. So, no, it wasn't harassment. It was routine police work. But Ray was ashamed to say that that particular police work might have been a bit too routine.

It wasn't because the young man refused to sell, nor was it his known drug problem or his popularity in spite of it. Ray had suspicions it was mostly because Ranse hired Mexicans and Blacks, two types of people that Maxxy hated.

Truth was, Maxxy was a known racist and a closeted Klansman. If it were still socially acceptable, and if it wouldn't harm his business, he would have been over at the Everly Ranch a long time ago draped in his wife's best sheets and erecting a burning cross. Ray's suspicions took over again, and he figured the real reason he wanted to buy out Everly Ranch was to shoo all the beaners and jigs out of Maldus. By force, if necessary. If Everly ever hired a Muslim, it would be the Range Wars all over again.

A searing hot pain shot its way across Ray's asshole. He shifted in his seat. God, all he wanted was some damn Prep H. At home, his wife Jan would have lunch ready. He would devour it, greedily, only after taking care of the blistering pain, of course. Those lunches, however, would go the way of the buffalo if he didn't finish this patrol. Drive by Wanda and Henry Stafford's house. Slowly, to make sure they saw him.

Dick Halpurt's dairy farm. Down Main Street on his way back. Make sure they all see him. Smile and wave between grimaces. Play the game, Ray, play the game. Small-town politics.

First thing's first, Ray thought as he cruised past a long, barbed-wired fence, *do the normal turnoff at Everly's place.* A remnant of his past routine police work. He wouldn't get that far.

Ray, a devout Christian man, held firm to the belief that God had a plan for everyone, that their lives were predetermined for them by the Lord Almighty and that there wasn't a thing they could do to change it. That being said, and he would never admit this to anyone, God could be a bit of a sadist, as evidenced as the haggard mongrel crossing the highway a few hundred feet in front of him.

"Holy Shit!" Ray slammed on the brakes. He came within feet of hitting him, but it didn't seem to bother the vagrant. He was acting erratically, weaving and swaying as he walked like a drunkard after single's night at the Bar. The vagrant turned and looked at Ray's car curiously as if he'd never seen one before. Ray noticed that the vagrant seemed to be sniffing it, or the air around it. Rolling his eyes and grimacing as a fresh streak of pain ran up his backside, Ray flipped on the lights of his cruiser and got out of the car.

"Mornin', sir," Ray said, holding out a hand and giving the vagrant a friendly wave. A distraction. His other hand was hidden behind the door of his cruiser, unbuttoning the strap on his holster. Something about this fella didn't sit right with him. Call it cop's intuition, human intuition or plain common sense. In either case, the facts were the following:

One: A man was wandering in the middle of a nearly deserted highway, wearing nothing but a few measly scraps of fabric. Two: He was acting awfully funny like he had a concussion, or he was sick or something. Hell, maybe it was rabies. Ray didn't know or care. The third, and the important one as it always was in small towns: Ray had never seen this man before in his life. As a life-long resident of Maldus, he knew the chances that some stranger wandering around town with no car in his condition wasn't up to anything shady were slim to none. Ray wasn't taking any chances.

Cautious courtesy was a mantra Ray lived by. He took that attitude with every person he stopped unless Maxxy or Richmond told him otherwise. He slipped his hand over the butt of his pistol and smiled. "Would you mind coming over to the hood of my car?" he asked, changing his wave to a beckon. "I'd like to have a little word with you if it's not too much trouble, and I would rather not stand in the middle of the street while we do it. Those Tyson truck drivers are a buncha crazy assholes if you ask me. They'd mow us down the same as they would an armadillo or a raccoon."

Cop. The word sprung into the man's rapidly dwindling consciousness. The words were nothing but gibberish to him, but he could understand the movement. The cop wanted him to go over to the car. The man supposed he could do that. He looked friendly enough, all but the right side of him. The right side of the cop was situated in a defensive flight or fight position. The man didn't know what the cop was hiding behind that door. He supposed it was a gun. There was still enough human in him to be wary of cops.

The disoriented man staggered over to the cruiser. Ray looked down and saw the man's feet were nearly as tattered as his clothing. The cause of this man's condition was obvious. He'd seen it a hundred times before, only then it had been Ranse Everly.

"You have a rough night with the bottle, sir?" Ray asked.

The man said nothing. He just sniffed the air and licked his lips.

Ray nodded. Definitely drunk.

"Musta been one doozy of a night, considerin' the look of ya," Ray said, trying but failing to goad a response. Pleasantries made what was about to come much more bearable. He let go of his pistol and grabbed the cuffs on the back of his belt. "Well, sir, I can't have you running around out here. Like I said, Tyson drivers are dangerous fuckers on the road. You're liable to get yourself kilt." Slowly, methodically, he took the man's arm and moved it closer to the cruiser. He turned him around and leaned him against as gently as possible, making sure not to get rough with him. The quiet ones were apt to snap at the first sign of force.

Cautious courtesy.

"We'll let you sleep it off at the station then you can go on your way," Ray said, not hearing the low growl forming in the man's throat. If he had, maybe things would have turned out differently. Maybe he would have let the man just keep on his way. He would go home, smear some ass-cream on himself, eat chicken salad with Jan, and go on back to the station. Instead, he kept on with his hospitable banter. "I'm gonna search you now." He took a look at the man's rags and was lost as to where to start. "Um, you don't have anything on you that's gonna poke or stick me, do you?"

The man didn't answer. Ray's frustration got the better of him.

"Goddamnit, boy, you sure keep a tight lip." He caught himself before he could go any further. He shook his head and smiled, the hospitality returning. He began his pat-down. "So, is this your first time in Maldus?"

Unsurprisingly, he was met with more silence. Ray returned it in kind and continued his search.

No ID, no wallet, no drugs, no stench of booze on his breath, nor even a few loose bottle caps. The man had nothing on him. Ray figured as much. Judging by the look of his clothes, he didn't know where the guy would keep anything. He flashed him the handcuffs.

"I'm gonna put these on you now. For your protection, and for my own. Do you understand?" He didn't wait for an answer. Not like the guy would give him one. He pressed one cuff against his wrist.

No killing during the day. That was a treaty the man had made with himself a little before the animalistic side took over. It had ingrained itself in his mind, had become a compulsory behavior like breathing, eating, and shitting. But like the man last night, this cop had to go and put him in a corner, driving him to his baser instincts. Last night, it had been a gun—kill or be killed. This, however, was a case of pure provocation. He wanted to be left alone, but the cop had to pull over with the intention of taking him somewhere, like a child picking up a turtle crossing the street. He just wanted to be on his way. He wanted to find some nice little hidey-hole and rest until night. Nothing had to die during the day. At least, not until now.

The sun glinted off the steel of the cuff. Ray didn't see the man snap his head around and take a chunk out of his hand, but damned if he didn't feel it.

"Christ!" Ray cried, pushing himself away. He looked down at the bloody mess of webbing between his thumb and forefinger. "You bit me!" he declared, as if to convince himself that it actually happened. He reached down for his pistol, taking his eyes off the man for the tiniest fraction of a second. What he didn't realize was that he wasn't dealing with a man, but an animal. And with any animal, all they need is a fraction of a second.

The man let out a noise that Ray had never heard come from any drunkard or stew-bum in all his years on the force. It was a roar. A god-honest, true to form, animal roar. He looked up from his hand just in time to see the man leap through the air, a thick pink foam spraying from his mouth. The man wasn't drunk after all. He was crazy. Ray pulled his gun as the vagrant landed full on top of him. He fell to the ground with a heavy plop. The gun skittered away from his fingers.

The vagrant sunk his teeth into Ray's left shoulder. Ray hollered as the tiny saw blades broke through the skin. His undershirt and uniform changed color—from beige and white to a muddy red. Whatever sickness this man had, whatever little bug or psychosis, was urging him to kill. The man raised his head; the foam dripping from his mouth had gone from pink to a dark crimson.

Ray brought up his knee and planted it squarely into the man's balls. The man let out a short, sharp yelp. It was inhuman, but there was pain in it. Human or animal, balls are balls. Ray felt the extra weight slip away. He scrambled for his gun.

Ray picked it up and whirled around to shoot. The man was already on his feet. He snarled and growled at him, the thick foam dripped from his gaping maw and plopped to the ground with an audible hiss. Ray had just enough time to flip the safety off and cock his weapon before the vagrant went airborne again. Time slowed down. Ray lay on the ground, looking up in awe as the man went what seemed to be a hundred feet in the air, his forward trajectory was aimed right at him with lethal accuracy. The Glock seemed to weigh a hundred pounds. Ray hefted it up and leveled it at the feral man's chest.

The quiet valley was rocked by three thunderous cracks. If there were birds roosting in the high grass on either side of the highway, they would have taken flight. But there weren't any birds. The valley was empty, void of any life, human or animal, save for those belonging to Ray Logue and the crazy man he just shot, the latter's slowly slipping away with every passing second. Going, going, a gasp of air, a shake, a rattle, gone.

Ray stood panting over the corpse of the vagrant. His hand and shoulder throbbed like they had been bashed with a hammer, a hammer coated with some sort of thick, volatile venom. He didn't have time to fully examine it earlier, but he now saw that the huge chunk the man had ripped from him also included a bit of muscle, tendon, and a bit of his index finger. He wondered if he'd be able to use it regularly ever again. His mind turned to his shoulder that burned with pain so vile and evil he'd never felt it before, which included the ten kidney stones he had passed and the hemorrhoid he had forgotten all about.

"Goddamnit!" Ray shouted to the empty valley, then a bit softer to the corpse, "What did you give me?" There was a hint of a sob in his voice. He reached into his cruiser and grabbed the radio.

"This is Sheriff Logue in Car One," he announced between heavy, ragged breaths. "I had an altercation up here on Highway 65, just north of Everly Ranch. Shots fired. Send a backup unit…" He looked down at the vagrant, studying it for any sign of movement. After a moment, he went back to the radio. "And send Doc Wyatt. We have a dead body." He let the mic fall from his hand and clatter back to the dash. He grabbed his shoulder, wincing at the pain. He looked down once more. The vagrant was still.

Ray ticked off the times he had to discharge his firearm in the line of duty. To the best of his recollection, there were three over the course of twenty-some-odd years. Once, on a pack of coyotes harassing Miss Pertree's chickens, once on a rather large, rather ornery eastern diamondback rattler, and once to scare off a pack of buzzards that had settled around a cow keeled over on the highway. But never once had he used it on a human being. Never.

Cautious courtesy. What the hell had that gotten him in this case? A gimp hand and a shoulder throbbing like a horndog's pecker, that's what. His heart beats a mile a minute, his leg's trembled like a bounce-house, and involuntary tears trickled down his cheeks. He leaned back against his cruiser and waited for backup to arrive.

Overhead, birds began to flock back into the high grass.

Chapter 4

<u>Game Trail</u>

The path that they followed was there long before Everly Ranch was even thought of. It had been padded and pressed down by buffalo, elk, deer, and the predators that pursued them. Animal and man. Mick supposed that it had to do with the watering hole a mile or so down the way. Back then, he assumed that this trail would be filled with sights of carnage and bones drying out in the sun, but he doubted it would be on the same scale as what he was looking at now. He shivered. Maybe it was the chill in the air, but he thought not.

He, Molly, and Ricky Lee Webster, one of the more formidable and intelligent hands, stood off to one side of the trail, waiting for the dust cloud in the distance to catch up. Ranse had called him a few minutes earlier. He and Grant Riddell made it back to the ranch and had already looked at the maimed heifers. His assumption was correct, and they were all suffering from snakebites of varying degrees of nastiness. One might have to be put down, but Grant told them he would monitor it. When Mick mentioned the few missing cows and the evidence of a large predator, Grant wanted to come see for himself.

"What do you think did this?" Ricky Lee said, still staring at the hump of slaughtered meat with a look of both awe and revulsion.

"Something big," Molly said.

"Mountain lion?"

She shook her head. "Na, I've seen their damage before. They're more precise. Whatever did this, was brutal. This heifer was ravaged." She pointed around to different spots on the ground, both nearby and further away. See all the blood? Mountain lions go in sneaky, they will snap their prey's neck." She snapped her fingers as if to illustrate. "Quick and easy. Whatever did this shook this cow and beat it like it was tenderizing its meat. Plus, there's no smell."

Ricky Lee nodded. After a call, big cats usually sprayed to ward off any would-be thieves. "Doesn't smell like cat piss."

"Bingo," Molly said. "My best guess would be a bear. A really fucking big bear. What do you think, Mick?"

Mick didn't answer. He had turned from Ranse and Grant's dust cloud and was now facing the opposite way where another cloud was coming toward them. This one, from Maxxy's ranch. "I think that if that cloud belongs to who I think it does, then we are about to be in for a show."

Ranse and Grant were the first to arrive. They had just enough time to take one good, horrified look around before the other dust cloud arrived. Mick was right. An oversized, decked-out Dodge Ram crew cab truck rolled up, skidded to a halt, and out popped Warren Maxxy. His face was as red as the paint job on his Dodge. Angry sweat puddled and stained the underarms of his shirt, between his ample bosoms and left a trail down his back. He was pissed; a pygmy rattlesnake ready to bite the first thing he saw. It just so happened his eyes landed on the object of his discontent: Ranse Everly.

"Anything I can help you with, Warren?" Ranse asked. Warren hated that Everly used his first name. That was reserved for deal-makers, backroom political parties, and drinking buddies. That was reserved for folks that could do things for him. Ranse, this piss-ant, had done nothing but cross him every chance he could. "If it's not very important, maybe you could come back later." Ranse pointed to the carcass on the trail. "Kinda busy at the moment."

"I want to know which one of your men did it," Warren barked.

"Did what?" Mick asked.

Warren studied the people there. The lesbo sheep-farmer, the vet, Ranse, and his cronies all looked at him like he was not a threat but a minor annoyance. Typical disrespect. He straightened up, and with a more authoritative voice, repeated himself, "I want to know, which one of your men came onto my property and killed some of my herd."

"Don't be ridiculous, Warren," Ranse replied. "I'm sure you can see that we're dealing with the same thing. Molly's place got hit too, isn't that right?" He turned to Molly, who opened her mouth, but it was Maxxy's voice that came out.

"I don't give a good goddamn what you're dealing with, Everly! All I know is that when I got home last night, I had a full herd. What's more, is that I saw a man crossing my field heading in the direction of your property. And when I woke up this morning, wouldn't you know, I'm down three heads. Three fucking heads, Everly! You know how much three heads of prime cattle are worth?"

"I'm aware," Ranse said. "What I don't understand is how you can say that a 'shadow' you saw is one of my men without any evidence and keep a straight face."

"Well, why the hell wouldn't it be?" Maxxy demanded. "I've seen the men you hire. I know where they come from, their heritage."

"Easy, Maxxy," Mick warned. "You're treading on awfully dangerous ground."

"I don't give a shit where I'm treading!" Maxxy spat back. "All I care about is who killed three of my stock and what you're gonna do about it, Everly!"

"Warren," Ranse said in a cool, even tone. "Whatever killed your cows did the same thing to mine and Molly's goats. We're trying to figure it out too."

"We think it might be a huge bear," Molly said. "Something bigger than a cougar, at least."

"A bear?" Maxxy said. "Did this bear have a name, perhaps? Maybe Jose or Juan? Or Leroy fucking Jenkins?" He shot his eyes to Ricky Lee. "And where were you last night, boy?" If it were any other white dude talking to him, Ricky Lee would have told him to go fuck himself, or maybe popped the asshole right in the teeth if his cooler head failed him. But this was Warren Maxxy. Ricky Lee knew well what the ramifications would be if he were to cross this man. Civil rights only got you so far in small-town Arkansas, at least, when fellas like Warren Maxxy were concerned. Rick shrugged his shoulders. "I was sleeping, sir. Had an early shift this morning."

"Oh, I'll bet you were," Warren hissed. "I'll bet you sleepwalked your black ass out of that welfare house your boss set up and right over to my land, too, didn't you boy? I bet you went over there and did some voodoo ritual on my cows, so they'd grow thin and wouldn't sell for much. Then right before you ate them, you stuck that pecker of yours right into their—"

"All right," Ranse barked, "that's more than enough. Get the hell off my property before I throw your fat ass off."

Warren whipped around to Ranse. "I can't believe you're protecting this animal, Everly! Him, and the rest of the garbage you have working for you. You know what they are, don't you? They're an invasive species, creeping into our land and taking it bit by bit until we lose all our culture, beliefs and morals!" Ranse reached back and sent a hard fist into Warren's cheek. He reeled backward and fell ass-first into the pile of cow guts. A shriek escaped him of both pain and disgust. With one bloody hand, he reached up and cradled the already swelling jowl. It smeared, giving him the visage of a demented sad clown. Words formed then fell away. He stumbled for something to say. For a moment, Ranse thought the racist prick might cry, but the look of shock fell away like a dancer fading into the background before a new look took its place. Rage.

"Do you know what you've just done?" Warren demanded. "Do you know what I can do to you?"

"I really don't give a flying fuck, Warren. You're on my property, threatening one of my employees. I can defend them and myself anyway I see fit. You're lucky I didn't shoot you, you racist, fat, old motherfucker. So why don't you do what I asked you to do and get the hell off my land before I give you another welt to match the first one?"

Warren scrambled up to his feet, trying to preserve what little dignity he had at the moment. "I'm calling Jim Richmond," he said. "I'll have your license revoked, Everly. Then I'm calling Ray Logue and having your little pet nigger thrown in jail for theft, vandalism, and bestiality!"

Ranse started to charge him and Maxxy hurried to his truck. He wasn't done though. "Then I'm making a call to the INS and have all your amigos thrown back over the border just in time for them to build the wall. This sort of shit might've flown with ol' president big-ears, but not in Trump's America."

"Get your fat ass in your truck and never come back on my property, Maxxy," Ranse said. "If I see you on here again, I'll shoot you. My men will have orders to do the same thing."

"Same goes for you and them, Everly. You shoulda sold to me when you had the chance because when I'm done with you, you won't have a pot to piss in!" He got in his truck, closed the door, then shot a finger out the window. He pointed at Molly. "Then I'm coming for you, carpet muncher."

"Fuck you!" Molly said with the same annoyance she would speak to a cat-caller.

"That's it!" Mick growled. He charged over to the truck, but Warren was already speeding off. Ricky Lee grabbed his foreman by the back of his shirt and pulled him back just as the Dodge darted by.

"Well," Grant said after a stunned, drawn-out silence, "I guess we know who he voted for." It was Ranse who laughed first. Mick and Molly soon followed. Grant finally allowed enough time to pass to join in on his own joke and soon the valley was filled with the echoes of their raucous laughter. The only one who wasn't laughing was Ricky Lee.

Ranse went over. "I wouldn't let it bother you," he said to Ricky. "You and I know Warren Maxxy is nothing but a sad piece of racist shit hiding a little dick behind his sheet."

"I know," Ricky said quietly. A rage was burning underneath him, dulled only by a new feeling of fear that had only just returned.

"You all right, Rick?" Ranse asked. "You're not looking too good."

Rick forced a smile at his boss. "Guess I'm just a little woozy, is all."

"Why don't you take the rest of the day then?" Ranse said. He looked at Mick. "That all right with you?"

Mick nodded and said, "Diego was looking to pick up an extra shift today. Go on home, Ricky. Get some rest."

Ranse turned back to him. "Don't worry about Maxxy," he said again. Ricky wondered who his boss was trying to convince. "He can't do anything, and as long as you're here, you're protected."

Ricky nodded and smiled again. He wanted to tell his boss that he didn't need some great white savior and that he sure as hell wasn't scared of Warren Maxxy. But he didn't. No, he wasn't thinking of any of that at all. What he was thinking about, was crossing this very game trail not six, maybe seven hours ago.

On numerous occasions, Ricky Lee wondered if Warren Maxxy's disdain for people of darker color was due to his wife's unbridled lust for them. He knew of five different dudes that had come to know Regina Maxxy in the biblical sense. Five different dudes and not one of them was a shade lighter than dark caramel. Diego, one of Ricky Lee's coworkers, came into the mobile home they shared not three months ago, bragging about the ride of his life with Geena. "Rode me raw, ese," he said with a shit-eating grin on his face. "I'll be walking bow-legged tomorrow!" And wouldn't you know it, the next morning he came out of his room walking like some gunslinger in a spaghetti western.

Part of him felt that Warren had to know. What else could inspire such vitriol? But despite Geena Maxxy's almost blatant infidelities, they remained married and the two seemed happy on the rare occasions they were spotted around Maldus. So, unless he was an unrepentant cuckold, that must mean he didn't know or at least didn't have any proof.

But there was that one guy.

Ricky thought his name was Archie. They had met in passing a few times at county fairs or at the Mercantile. Contrary to what most in Maldus believed, there wasn't some secret club all the local black guys hung around in. A couple of years ago, Archie started fooling around with Geena. He was all about town with it, too, bragging to anyone who would listen how he fucked that white girl better than her rich hotshot husband ever could; that it served him right for being a racist, no-good peckerwood.

The affair went on for a few months, but one night, while ol' Archie was balls-deep in Geena Maxxy, who walked in but the rich, hotshot husband himself. There was yelling, there was threatening, and before Warren Maxxy could get up the stairs to his gun cabinet, Archie was streaking his black narrow ass clear across Maxxy's ranch.

If his racism wasn't enough, word around Maldus was that Maxxy had one hell of a mean streak in him. Ricky supposed that's why Geena did what she did; out of fear. Instead of owning up to her adultery, she claimed that Archie had sexually assaulted her. From then on, Ricky Lee hadn't seen hide nor hair of his fellow black man.

Word got around, as they do in small towns, that Maxxy had Ray Logue take Archie into the woods and lynch him. Ricky Lee knew better. First of all, despite his continued harassment of Ranse Everly, Ray Logue was pretty much harmless and didn't have a racist bone in his body. Ricky Lee shot pool with him from time to time and the guy bought him several rounds. Second of all, Warren Maxxy wasn't powerful enough to have such a crime pulled off at his will although he liked to think he was. He did something to Archie, though. Sometimes Ricky kept himself up at night thinking of what it could have been. He vowed the next day to never to get caught up with Geena Maxxy.

He made a good effort too. He lasted a little over a year.

They saw each other quite a bit, being neighbors and all, and they did exchange glances from time to time, heavy with implication, but Ricky Lee and Geena Maxxy never said a single word to each other up until last night at the bar. As it turned out, Warren was out of town for a bit, staying overnight as he brokered a new deal with Tyson Foods. Geena took this as an opportunity to peruse some of the local talent, and peruse she did, settling on the tall, lean, good-looking black man enjoying a few beers on his night off.

Ricky Lee saw her watching him from across the room. He tried to pretend to be interested in the St. Louis Cardinals game on TV, but his eyes kept being drawn back to her. Though his mind screamed for him to pay his tab and get the hell out of there, something kept him planted in his seat. There was plenty of tail in Maldus, after all, and Ricky Lee got his fair share. Besides, Geena Maxxy was dangerous.

But wasn't that the exciting part of it all? Didn't the taboo, the danger, make it all the more exciting? Before he could debate it further, Geena was crossing the bar and heading right for him. "Aw shit."

Geena was half her husband's age, but she looked like she could be his teenage daughter. She had dark red hair that outlined a perfectly sculpted face, straight teeth that she ran her juicy tongue across like a hungry wolf. The curves of her hips were peeking just above the tight black jeans she always wore on her nights out. She wasn't wearing anything underneath, he concluded. Her dark green eyes were locked onto Ricky and he felt a slight tightening in his groin, one of both arousal and fear.

"I've seen you working at Everly's before, haven't I?" she asked when she approached Ricky's table. Ricky could do nothing but nod. "Well, how come you don't ever say anything to me?"

Ricky thought of a million cool things to say, things that would normally have any woman's panties on the floor, but this woman wasn't wearing anything under those tight hip-huggers, and the only thing that came out of Ricky's mouth was, "Honestly, ma'am, because you scare the shit outta me."

Geena Maxxy threw her head back and howled with laughter. "I scare you, huh? I like that. I like it a lot." Her hot breath hit Ricky Lee's neck and he shifted uncomfortably in his seat. She ran her fingers across his back. "Don't worry, honey, I'm not gonna hurt you.

I promise I don't bite." She leaned in and her tongue lapped against Ricky Lee's ear just barely. "But I do want to know what you taste like."

For the first time in his life, Ricky Lee was at a loss for words.

"You know where I live," Geena continued. "Why don't you come over in an hour? I'll leave the front door unlocked." She took her hand off his back, and pushed herself away from the table, using Rick's thigh for leverage. The tips of her finger glanced across the tumescence running parallel to it. Geena flicked her eyebrows, impressed. Ricky looked down and saw a slip of paper on the table. Numbers were hastily scribbled on it. 0867. "Don't keep me waiting." With that, she turned, and Ricky watched as she exited the bar.

It didn't take him long to decide on his next course of action. Ricky Lee Webster was a man, and when propositioned by a beautiful woman, he was a feeble-minded man at that. His mind was screaming fire alarms, air-raid sirens, tornado warnings, but the slow and heavy thrum of his hormones drowned them all out. He wanted, and want almost always outweighs logic.

It didn't take much to attribute the numbers she'd given him to the numeric keypad that opened the large gate surrounding the Maxxy house. True to her word, she left the door unlocked. Ricky let himself in. The Maxxy household was a huge, gaudy monstrosity that he had only seen from a distance. Up close, it was adorned with high-end replica paintings of the masters, thick tiled floors, and furniture made of hard oak. It smelled of stale cigar tobacco and cedarwood, with just the tiniest scent of perfume. Chanel. *Her* scent. There were five bedrooms in all, a large office he skirted by on his way to Geena, a chef's kitchen, and a garage large enough to house a fleet of tanks. Just outside the living room was an indoor pool so they could swim during the cold mountain winter in Maldus.

She was waiting for him in the master bedroom. When he found her, she was dressed in a getup comprised only of straps and thin lace. She lay sprawled out on her California king, almost floating over the thick and fluffy duvet. Her legs twitched when she saw him enter, a jump, but the good kind of jump. A jump filled with anticipation. She got up in a seductive, cat-like way, and walked over to him. Ricky grabbed her waist and pulled her in. They kissed. She sucked and nibbled on his lips while undoing the clasp of his belt. Ricky heard his pants fall to his ankles.

He was off-balance, and with one tiny shove, Geena knocked him onto the bed. He felt the smoothness of her hands course their way up his thighs, down his chest, and finally settled on his now engorged penis.

Their first encounter lasted a total of three minutes. Months of want and desire, of denied satisfaction from both parties, resulted in clumsy and quick fuckery. Ricky could tell that Geena hadn't gotten what she wanted, and sheepishly asked for just a few minutes and then he'd be able to go again. He only needed one.

While Cole Vaughn was being mauled to death only a few hundred yards away, the two of them went back at it. They were more attuned to each other now, Ricky's organ more desensitized. The real fun could begin. They moved as one, stuck in a sexual trance like two cobras dancing to a pungi. Buzzes of pure gratification rang through their bodies. Their mutual orgasm would be intense and so loud it would echo all the way through the house and out to the driveway. But that would never happen.

Just as they reached the pinnacle of their love-making, a pair of beams broke through the bedroom window, casting shadows on the wall and illuminating their sweaty intertwined bodies. Ricky got a good look at the two of them, and the scope of the situation dawned on him. "Shit," he groaned, pulling himself away from Geena. He got up from the bed and found his clothes piled in a corner and started pulling them on. The lights were still on, aimed at the window, which meant that the person behind them was still outside. Which meant he still had time to get the hell out of here with his existence intact.

"What is it?" Geena said? Noticing the lights, "That's just someone turning around in the driveway. Come back to bed, baby. Finish me off."

But Ricky knew better. Everyone in Maldus knew that the two driveways leading to the Maxxy house, one in the front and one in the rear, were surrounded by a large wrought iron gate and unless you had the code, you had to buzz in to visit. Ricky knew the code, but he didn't know how many others did, other than Archie, but he wasn't around to turn around in the driveway, was he?

His mind settled on only one possibility. The lights in the driveway belonged to nobody other than Warren Maxxy. It dawned on him that this could all be some sort of game the two played. Draw in a horny, unsuspecting black man, get caught, and lock him up in a dungeon somewhere in the house. It would certainly explain what happened to Archie. Geena was still urging him to return to the bed. She wanted him to get caught. She got off on this.

The lights still burned outside. Ricky pulled on his pants, his shirt, but he couldn't find his socks. "Come back," Geena cooed. "They'll be gone in a second.

Come on and fuck me!" The lights outside still burned. Ricky thought he could hear a scraping in the wall. Archie, perhaps, trying to claw his way out to freedom. He was crying, screaming for anyone to help. For mercy.

Slipping his boots on over his bare feet, Ricky shook his head. After a long and arduous battle, logic finally won the day. "I gotta go, Geena," he said. "I don't know who those headlights belong to, but I don't want to be here to find out."

It was then, Geena's sultry attempts to lure him back into bed turned to anger. She whipped the covers up to her, folding her arms around her chest.

"You're just gonna leave like that?" she demanded. "You bust in me after two seconds and you won't even do me the service of making sure I get mine?" Ricky pointed to the lights outside once more. "Fuck the lights!" she screamed. Ricky Lee cringed at the volume. "That could be my husband, the president, or the second coming of Jesus Christ for all I care. I'd still keep fucking and wouldn't stop. I want mine!" She reached over to her nightstand and picked up a small mirror. She flung it at Ricky. It missed and shattered against the wall.

He realized then that Geena Maxxy, despite her beauty and youth, was not some seductress after all, but simply bat-shit insane. "Fuck this!" he cried, as a hail of makeup, perfume, booklights, and glasses flew toward him. Ricky scurried from the room, down the stairs, and out the backdoor. As he exited, he was certain he could hear the door at the front entrance open.

He ran clear across the back fields of Maxxy's ranch, passing shop buildings, storage sheds, and cow, after cow, after cow. He didn't stop until he reached the game trail, its beginnings barely visible in the night. And that's when he heard it.

Any thought of Geena Maxxy, her fit of insanity, Warren Maxxy, or what happened to Archie because of him, left Ricky's mind as a murderous howl ripped through the air. No, it wasn't so much a howl as it was a roar, a weird hybrid of a wolf and a tiger they kept up at the big-cat sanctuary in Eureka Springs. It was the roar of a monster.

He didn't make it back to his trailer until close to dawn. He had stuck to the trees, wanting to be near them in case some beast popped up in the distance and came charging in for the kill. Several times he scrambled up a limb, sure he heard something stalking close by. The light of the moon made it easier to see in the dark, but it also played tricks on the minds of the poor souls caught wandering around in it. He never felt so alone as he did on his way home that evening. He prayed, he reasoned, he explained the roar away as some trick of the wind. But there was no wind that night. And all his prayers and reasoning did little good to quell the fear that had risen in him with such ferocity that it was roaring, too.

"Ricky," Ranse said, ripping him mercifully back to the present and away from that god-awful noise that haunted him. Ricky looked up and saw his boss, his friend giving him a concerned smile. "You all right?"

Ricky Lee forced a smile in return. "Yeah," he whispered. "I guess I let Maxxy get to me, is all."

"Why don't you go on home," Mick said. "And tell Diego to meet us over at Ranse's house."

Ricky Lee did just that.

After a few minutes, they turned their attention back to the pile of cow guts on the ground. "So, what do you think it is?" Molly asked Grant.

Grant, who had, for the most part, been studying the remains all through the confrontation, was perplexed. "I really don't know," he said. "Maybe if the animal was a bit more…in one piece, I could make a more educated guess. Whatever it was, it was big."

"We've established that," Molly said.

"It would have to be to leave this mess behind and eat Molly's animals whole," Ranse added, still watching Ricky walk off in the distance. "Come on, Grant, best guess."

"What do you think I am?" Grant asked, "Ace Ventura: Pet Coroner?" That got a small laugh, but the unease had never left. They all knew what would happen next. They would have to go to Jim Richmond and try (and fail, more than likely) to obtain an off-season hunting permit. Those were only issued in the case of a nuisance animal. While they obviously had one, the real nuisance was Jim Richmond. He and Maxxy were as thick as thieves and he wasn't fond of Ranse, Molly, or anybody who worked for them. The best they could hope for would be that Maxxy saw reason and applied for the permit himself. "If you really want my guess," Grant said, "I would say that it was a wolf-bear."

"A wolf-bear?" Mick grumbled, clearly not amused.

Grant nodded. "Just a cute name to tell you that I have no fucking clue. It could be anything in between a wolf and a bear."

"But do wolves get that big?" Ranse asked, "Big enough to do this type of damage?"

"I suppose they could," Grant said. "I read an article not that long ago of wolves the size of grizzlies up in the Rockies. But the important thing to remember is that there are no wolves in this region. There aren't grizzly bears either."

"Well it damn sure wasn't a coyote or a bobcat that did this," Mick said. Grant shrugged his shoulders, neither confirming nor denying anything at this point.

Ranse's eyes widened as a thought occurred. "Hey, could it be that one of the lions or tigers escaped from the sanctuary up north? I took Noah there a while back. They have these animals called ligers. A mix between…well, you know. Anyway, these things are huge!"

"I doubt it," Grant said. "I usually get alerts if something like that were to happen."

"Plus," Molly chimed in, waving her finger around in the air, "no cat piss."

"So, we got nothing," Mick said, kicking at a patch in the ground. No dust flew up. The ground was still too chilly for there to be dust.

Ranse pulled out his phone and took a picture of the mess and the surrounding splatters of blood. "I'll take these to Jim Richmond. We might not know what the hell we're about to hunt, but we'll need to hunt it anyway. I just hope the crooked bastard will issue a permit."

"That's not likely if Maxxy already went bitching to him about that love tap you gave him," Mick said.

"Well, with any luck Maxxy already applied for a hunting permit and he'll do all the work for us," Ranse offered.

"But if he hasn't," Molly said, "I think you'd stand a better chance with Richmond if we presented a united front."

"I should go too," Grant said. "I can give him my expert opinion, or maybe just confuse him into issuing a permit."

Ranse nodded. "Sounds good." He turned to Mick. "Will you gather up some of the guys and split them into teams? One will go out tonight and look for whatever did this and the other can get the boat ready to drag the watering hole."

"Why do we need to drag the pond?" Mick said, forgetting all about the festering boils on the still living cows. It came back to him presently. He clicked his tongue and scolded himself inwardly. "The snakes…"

"Yeah," Ranse said. "We still got a ranch to run."

Chapter 5

<u>Warren Maxxy Lays Down the Law</u>

Warren didn't need to go see Jim Richmond. A quick phone call sufficed. In his present state, he doubted he could stomach seeing anyone. His head throbbed and ached and the spot on his cheek where Ranse Everly's fist connected was now the size of an orange. Halfway back to his house, Warren afforded himself a few quick and secret sobs.

He was angry, he was hurt. He wanted nothing more than to go upstairs, get one of the rifles from the safe in his office and go marching back to that shithole ranch of Everly's and blow the little snarky prick away. Jim Richmond promised he would take care of it, though, and that would have to do. Warren decided to go upstairs with an icepack and lay down, maybe watch some golf until he fell asleep. He hadn't slept the night before, something kept him awake. The night just didn't feel right. He spent the night in his office, going over business deals, examining, and re-examining his ledgers. He hadn't been in his own bedroom since he got home, didn't want to wake up Geena. She could be a downright bitch when she was just waking up. Warren could be the same way after being deprived of sleep. Maybe he would feel better after a nice nap. Then he could deal with Everly on his own terms.

But what's this? He surveyed the room with growing unease. It was wrecked. Broken glass, smeared and leaking makeup bottles, and other bric-a-brac littered the normally impeccable hardwood floor. Warren would have thought his wife abducted if he hadn't seen her lying naked in bed, snoring the day away perhaps fighting off one of her chardonnay hangovers. This mess was her doing. But what could have caused such a fit? Grumbling, and making a mental note to chastise her later, he began to clean up the mess, an almost insufferable chore with his head pounding the way it was.

And what's this? He almost missed them, hanging halfway under his dresser. Almost swept them up with the rest of the mess. A lone pair of socks. Not just any socks, but a workman's socks. They were gray with little strips of yellow at the tips. They stunk of sweat, hard work. They stunk of men beneath him. Most importantly, they did not belong to Warren. No sir, he only had two colors of socks in the top drawer of the dresser. Black for business, white for play, separated by color on either side. The way God intended. He never wore gray socks, and he certainly didn't leave an odor behind in any of them. He didn't know who they belonged to, but he was sure that he knew somebody that did.

He squeezed them hard in his fist, wishing that whoever they belonged to could feel it deep in his gut, wishing he could draw blood. He stared at the slut in his bed. He would let her sleep for now. Once she was awake, he would question her.

This happened before. That jig whose name he couldn't remember. The one he ran out of town after catching him raping his wife. Rape. That's what Geena claimed. But when he caught the two of them that night, something told him that it was anything but. Maybe it was the way they were moving. Maybe it was the look of sheer pleasure in his wife's eyes. That time, though, Warren was forgiving and willing to believe her. Belief was so much easier than coping. But you know what they say: "fool me once…" Warren left the mess in the room and went back to the office where he stewed for the better part of the day.

Geena Maxxy woke up not long after, her head and loins both throbbing from last night's adventure of which she remembered only the dimmest of details. She was nauseated and felt a fleeting rush of panic. Was she pregnant? No, only hungover. It could only be a hangover. Ever since her wedding night, she had been vigilant about birth control. She considered going back to sleep, to spend what would be the worst hours of recovery in dreamland, but then she got a look at the room.

She blinked a few times, hoping that what she saw was only a mixture of blurred vision and an even blurrier mind. She sharpened her focus—god that hurt— and with a sloppy, pickled groan, realized that what she saw was true. The room was in shambles. She'd have to clean it up before the hubby got home. If he saw it in its present state, there would be questions. Questions she would rather not answer.

It was tough keeping up the façade of a doting wife. Tough and miserable, if she was being honest. Marrying Warren Maxxy was more a decision of business rather than the heart. He was twenty years her senior, and when they began their courtship, she was barely out of high school. But he was rich, and in Maldus, marrying rich was the equivalent of making it in Hollywood. Regina Maxxy came from the far side of town, where the mobile homes were. No, there she was being dishonest again. They weren't mobile homes, they were trailers. They were sat up on concrete blocks, screen doors hanging askew on hinges, linoleum-lined trailers.

Growing up, Geena played with dollar-store versions of Barbie Dolls, wore holey shoes and stained blouses, and slept in a bed crawling with bed bugs. She ate things deep-fried and smothered in ranch or cream gravy for every meal, that is if her mother could afford it after securing a carton of Winstons and a case of Keystone Light.

Her daddy wasn't around much, and the job he had working on a farm down in southeast Arkansas earned him enough money to keep them firmly in the welfare state and little else. Every now and then, he would come home long enough to smack around her mom, get drunk, and pass out in front of the television. That, as terrible as it was, would have been survivable, but he never stayed asleep for long. Every night that he spent at home, he would get up from his perch on the couch and come to her. She would be asleep, but the rough, calloused touch of his hands would wake her up. "It's okay," he would coo into her ear. "It's okay. Daddy just wants to love on you a little."

She would lay down, ashamed and trembling, while he diddled her and panted things like "Your momma won't let me do this" or "she's not pretty like you. She's fat and ugly," and he would go on touching her until he seemed to cramp up. Then he would stumble out of the room to fall back into his drunken sleep once more.

It only got worse as she grew. Once she was near high school age, Daddy began to put his thing in her. The shame grew, too. Every now and again she was horrified to find that it felt good. She took to falling asleep in different parts of the trailer. Sometimes, if the air was good, she would sleep outside. She didn't like the way he touched her, never did, and she hated herself even more for letting it happen. But no matter where she slept, he would find her. And it would happen over and over again. She decided then, at such a young and tender age, that she would never love a man.

When she met Warren Maxxy, she was twenty. Her father had been in the ground for nearly five years by then, and Geena was opening up to the idea that men, despite her hate for them, could be useful. She found pleasure in fucking them consensually and found they saw her as attractive. They gave her things. Things like jewelry, and clothing, took her to nice dinners. When she agreed to go out with Warren, he bought her a beautiful diamond-encrusted watch and took her to her first-ever steak dinner. It was their first date, and it made such an impression on her that she agreed to another, then another, until finally, she agreed to marry him.

But once he said, "I do," Geena was chagrined to find that it also meant "I don't," as well. As in, I don't buy expensive things for you on a whim anymore, I don't acknowledge your presence, and I don't really care what you do as long as you're right here when I need you.

Geena learned that she could live without the gifts. She had so many expensive baubles that it would make Kim Kardashian green with envy. She learned she didn't care about the sex either, at least with him, she didn't. Warren had a pathetic tool and barely knew how to use it. When he was able to get it working properly, he was a two-pump chump. No, she could live without all of that, but what she did crave was the attention. After she took her vows, she had become invisible again, locked up in her own home and forgotten, like some damsel in a fairytale. If Warren gave her security and financial stability, but not much else, that was swell; she could cope with that. But she would go after the attention on her own.

What followed was a revolving cast of men. She began with some of the more prominent residents of Maldus, some ranch-owners and members of the AAA. She gave Jim Richmond a blowjob in the back of his offices, and Ray Logue a handy at the sheriff's station on St. Patrick's Day when Warren was down in Hot Springs officiating the parade alongside people like Jerry Van Dyke and Ted Danson. The men were more than willing to give it up to her. The only one who ever turned her down was Ranse Everly. He was freshly married, but Geena still took it as an affront. She began to whisper into her husband's ear about the dirty dealings going down at Everly Ranch.

But despite all the attention she got from the men around town, she still didn't feel satisfied. It wasn't until, in a rut, she gave one of the ranch hands from across the way a go. His name was Desmond Yates, and he worked on the Everly Ranch. He was twice the size of Warren both in height and weight, sturdily built with muscles upon muscles from his labor. And when he fucked her, she felt like a queen. The man worshipped the ground she walked on. The laborers had never been with a woman of Geena's esteem before. They'd been with plenty of women whose lifestyles, if she had not met Warren, she would still share, but never a rich, hoity-toity as she was now. The mere fact that she would cast her gaze upon them made them hers to play with. She liked that. She needed it. It was the total opposite of how she felt with her dad. Now, she had the power.

The trouble came when Warren caught her in the throes of passion with that one black man from Standard Breed Ranch across town. Geena couldn't remember his name, but she did remember his face, his body, and the way he made her feel.

Warren came in, screaming and hollering, demanding that they explain just what the fuck was going on. In that instant, Geena saw her life crumble before her eyes. Gone was the jewelry, gone was the cash and the big house, and with it, the prestige she had gained. She saw herself in the trailer park once more, slinging beers at the Bar or waitressing at the Diner. She couldn't have that. The man stumbled for an explanation, and in that brief gap, Geena saw her out.

"He raped me!" she screamed, manufacturing some phony tears. "He came in to rob us, and he found me and raped me!" She saw the disbelief in her husband's eyes, boiling there with betrayal and anger. *You were supposed to be out of town,* she thought with a fair share of betrayal and anger as well. *You were supposed to be gone until tomorrow! You weren't supposed to see this!*

She thought of the trailer park once more, and with the future she faced so clear and present in her mind, she threw herself into hysterics. She accused the man, now shaking his head and vehemently denying everything, and she saw Warren's expression break. His anger was not directed at her but at him. He crossed the room and grabbed the man by the shirt collar. They disappeared. Only Warren returned. She never saw that man again. She didn't know what happened to him, nor did she care. All she cared about was that her position in life was safe.

But it wouldn't be if Warren were to find this mess. Forcing herself up, Geena got to cleaning. Luckily, the broom and dustpan were in her bedroom. She didn't know if she would survive a trip to the pantry to fetch them, but were they here last night? She didn't think so. But if they weren't, how did they arrive here?

That's when it all came crashing back: the headlights and the fight she had with the black man from Everly's whom she had brought home. How he was certain that it was Warren arriving home, and how he had denied her when she tried to assure him it was not. Warren never came home early save for that one time, and lightning never struck the same place twice. Did it? Looking at the dustpan and broom and the partial mess swept into it, she began to think that it, in fact, did.

"Warren, honey?" There was no reply. If he was home, he would be in his office. She stumbled out of the bedroom on wobbly legs, going to face the questions, and wondering what she could say to keep her place in the world safe.

Warren looked up from his desk when he heard his wife's voice. For the last hour, he'd been staring at the paperweight he received from the Maldus Chamber of

Commerce, an award given to him just a few months ago. "Man of the Year," it read. It was a gold obelisk meaning to represent the highest prominence one could hold in town. People respected him, feared him. They adored and admired him. Only a very few were impertinent. Everly, of course, who refused to call him "Mr. Maxxy," or "Sir," but instead used a first name basis that drove Warren crazy. Then there was the rug-muncher that lived next to him who always looked at Warren like he were some disgusting slithery creeping creature. And of course, there were the blacks and Mexicans. Now, he was ashamed to admit that he would have to add his wife's name to the list. "I'm in my office," he called back, coldly.

He watched as the door to his office creaked open, and Geena stuck her puffy, hungover face into the crack.

"You can come in," Warren said, baring his teeth in what he thought was a harmless smile. "I'm not gonna bite."

"You're not busy?" Geena asked, second-guessing her decision to face this head-on. "I could come back later if you are."

"Not at all," Warren said, waving her in. He motioned to the chair, so much like a businessman rather than a husband. "Take a seat, hon. I wanted to talk to you." Geena did as he asked, more flopping into the seat than sitting in it. She rubbed her temples, willing her mind to clear itself. "Have a little too much to drink last night?" Warren asked, his voice bright-eyed and bushy-tailed.

"I suppose I did," Geena asked. "I was bored."

"Yeah, well I'm sorry, darlin'. I know I go out of town a lot, but it's so you and I can enjoy the life we have. If it makes you feel any better, I spend my nights knowing that I will come home to my beautiful wife that loves me, that's faithful to me, and I to her." He smiled at her again.

Geena smiled a crooked smile back and rubbed her temples some more. "I know," she said. "And I love you for that."

"Good, good. So, I was wondering if you wouldn't mind telling me what happened in our room last night. It sure was a mess in there. Was it because you were mad at me? Or was it the chardonnay?"

Geena's heart began to bounce in her chest, making her head hurt even more. She forced herself to think of something. It nearly killed her. "We were robbed!" she cried. "There was a man in our room last night. I started throwing whatever I could at him, and I guess I scared him off. I'll clean up the mess. I promise. I didn't want to tell you because I thought you would be worried."

"Well I am," Warren said, though not about the robbery. He remembered seeing the shadow crossing the backfields last night. It was running like an intruder, but he was certain that the house was not the thing being intruded upon. "Tell me something, hon', did you get a good look at this robber's feet?"

Warren got up and began to pace the office. Geena's heart was like an IndyCar engine revved to full torque. "I don't understand," she said.

"I'm just curious," Warren told her, "because I can't help but wonder why a robber would come into our home, take off his shoes and run around barefoot." He tossed the socks, now wadded up, into her lap. "Cause, honey, those aren't my socks."

Geena's heart stopped cold then. "I-I don't know why they would do that either," Geena stammered. "I suppose they didn't want me to hear them and when I started throwing things, they just forgot them."

"You can stop now," Warren said. His pacing quickened, his feet coming down harder on the hardwood. A little more of it and Geena thought she would go insane. "You know, I often think about that night. You know, the night you were, 'assaulted.' I wonder if it was really an assault at all."

"It was!" Geena cried breathlessly.

"So, you say. But I replay that night in my head, you see. I remember everything about it. The smell…vodka, wasn't it? The sights…both of y'all were ass naked, rapists don't really wait for people to take their clothes off. And the noises. Those weren't the noises of someone being attacked. They were the noises of someone who was enjoying themselves."

"But I wasn't!" Geena cried. "I wasn't! I promise!"

"You never made those noises with me before," Warren mused. "So, I guess the question is, how many men *have* you made those noises for?" He pointed to the socks. "And was he one of them?"

Geena was sobbing now. Not from guilt or remorse, but from selfishness. Her whole world was going away. "We…were robbed, Warren. I swear!"

"Oh, shut up you lyin' heifer!" He reached out and popped her upside the head then continued his pacing. "You know, I'm a well-respected guy. People in Maldus love me. Tyson loves me, Wal-Mart loves me. There's only a handful of defiant fuckers that don't." He stopped in front of her chair, grabbed the armrests and leaned in, looking her deep in the eye. "I just never thought you would be one of them."

"I do love you, Warren!"

"Admit it then!" he screamed so loud that the gun cabinet shook. "Say that you weren't raped. Say that we weren't robbed! Admit that you disrespected me, that you were unfaithful!"

After a long silence, broken only by her quiet sobs, Geena Maxxy nodded. "I admit it, Warren. I'm sorry."

"That's what I thought," he said, then spat in her face. Geena cried out and pawed at the loogie. "How many then?"

"I don't know," Geena said.

"See, now you're lying again. Let's start again. How many? How many of those jigaboos did you have inside of you?"

Geena hid her face and wept uncontrollably. "I'm not sure."

"How many, Regina?"

"I'm not sure!"

"More than these two?" he asked. She didn't answer. "More than five? More than ten?"

"Yes! More than ten! Are you happy now? Yes! I've fucked way more than ten! And it's your fault! I wouldn't have done anything if you'd only given me the attention I need—" Her cries were stymied by a loud, thick thud. Geena looked up at Warren, at the obelisk paperweight in his hand, the chunks of hair and a bit of scalp dripping with blood. The last thought she had before her whole world went dark was: *scalp wounds always bleed so much, I'm going to make such a mess.* This was not the kind of attention she wanted.

"See what happens when you defy me?" he yelled at her. "Do you see what happens when you go flaunting your pussy around town?!" It took her falling to the ground with a dead thud for Warren to realize what he had just done. Geena's eyes fluttered in their sockets then disappeared towards the top of her head. Only the whites showed.

"Oh…oh no." He bent down and slapped Geena's cheek. "Baby? Come on, now. Wake up. I'm sorry. I didn't mean to hit you so hard, I was just mad is all. Wake up now." His hand stopped its rapid tapping and found her throat. He felt for a pulse. It was there, but faint. "Oh, thank you, Jesus," he said. "You just need to sleep for a while, that's all." With all his might, he hoisted her from the floor. "Some sleep will do you some good. Tell you what, I'll lay down with you, okay? And when we wake up, I'll make you some dinner and we can discuss this in a calm, adult manner. I'll forgive everything, Geena. I'll forgive everything if you wake up."

He hit her with all the anger and frustration that was festering in him since he could remember, at least from the night he caught her with that black fella. He hit were with all the anger he felt for Ranse Everly, for his disrespect and his refusal to sell his land. He hit her with all the rage that he had for his own body, his small penis, his bulk, and his jowls. For his ugliness. For the looks she had given the Mexican men and the black men around Maldus that she tried and failed to conceal from him. He hit her with all the rage he had for his failure as a man. He hit her, intent on killing her.

Warren Maxxy failed in that regard, too.

He took her to bed, laying her down gently and pulling the covers up to her chin. Her breathing was ragged, but he took comfort in knowing that she was still able to do such a thing. He kissed her forehead, the sticky blood from her scalp coming away on his lips. He licked at it, the way he had done with her rouge when she kissed him before. Kisses that were lies. He lay down beside her and allowed himself to cry.

Chapter 6

<u>Homecoming</u>

Ranse arrived back at his house as the odd summer sun just began to set. It was still rather early, but night came early in the Ozarks. He was enraged. Not only had Jim Richmond pishposhed his call for an emergency meeting, arriving an hour and a half late, he found their claims of a rogue animal utterly laughable.

"Your request for an off-season hunting permit is denied, Mister Everly," Jim said. "I can't believe you called me away from my dinner for this. Your claims are silly and unwarranted."

"How could you deny the evidence?" Molly chimed in. "Doctor Riddell showed you the proof. Something tore Ranse's cows apart, and whatever it is took two sheep and a goat from my ranch as well."

"Be that as it may," Jim continued, "for all we know, one of your ranch hands wasn't looking where he was going while driving a tractor."

"Oh, bullshit!" Ranse cried.

Jim Richmond, who reminded Ranse of a cross between Terry O'Quinn and Kurtwood Smith, held up a hand. He was getting perturbed, his face and the bald patch on the top of his head-turning a light shade of red. "That's enough of that, Everly. I won't have you swearing in my office. Especially not when women are present."

"I can take it," Molly said. "I don't need you to protect my feminine sensibilities, Jim. I need you to let us do something about whatever it is that got loose on our ranch."

"Maybe if you'd just look at the photos again," Grant said, approaching Richmond's desk. He pulled out his phone and opened up the camera app. "As you can see, whatever did this was much more powerful than a tractor. Not to mention, that if someone ran over a cow with a tractor, they would feel it."

Richmond handed back Grant's phone.

"This could be a hoax," he said bluntly. "For all I know you doctored this photo. I know you don't think highly of me, Everly. You and your pals could have come up with a phony wild animal story to make me look like an idiot."

"Jim, we wouldn't do that," Ranse said, rolling his eyes at the sheer absurdity of the claim.

"Furthermore," Richmond went on, "I won't issue a permit to someone whose license is under review for revocation."

Ranse stopped cold. "What do you mean?"

"Warren Maxxy called," Richmond said, leaning back in his chair with a smug grin on his face. "Told me the two of you exchanged words, and that you exchanged a little more than that. Why would I issue a hunting permit to someone so violent? Who could easily use the gun on his own neighbor and claim it was a hunting accident?"

"You've got to be kidding me," Ranse said.

"I assure you that I'm not. Nor could I in good conscience allow someone with such anger issues and a history of drug abuse to continue to do business in this town. The AAA board will consider your license and make its decision within a week or two. For right now, you're on probation. Consider that the stretch of the board's goodwill."

Ranse was shocked. The punch he gave to Maxxy was one thing, but to bring up his past? Threaten his business license? His livelihood? He wanted nothing more than to cross the desk and wring Richmond's neck. He got close, too, but stopped just short. He held out a finger and jammed it in Richmond's face.

"This is ridiculous, Jim," Ranse argued. "I'll keep doing business in this town. You can make it hard on me, and I might lose a couple heads of cattle in the process, but I'll keep doing business. My ranch won't close, but I want you to remember this conversation once your term is up and it's time to vote on a new head of the Agricultural Association. I want you to remember it well." He turned and stormed out of the office. Grant followed closely behind.

"Threatening me won't win you any favors, Mister Everly," Richmond called after them.

Molly remained behind. She stared at Richmond, crossed her arms over her chest. The two were silent for a moment before Richmond asked, more out of nervousness than anything, "Is there anything more you'd like to add, Miss Hyndman?"

"Ranse Everly is a decent man," she said, "flawed, stupid sometimes, but decent. And I can't fathom how you, *in good conscience,* could threaten him but let that racist piece of shit Maxxy get away with murder if he so chose."

"Now wait a minute," Richmond began.

"No, you've had your turn to speak. You and Maxxy are dinosaurs, Richmond. And sooner or later, this whole town is gonna realize that they'd be better off with someone like Ranse in your chair than two corrupt rich-boys who have never so much as picked up a sack of feed." She turned and stormed off as well.

Mick met them on the porch. "That bad, huh?" noting the dour looks on each of their faces.

"Yeah," Ranse said. "That bad." He filled Mick in on the meeting.

"You know, technically," Grant said, "you really don't need a permit from Richmond. Arkansas law states that you can defend your land and everything on it. I didn't want to bring that up at the meeting for obvious reasons."

Ranse flicked his eyebrows up "That so?"

Mick and Molly both nodded.

"I didn't think it would come to that," Mick said, "but he's right. If Warren Maxxy rats you out, you might have to take him and Richmond to court to keep your license and for whatever else you might feel like suing them for, but you are well within your rights to discharge a weapon on your property."

"Can you round up a crew?" Ranse asked him.

Mick nodded. "Diego, Ricky Lee, and Pike are ready to go when you say so."

"Send 'em out," Ranse ordered. "I'm thinking they should use the deer blind further up the game trail. Make sure they have everything they need and to be safe."

Mick nodded. "I'll get on it." He turned and headed off to the mobile homes. A few moments later, he saw a group of men head off in trucks and carts loaded down with rifles.

Ranse turned to Molly and Grant. "I appreciate the help with Richmond," he said. "I know it's hard to throw in with someone with such a questionable past."

"You're a good man, Ranse," Molly said. "Even when you were fuckin' up, you were still a good man."

"She's right," Grant said.

"I appreciate it, but facts are facts. You put your reputations on the line for me, and I can't thank you enough."

"Don't mention it," Grant said, patting Ranse on the back. "I gotta head home. It's been a long day and since I've spent all of it playing with y'all, I'm sure it will be an even longer tomorrow." He smiled and said his goodbyes.

"I guess I should go too," Molly said. "Though I don't know how I'll be able to get to sleep, I'm so pissed."

"Try a tall glass of whiskey," Ranse told her, it always did the trick for me.

Molly laughed. "I might have to do that." She turned and walked down the stairs of his deck, heading for her house. Ranse would have offered her a ride but knew she wouldn't accept it. Her house was only a quarter-mile away and Molly Hyndman was a walker. She walked a few feet before turning back to him. "How did it feel?" Molly asked, "Punching Warren Maxxy like that?"

Ranse thought about it, then smiled. "I used to be hooked on crystal, Molly. I used to get blazed out of my mind, all spun up and high. But nothing could compare to the high of cracking that motherfucker in the mouth. *Nothing.*"

Molly laughed. "That's what I thought. I practically had an orgasm watching that. Have a good night, Kid. Have Mick call me."

"I'll do that, Molly. Goodnight."

And then he was alone. Molly disappeared into the darkness, Mick had followed the crew out to the deer blind. Probably to make sure they were all settled for the night. Ranse wondered when the last time was when he was purely alone with his thoughts, or when he actually had thoughts to be alone with. But before he could delve too deep, he found that he wasn't alone anymore.

With all the excitement, he had forgotten the most important thing. That is until he heard the crunch of car tires coming up the gravel road to his home. Sarah was coming and bringing Noah with her.

The excitement and happiness didn't hit him until he saw his son dart from the car, carrying an oversized Batman action figure. He had grown quite a bit since Ranse last saw him. Not so much in height, but he gained some pudge. Sarah had gotten his hair cut short, almost buzzed.

"Daddy!" Noah cried, running across the lawn. Sarah was slower to come out of the car, but when she did, and he saw the two of them back home, he seemed to melt into the deck.

"Hiya, kiddo!" Ranse said, opening his arms as Noah approached. He wrapped his son up in his arms, squeezing him tight. "You've gotten so big!"

Noah's Down's syndrome never affected his comprehension. "Momma says I'm growing," he told him. "That I'll be bigger than you."

"I'll bet you will," Ranse said. "You might wake up tomorrow and be a giant!" He tickled him, and Noah laughed. "God, I missed you, son."

"I missed you too, Daddy," Noah said.

"He really has," Sarah said, climbing the stairs. She was struggling with a suitcase and an overstuffed *Ninja Turtles* backpack. Ranse let his son go and helped her. "Thanks," she said, out of breath. "Guess I didn't realize how heavy they were."

"How are you, Sarah?" Ranse said. "For real, this time?"

"We can talk about me, later," she said, motioning to Noah who had now gone off running around the large area that served as Ranse's backyard. Ranse didn't like that at all. It didn't sound like her. "Why don't you fill me in on what's been going on around here?"

"I'd like that," Ranse said, "but first…" he held out his arms. "It's good to see you, Sarah. Really good." She came into his arms willingly, but coldly. He wasn't surprised. His actions and habits had hurt her, and there was nothing he could do to ever make her feel the way she used to. He had broken her in that regard. Snapped her in two like a twig over his knee. He hated himself for that. After a moment, he let her go and filled her in on all the happenings in Maldus, including the animal attacks from the night before, and his encounter with Warren Maxxy.

"God, I've always hated that prick," she said. "Even when you were…not all there, he had no reason to bully you."

"Well, I suppose some people are just mean," Ranse said, looking out at his son going after some very sluggish fireflies and thanking God that Noah was not one of them.

"I guess you're right," Sarah said, "And you're not worried about losing the ranch?" Ranse shook his head. "And Noah's safe here, right? With the animal out there and all?"

"As safe as he would be in Little Rock," Ranse said. "Animals won't come this close. They can smell us. Plus, I got some guys out there looking for it. They'll get it sooner or later."

"Hopefully sooner," Sarah said. "I don't feel good about there being an animal on the loose. Especially one that could take down a cow."

"He'll be fine, Sarah."

"He's been sleepwalking," she said quickly. "I caught him going outside well past midnight a few weeks ago. When I asked about it, he couldn't remember a thing. So, watch him carefully."

"I will," Ranse said. "Was that the only time he's sleepwalked?"

"No. There have been others, with varying degrees of roaming. Once he got into my parents' neighbor's house and crawled into bed with her. She about had a heart attack, but when she realized it was Noah, she woke him up and brought him home."

"Jesus," Ranse said.

Sarah nodded. "It's not an everyday thing, though. You just have to watch him."

And watch him, Ranse did. He was so happy that his son was home he thought he would never take his eyes off him. He watched Noah prance around catching fireflies in his hand then letting them go until he tired himself out. They took him upstairs and put him to bed. Ranse hadn't changed his bedroom one bit.

"Thank you for this," Sarah said, as they climbed down the stairs and headed into the kitchen. "You don't understand how much this helps."

"Maybe you could help me understand," Ranse said. "What's going on, Sarah? Why do I suddenly get custody of our son?"

Sarah laughed, "First of all, you don't get custody of our son." They both shared a laugh, though it did sting a little. It stung both of them.

"Well, what about you?" Ranse said. "You could stay here for a while. We could work on this together, make things how they used to be before I fucked up. Please, Sarah, I've changed. Really." He could see in her eyes that hint of disbelief. "I promise that I've cleaned up. We can make this right. For all of us." The siren song of the recently and wobbly sober. No matter how good their intentions might be, all it takes is just one little hiccup and then…

Sarah sighed, blowing a loose strand of mahogany hair out of her eyes.

"I think it may be a little too late for that, Ranse." She chuckled bitterly.

Ranse was confused.

"What do you mean?" he demanded. "I know I don't deserve it, but can't you give me another chance? Can't you see that I'm trying?" The truth was, she did see. She could tell by his eyes that he was sober, by the thin layer of muscle he'd grown back and by the thick blonde swatch of hair that had taken root once he kicked his habits. He was sober, and maybe it would stick, but the chances had run out a long time ago. Somewhere between the fifth or sixth time she'd found his pipe after him profusely swearing to God that he was clean. He was being honest now, for the first time in a long while. Now it was her turn to be honest with him.

Of all the monsters in the world that barked and bit and howled and roared, it was nothing compared to the stealthy, sneaky ones. It was those that lay in silence that scared Ranse the most. The things so lethal in their undetectability. There were plenty of monsters in the world but not all of them needed teeth and claws.

Sarah was diagnosed with ovarian cancer a few months after he'd last seen her.

It explained the span of a few weeks where he had absolutely no contact with her, her parents, or Noah. It explained the reason behind this visit, whereas only a few months ago, she would be damned if Ranse spent even a millisecond alone with their son. It explained the lack of malice on the phone this morning. What it did not explain, however, was why she couldn't stay here. There was a very reputable hospital in Fayetteville. One that specialized in cancer research and treatment. Ranse would have no problem driving her there every morning so long as she got what she needed.

"I start chemo in two days," she answered for him. "My doctor referred me to Saint Mark's. Apparently, they have one of the best cancer programs in the state, and it'll be much more affordable since it works in conjunction with U of A. He wants me close so that he can consult."

Ranse's soul came crashing down on him. He hated himself for this. He broke her heart and all she got in return was cancer. He was so busy trying to convince her to come home that he couldn't see the reason written all over her face as he could now. God, he was a selfish asshole sometimes.

"Sarah, I had no idea. If there's anything I can do…"

"You can watch over our son," she said without hesitation. "You can love him and care for him like you're supposed to."

"Of course, Sarah, but that's not what I meant."

Sarah shrugged. "I know. And I didn't mean it that way…"

"Really?" Ranse cocked an eyebrow and smirked.

"Maybe a little," she said. He could feel her beginning to loosen up slightly. "It's just that with the sleepwalking, you know? It makes me worry. And he's been acting out too. There was a rash of him pulling his classmates' hair at day camp, hitting some of them, pinching…"

"Normal stuff for normal kids," he reminded her. "I'm assuming you taught him better? Told him that it wasn't nice to bully?"

She looked like he had just slapped her in the face.

"Of course! Lately, his teachers have been telling me his temperament has cooled. I think taking that X-box away helped."

"You took it away?" There was some anger in Ranse's voice, mixed with the slightest bit of hurt.

"As punishment," she said diplomatically. "Not to make him forget about you, Ranse. He misbehaved, and he had to learn that there are consequences for that. I wouldn't ever let him forget about you even if I wanted to. You're his daddy. He worships the ground you walk on. Look, I brought him all the way up here, so he could be with you."

"Not as a last resort?" Ranse asked as if wanting to be absolutely convinced. Although, if that were the case, he doubted it would change anything.

"No," Sarah said, the emotion in her voice true. "It was my gut reaction. He needs you just as much as he needs me. And assuming you're telling the truth about your sobriety, at least *you* have your health."

Ranse winced. "How's his speech?"

"He still has trouble pronouncing his M's, but his R's and G's have gotten a lot better."

"Sarah," he asked, his voice frail and devoid of all pretense, "how bad is it?"

But before she could answer, Noah's little voice called from upstairs. "Bobba!" his word for momma. Sarah flicked her head upward. "Go check on him," she said.

Ranse went up to Noah's room and found that in the seconds between him calling for his mom, and Ranse arriving, Noah had fallen back asleep. He pulled the sheets up to his son's chin and kissed him on the forehead. At least he had *him* back. That was a start.

He'd openly admitted to hating himself for losing his family in the first place. There's been a shift in his demeanor, too, especially when the constant high he'd been suffering from wore off. He'd become more subdued since Sarah took Noah and left. Once bright and cheery, a fog had settled over him. As he flicked the bedroom lights off once more, he felt as though the fog was beginning to lift a little. He chanced a genuine smile. If he had known that it would be one of the last smiles he would ever make, maybe he would have let it last a little longer.

He went back downstairs and wasn't surprised to see that Sarah was gone.

Chapter 7

<u>Blue Moon</u>

Warren Maxxy woke up in complete darkness, but he wasn't alone. As cold as she had become, he could still feel Geena next to him, hear her shallow breathing. She made a mess in the bed.

"Don't worry, darlin', I'm still here beside you," he told her, wondering if she could hear him while comatose. His wife was somewhere between the present and oblivion, stuck there by his rash actions that, despite his regret, he still felt were justified. Now was the time for amends. He got up, walked to the window, and pulled the blinds, bathing their bedroom in the eerie, soft blue of twilight. "Would you look at that?" he said. "Another full moon tonight!" He turned to the body lying in his bed. "Did you know it was a blue moon this month?" He waited, and she didn't answer. What he did hear, somewhere in his delusional scattered mind, was his wife beckoning him back to bed. Warren sparked a foxy smile. "Oh, Geena, you dirty girl! I got company comin' over. I called Jim Richmond a while back and he should be here…" he checked his watch, "…any minute." Still, the soft, spectral voice of his wife, powered by his guilt, shame, and grief, floated to him.

Come back to bed, Warren. I want you. I need you.

Warren shivered, and gleefully tiptoed back to bed. He slipped beneath the covers, his hand grazing his wife's crotch. There was heat there, still. Just like there was heat left in her body as it slowly drifted away. Something stirred in him, and he reached between her legs. He could feel her pulse, barely there, shallow.

"I really shouldn't, baby. Jim will be here any minute. I don't want him interruptin' our…" he slipped his hand inside, "our fun."

He molested her, every so often looking over his shoulder at each creak and knock in the house. Waiting, like a child in the throes of a masturbatory act, to be caught. And a masturbatory act it was. The vileness turned him on, for what else would turn on such a vile man?

Outside, the moon glittered in the sky.

***

While Warren and Ranse were getting reacquainted with their wives, Ray Logue was on the verge of killing his. She'd been hounding him ever since he came home sweating and flush like he had just come down with some awful strain of the May flu. But how could he explain to her, without drawing the appropriate panicked reaction, that he'd just been attacked and bitten by some strange vagabond out in the country?

All he wanted to do was eat. Jan made him a plate full of tuna fish sandwiches, but that sounded as appetizing as licking a public toilet seat. No, what he wanted was fresh, bloody red meat, and it just so happened that there was a pile of it in their freezer.

Ignoring his wife, Ray went straight for it, the low hum barely audible to him days ago, was as loud as cannon fire now. He could smell it sitting there, going to waste and gathering frost. His lips began to moisten. He licked them hungrily and ripped the package from the freezer.

"Ray," Jan scolded, "if you wanted venison, all you had to do was say something! What are you doing?"

Ray waved her away, pulling the wad of frozen meat out of her grasp. "Go away!" he growled at her. "Damnit, Jan, you mind me now. I'm starved and I wanna eat in peace. Go on and watch *Wheel of Fortune*."

"It's not on right now," Jan informed him. "It's one of the Judge shows. *Joe Brown*, I think. Why don't you let me thaw that and cook it, so you don't get the worms?"

"I don't want it cooked, Jan! I want it tartare. Now leave me alone or so help me…" There was a look in his eyes that told her he wasn't messing around. That had been a running joke in their marriage, though a distasteful one. This time, however, there was no joking. This time, he meant to harm her if she didn't let it go.

Her husband's face reminded her of a time when her old pooch, Scout, caught a rabbit in the backyard. She wanted to take it away, end its suffering, and get ol' Scout a few more precautionary shots, but Scout wasn't having it. The dog stared at her wide-eyed and afraid of losing its quarry. It gave her a low growl, a don't-you-dare growl, much like the one her husband was making, though he didn't realize it. Jan took a backward step out of the kitchen.

"I'm going to go watch TV," she said. Ray grunted his approval, content to be left alone to eat his meal in peace.

But that peace didn't last long. He'd made a good go of the meat, only breaking a few teeth in the process, but only a few scraps had come loose enough to swallow. Ray's patience was wearing thin. He was determined to gnaw at it until he had his fill. Whenever that might be, he wasn't certain. A few more scraps came loose when the swinging door to the kitchen burst open and Jim Richmond, the officious little cocksucker of Maldus, barged in. Ray saw his wife a few steps behind him, wringing her skirt in that irksome little way she did when she was worried. He wanted to rip her throat out just then. Suddenly, the venison didn't sound so appetizing.

"Ray, just what the hell is going on?" Jim stood with his hands on his waist, the way all officious little cocksuckers did when they thought they had power.

"M'hungry," he said through the raw meat. "Leave me alone. Both of you."

Jim shook his head like a disappointed father catching his son spanking it to online porn.

"We don't have time for whatever this is," he said as he whirled his hands. "If you're suffering a breakdown, do it on your own time. I need you to go and pick up Everly for assault. Seems he got into a tussle with Maxxy over some dead cows, and he smarted off to me when I brought it up to him. I can't let that pass. I'm going over to Warren's right now to get a formal statement."

"Do it yourself, you prick," Ray said. It felt good to call him that. It felt almost as good as eating. Almost as good as it would feel to rip both his and Jan's throats out.

Jim's face turned a bright pink. Nobody talked to him this way. Nobody except Warren Maxxy, but even then, he was usually joking. Warren's threats were subtle. When Ray raised his head to speak, Jim got his first look at what he was eating. Ray's teeth were bared in a menacing grimace, and Jim saw that some of them were cracked, chipped or just plain missing. He wasn't angry anymore. He was concerned.

"Ray, what the hell is going on here?" Jim asked with horror. He hitched a thumb towards Jan. "You're scaring your wife. Hell, you're scaring me!"

"Nothing," Ray replied. "Leave me alone." He went back to the meat, though his eyes never left the two interlopers in the kitchen.

"I've had just about enough of this," Richmond huffed. "Give me that fucking steak and start acting right." He took a step forward, his arm outstretched, meaning to grab the meat-wad and take it away. Ray retreated, scooting backward on his ass to a far corner of the kitchen.

"Leave me alone," he repeated, but Jim Richmond was a stubborn man. The hand came out again, a finger grazing the slightest bit of the cold hunk of deer meat, leaving Richmond's stench all over it. Ray lunged forward and nipped the man's finger.

"Jesus!" Richmond shouted. Behind them, Jan let out a startled sob. "Look at that, Logue! You broke the skin! I'm bleeding! What are you, rabid or something? That fucking hurt, you bastard!" Jim stomped around the kitchen looking for a paper towel, or a napkin, anything to staunch the bleeding. He settled on an old stained t-shirt and wrapped it around his finger. When he turned back to the sheriff, he was still gnawing on the venison like a cranky old mutt with a bone. "You're on notice," he said, wishing he could stick out an official finger like he always did when he was angry. "Come this time next week, we might have a new sheriff. Is that what you want, Logue?" Ray didn't answer. "Yeah," Jim said, nodding his head, "I didn't think you wanted that. You better get your ass over to Everly's and bring that sumbitch in, do you understand?" Still no answer. Jim waited there for a moment, shook his head in disgust and frustration and stormed out of the house. On his way out, he turned to Jan. "You either need to have him committed or go spend the night at your sister's house," he told her. "Cause something ain't right with him." He waved the bloody shirt in her face. "I'll have this returned to you."

Ray could hear the front door open and slam shut from his nook in the kitchen. He looked down at his meat. Richmond's touch didn't just spoil it with his scent, it infected it, contaminated it like it was E. coli or salmonella. The meat was sour now, inedible. Ray let it drop to the floor with a frozen thud. It wasn't that great to begin with, cold and long dead. What he really craved was hot and fresh. He wanted the coppery taste of blood in his mouth, the heat from freshly worked veins and arteries. He wanted to taste the life force as he consumed it. The door to the kitchen squeaked open, but there was no one there. A shadow had fallen into the living room. He couldn't see his wife, but he could certainly smell her.

"Ray?" Jan called in that droning, irritating voice of hers. He could hear the ripples as she wrung at her skirt.

"Ray," she repeated, "Are you all right? I'm coming in there. I just want to check on you." He could hear her heart going a million miles a minute. He could smell the fear on her coming down in tiny beads of sweat. She smelled delicious.

Ray's lips peeled back into a toothy grin.

"I'm in here, darlin'," he said. "I'm sorry, I don't know what came over me. Come in here where I can see you. I promise I won't bite…"

***

By the time he reached Maxxy's, Jim Richmond was pouring sweat. His perspiration, he thought, was a byproduct of the hot and cold flashes he'd been suffering from since that goddamned Ray Logue bit him. Like when a hot-air and cold-air mass collide, but it was more like precipitation, condensation, then perspiration.

His stomach hurt, too. He was nauseous but hungry at the same time. His skin crawled like it was made of ants; it felt like they were slowly peeling it back to reveal the muscle and sinew underneath. What the hell had Logue given him? Some sort of super-flu? Jesus, he hoped not. Even a cold was amplified during the summer. A cold, mixed with his allergies, would put him out of business for at least a full week. And he had work to do.

The deal Warren had brokered with the Tyson Company would open not one, not two, but three plants just outside of Maldus. They would buy stock exclusively from Maxxy and Richmond, making the two men extremely, obscenely, and stupidly richer than they already were. But that's not what they craved. With the factories, came workers, and that meant expansion. That meant that other companies would come sniffing. Wal-Mart, Bass Pro, GameStop, and Apple would all come knocking on the door of Arkansas' newest boom-town. They would have to play ball with Richmond and Maxxy if they wanted to set up shop here. That meant power, and power was always more appealing than money. Sure, they would have to adapt. Warren would have to pull back on his...*alt-right* leanings a bit, and Jim would have to cool his tenacity, but it was all in the name of progress, right? Just so long as they kept the power.

He stumbled up to Warren's door and pressed the doorbell. After fighting with the intercom at the gate, he didn't know if he even had the strength to get out of his truck. He persevered. Warren answered the door, looking just as pale as him.

"Jesus, Jim, look at you!" Warren said, shocked. "You coming down with something?"

Jim waved him away, not sure if he could get a word out without barfing all over Maxxy's front porch.

"Need...to...talk," he panted.

"Yeah," Warren said, his demeanor turning from shocked to grim, "we do. Did you take care of Everly?" Jim nodded. It seemed easier than explaining the events at Ray Logue's house. He was sick, and if Everly wasn't taken care of by the time he was feeling better, then he'd go do it himself. "Good," Warren continued. "We...I have a bit of a problem, Jimbo. Geena, well, Geena had an accident. She's alive, but not doing too well. I got her in bed upstairs. Why don't you come up and look? Maybe you have an idea of what the next steps are."

Jim groaned inwardly. If the journey from the porch to the stairs didn't kill him, then the trip to the second story most definitely would. Warren noticed his trepidation and slipped a hand around Jim's waist. Warren, such a good friend. Jim's only true friend in this town. There would be more, though. Lots more.

"Come on, buddy," Warren said. "I need your help on this one." He led him to the stairs, closing the door with his foot, and up to the master bedroom. Jim had never seen Warren's room before. His dealings with Geena had always been under the guise of business dealings in his back office.

Jim barely registered the lump in the bed through his blurry vision, and he didn't know it was Geena Maxxy until Warren pulled the covers back. When he did, he had to let go of him, and Jim nearly collapsed on top of her. He had to grab onto the woman's body to keep from falling full on the bed, making the disturbing scene only that more offensive.

"Goddamnit, Jim!" Warren cried. "You're bleeding all over her!" He reached down and pulled Jim back up on wobbly legs. "What'd you do, cut yourself? Come on, I'll get you a bandage and we can go downstairs and discuss what our options are." He reached down and flung the comforter over his wife once more.

A few minutes later, Jim was sitting in an overstuffed easy chair. Warren had given him a glass of whiskey, a Band-Aid, and a Motrin. He was beginning to feel a little better. Well, enough to talk at least.

"What did you do?" Jim asked Warren, pushing the words out was a struggle, but an accomplishable one.

Warren was taken aback. "What did *I* do?" he asked. "I didn't do a damn thing! Geena was hungover, she fell on my paperweight."

"I might be sick, Warren," Jim said, nursing his freshly bandaged hand, "but I'm not stupid. If that was the case, you would have called someone other than me."

Maxxy grimaced. He shrugged his shoulders and let out a long, woeful sigh like a murderer might just before he confessed.

"She was fuckin' around again," he finally admitted. "I lost my temper. I don't know why she always felt the need to flaunt her pussy around town, fucking anything with two legs and a dick..." Jim didn't know if it was the bite from Logue or Warren's confession, but he suddenly felt sick again. Worse than he had before. "I guess I was still fuming from my run-in with Everly, and the sucker-punch." He gave Richmond a look that only a liar could give. "I snapped! It was passion, and nothing more! What do you think I should do, Jimbo? Should I..." he gulped, "should I finish her off? Take her out to the field and bury her? If anyone asks, I could say that she took off on me." He let out a disgusted grunt. "That's a pretty believable story."

Jim couldn't hear him. Warren's words, the sight of Geena, Ray Logue's bite, and the Tyson Company were all just a pack of distant, blurry memories. All he could think of was getting out of this place. He wanted to go home, go somewhere safe and quiet where he could be alone to suffer. God, was he hungry too? The thought of food both intrigued and repulsed him. He shot up from the chair and stumbled for the door. He was going to be sick. He knew it.

"Hey, where ya going?" Warren demanded. "We got a problem that needs solvin', buddy!"

The front door crashed open, and Jim stepped outside with enough time remaining to lurch into

Maxxy's azalea bushes. Warren didn't get up. He stared on in puzzled awe as Jim puked all the way across the lawn before finally making it to his car. He swerved like a drunk driver, nearly crashing into the front gate and sent the car fishtailing onto the highway.

Finally, Warren got up and walked to the front door. He'd never seen Jim that out of sorts before. He thought his old friend could be drunk. Yes, that would explain it. Jim had always been so composed before. Even when he was sick, the man would excuse himself to the bathroom before quietly puking into the toilet. This just wasn't like him. Something like this could only happen once in a...

He looked up at the sky.

A blue moon.

Chapter 8

<u>The First Hunt</u>

Ray Logue stepped out of his house, lapping at the blood splatter which made a perfect bib from his mouth all the way to the middle of his chest. He was full, there was the slightest bit of guilt, but he was full. That was all that mattered.

His gut instinct was to find a hole and crawl inside of it. To sleep off the meal until his wits returned, but something inside of him said that those old wits wouldn't return at all. That they were replaced by an all- new set of wits. Instincts. He looked up at the sky. The weatherman said there was going to be two full moons this month. The moon. It was so beautiful hanging there in the sky, like a giant marble. Ray felt as if he could reach up and pluck it from whatever perch it stood on. He wanted to pluck it from the sky; he *needed* to pluck it from the sky and shove it in his mouth, swallowing it whole. Without realizing it, he reached up and pawed in the air. Too far. *Of course, it was*, his rational mind told him. The thing is thousands of miles away! Still, he tried pawing again, but to no avail. Ray howled in frustration.

Suddenly, he didn't feel like sleeping anymore. He felt like running, hunting. He felt like fighting. The moon shone down its brilliant rays upon him, he could feel some sort of ambient heat. It felt good.

The change came quickly.

***

Jim Richmond made it halfway to his house before he had to pull over to expel another deluge of vomit. He'd served in the Persian Gulf War. He'd heard stories of the torture some of the older vets from older wars had endured. He was certain, though, that none of them had endured this. A raw, aching hunger coupled with crippling nausea. Torture by oxymoron. As soon as he pulled out of Maxxy's driveway, he shat himself. It was a fetid, foul stink that only made his stomach groan that much more. What was wrong with him? The only saving grace was that his vertigo, as well as the hot and cold flashes, had abated since he escaped into the fresh night air. Maybe Maxxy had some sort of air freshener or incense that disagreed with his allergies. He wasn't sure. He didn't want to be sure. To be sure was to accept that he was sick, and he couldn't be sick now. Not at such a pivotal moment for his town. Maldus needed this, he needed this, and whether Warren Maxxy liked to admit it or not, he needed this.

There was a meeting tomorrow afternoon. Two chairs of the Tyson Company would be here to discuss layout plans for their factories and discuss what they could give back to Maldus. What good would it do to have the two town representatives show up, one shitting his pants and the other a paranoid wreck? No, that wouldn't do at all. This had to be a united front. They had to show them that this was a decent town full of decent people. They had to show—

A terrible stomach cramp gripped Jim's guts and wrenched them this way and that. He seized up and fell from the driver's seat into the puddle of his own sick on the dark highway. He looked up at the sky. The moon shone down on him, cursing him, like the accusatory finger of God himself.

"Why?" he croaked. "What did I do to deserve this?"

But he had done plenty. In the part of his mind that wasn't rattled with sick, he ticked off exactly what all he had done to deserve such a penance: the constant persecution of Everly, selling his town out, his tolerance of his partner's blatant racism, and his acceptance of sexual favors from that same partner's wife. Jim Richmond had held this town ransom for years. Whatever plague he'd contracted was the town's way of paying him back. He hated this place now. He hated everything and everybody in it and wanted nothing more than to rip it to shreds. The rage came then. As his eyes turned from human to wolf, they saw nothing but red.

***

"You think we'll see anything?" Ricky Lee Webster asked his hunting partner, Diego Padilla. They were stuffed up in a deer blind crawling with early summer spiders, slugs, and cicadas, but thankfully no tics or mosquitos. Mick had left them with an ice chest full of beers, a thermos of his cocaine coffee, and a bag full of sandwiches that he'd made for them, and the two gnashed away, every so often scanning the horizon for something other than a rabbit or night bird.

"I dunno," Diego said. "I haven't seen a goddamn thing so far. Not even a rabbit."

"Weird," Ricky Lee said. Diego nodded in agreement. "So, what do you think did that heifer in?" he continued, hating the silence that came with activities like hunting or fishing. "Let me guess, you probably think it was the chapacabro or something. Am I right?"

Diego chuckled. "Ok, first, you're an asshole. Second, it's the *Chupacabra,* and not whatever the hell you called it."

"So what, then?" Ricky Lee asked. "A bear? Coyote?"

Diego shook his head and scanned the dark. "I think Ranse and Mick are going about this all wrong. I think it's something new."

Ricky Lee ripped a hunk off the sandwich and tossed it in his mouth. "So, you do think it's the chapacabro."

"God, you really are an asshole. Even if I did believe in the Chupacabra, which I don't, who's to say that it doesn't exist? Scientists are discovering all sorts of new species every fucking day, coño, so for all we know that animal isn't as mythological as we thought. Anyway, I'm not talking about that. I think that whatever is doing this, is as normal to this world as you or me, just not normal to this region."

Ricky Lee remained quiet, pretending to watch the distance, but he was secretly interested in what his hunting partner had to say. The two were friends, but to the uninitiated, their constant bickering, hostilities, and racist remarks might be considered a sign of shared hatred rather than a show of brotherhood.

"All I'm saying is that what if one of those big cats from up north got loose? Not all of them need to mark their territory, right? Or what if a rogue wolf came down from Minnesota or somewhere? What if someone was keeping it as a pet and let it go like those assholes with their big snakes down in Florida?"

"Invasive species," Ricky Lee grumbled.

Diego popped him on the arm as if to concur.

"It happens more than we realize, man," Diego continued. "I watched a documentary on Netflix about it not too long ago. You never think about it when you step into a pile of fire-ants or hear about some baseball park infested with killer bees, but those animals aren't supposed to be here."

"That's rich comin' from a Mexican," Ricky Lee joked.

"Fuck you, man, I'm being serious!"

Ricky Lee nodded in surrender, easing off on the racial humor a bit. "You might have a point, but how will we know if we don't see anything?" He thought of the reports he read in *Angler Quarterly* of giant great white sharks spotted off the Texas Gulf Coast. Driven in by rising oceanic temperatures, they had confused the warmer waters as normal hunting grounds. Could that be the case here? Could a grizzly or huge wolf have been driven south by rising temperatures in the Rockies or the Upper-Peninsula? He thought it possible, though not probable. Judging by what Mick told them about the damage, even a big bear or rabid wolf couldn't have left such carnage in its wake. The two remained silent for a while, scanning the dark for any movement until Ricky Lee once again got antsy. "What exactly is a chappy-whatever?" he asked.

"Chu. Pa. Ca. Bra," Diego said phonetically. "There are a lot of legends behind what it is. Different artists painted different pictures, different writers told different stories, and different crazies describe different encounters. Some say it's a vampire, others say it's like Bigfoot or something."

"What do you think it is?"

Diego shrugged his shoulders and peered through the night-vision scope mounted on his rifle. All quiet. Just like the *Night Before Christmas,* not a creature was stirring. He remained silent as well.

"Come on," Ricky Lee said, prodding his friend. "What do you think?"

"There's only one thing I can think of," Diego told him. "I think it's a werewolf." He cringed as he said it, thankful that the dark would conceal his cheeks and the blush that came to them once Ricky Lee started in with his braying laughter.

But the laughter never came. Diego peered over and saw his friend only nod in silent contemplation. What Diego didn't know about Ricky Lee was that he came from a place filled with folklore as well. Ricky Lee was from Lafayette, a place not too far from where they now sat, and there were plenty of stories of werewolves ranging from the absurd to believable. They didn't call them werewolves, though. They called them…

"Rougarou."

"What?" Diego said.

"Rougarou," Ricky Lee repeated. "That's the Creole Chupacabra. Swamp-Wolf."

"You believe me?" Diego asked, almost skeptical of the ease in which Ricky Lee accepted such a claim. "Did you see one or something?"

Ricky Lee shook his head. "When I was a little boy, me and my brother used to go frog-gigging at night. Used to fry their legs up, eat 'em like they were chicken nuggets. It was my favorite meal in the world. Don't give me that look, y'all eat rattlesnakes below the border. One night, I was down with the flu or something, and my big brother, Troy, went out by himself. It was my birthday coming up, see, and my momma wanted to make me frog legs for my birthday supper.

"I waited all night for Troy to come back. I planned on sneaking outside and chancing pneumonia just to see his haul. There were always a few snakes or swamp rats mixed in with the frogs. I was a kid, and I liked gross shit. But Troy never came back. The next day, my daddy and a few of our neighbors went out looking for him. They never found hide nor hair of my big brother, and I never had frog legs again."

"And you think it was a…werewolf?" Diego asked. "That got your hermano?"

Ricky Lee shrugged. "They said it was a gator, and I suppose that's the one explanation that makes sense. Other than a pervert or something. But the thing is, for some reason or another, gators didn't like that particular area of the swamp. I can tell you for certain that I never saw one growing up, and that swamp was my second home." While Diego mulled it over, Ricky Lee reached into the ice chest and rooted around. "Wanna beer?" he asked.

"Yeah," Diego whispered, but the thought of an ice-cold Coors only chilled his bones further. The two sat drinking, sharing stories of brighter subjects: sunny summer days, Christmases past, things so far from Chupacabra or the Rougarou that they began to feel a bit better, more comfortable.

***

She was certain that Ranse would try to follow her. Part of her hoped he would. That's why she stopped at the only place that he, if he was telling the truth, wouldn't dare think of entering. She sat at the Bar drinking draft Pabst Blue Ribbon from a red Solo cup and listening to the croons of old Dwight Yoakum and George Strait. Their heartache, mixed with the cheap beer, only served to darken her mood.

Cancer was survivable, but not in her case. Without so much as a, "how do you do, ma'am," it had spread to her lungs, her bones. She thought the doctor was just wasting time on such a futile thing like chemo, but the doctor reminded her that despair only served to hasten the inevitable.

Sarah knew that there was a chance, albeit slim, that tonight could very well be the last time she saw Noah or Ranse. Ranse would face the fires of hell before he let Sarah die without saying goodbye, and she loved him for it, but sometimes she felt that dying would be easier alone. It was going to be hard enough with her parents there. Yet, part of her held out hope that at least once she passed, the pain that had come on like tsunami in recent weeks, would end, only for the pain to begin for everyone else in her life.

She needed this beer, goddamnit. Alcohol was strictly verboten now that she was about to put up a fight against the big C, but she was supposed to remain stress-free as well and that went out the window when she called her ex-husband that morning. She figured one more night of rule-breaking wouldn't hurt, and only wished there was a friendly person with a spare cigarette, so she could complete the trifecta.

She got up and paid her tab after only two beers. An odd thing to the bartender. Most of the time when folks came in there, it was for the long haul. They didn't so much as leave, as they poured themselves out to the street. But then he remembered who this lady was, and who her ex-husband used to be, and he figured that Ranse did enough pouring for the both of them. Maybe she was only trying to restore balance.

As she waited for her change, the old George Jones song kicked on the jukebox, "He Stopped Loving Her Today." She kept her composure all the way to her car, only letting a sob out as she turned the ignition. That way, she didn't have to hear it.

She drove slowly through Maldus, certain that it would be her last time seeing this place. She marveled at the countryside bathed in the soft glow of the moon. Trees looked blue instead of green. The grass was a blanket of rich dark chocolate. The Ozark Mountains were now just looming shadows in the distance, pocked every so often by a halogen light, giving them eyes that could see in the dark. Soon, her only view would be the walls of a hospital room, the chair where she would receive that radioactive milkshake, and perhaps—if she was lucky—a courtyard.

The inside of a coffin.

She didn't stop crying until she reached the edge of town. Here, the only light was coming from her car. She slowed down, all too aware of the trucks and cars sent careening to the valley below by swerving to miss a deer or a maverick cow, and she had to laugh. What's the point? You'd just be speeding along the inevitable.

That was the last thought she had before her car went airborne.

Something smacked into the side of it, caving the driver's side door inward and shattering the window into a million fragments. Not another car, though it was just as powerful. She could have gone on thinking it was, though, if it hadn't been for the great roar she heard.

Sarah screamed as she went rolling down the embankment toward the valley. This was Jim Richmond's property, she thought fleetingly. Maybe he's outside on his porch. Maybe he'll see my headlights whirling around in the dark like two rabid lightning bugs, hear the crunch as my car comes to its final resting place, as I… She realized then, that despite the cancer, despite the pain that racked her body, she was not ready to die.

Sarah got her Nissan on insistence from Ranse that it was one, if not the, safest vehicles on the road. As it came crashing down in a gulley separating the embankment from Richmond's property, she was surprised to find just how safe it was. The car was demolished, totaled beyond all repair, but she was okay. There would be headaches, backaches, and all sorts of other aches, but nothing was broken, nothing was bleeding save for the slightest scratches from the broken glass. She whimpered in thanks and disbelief. She tried the seatbelt only to find it was jammed. The car's doors were obliterated, but she figured if she could get loose then it'd be possible to climb out through the hole where the windshield used to be. But maybe all she had to do was wait. If it took until morning, someone would find her out here.

She resigned herself to do just that, waiting, and in her waiting, her mind began to wander. Not to areas dealing with cancer, or losing her son, or even Ranse. She began to wonder just what the hell had hit her.

The answer didn't elude her long, however, as a great hulking mass fell upon the crumpled remains of her car. A small cry escaped her as she stared into the glowing eyes of a very large wolf. It was smelling her, taking in her scent, and something inside Sarah broke as she watched the monster lick at its jaws. It was hungry.

Since when do wolves wear clothing?

With one giant paw, it reached up and peeled back the roof of the Nissan like it was a can of tuna. The shriek of metal contorting was deafening, but still, she could hear the monster's breathing, a heavy pull and push of air that sounded more like the revving of a semi-truck.

The claw reached inside, its hooks ripping through the cloth of her blouse, cutting into the soft flesh of her breastbone like it was soft butter. Sarah cried out once more, through teeth gritted against the pain. The pain. It seemed like it would last a little longer now.

The thing that was once Jim Richmond stared down the interloper as it broke through the woods into the clearing where the car now sat. It dropped its quarry, the woman sniveling and pleading words that it didn't understand, nor did it care to. Sarah dropped back to the Nissan's driver seat clutching at her bleeding breast and sobbing like a sinner thrust into the face of God's judgment. Blood pooled in her lap, her head was swimmy, and she felt the distinct chill of someone bleeding out. Soon, she would be dead. Hopefully, she would be dead before whatever these monsters were, began to eat her. That death, she thought she could live with.

The two beasts locked eyes. They huffed and puffed, trying to scare one another off. The one on the car brought itself up to full height, blotting out the moon and casting Sarah in full dark. It pulled in air—it sounded more like a heavy-duty air compressor than the breathing of a living thing—and it howled. It was so loud that one of Sarah's eardrums ruptured. She clapped her hands over them before the other monster joined, but it did little to drown out the din of their macabre ode to the night. Then, the wolf in the clearing charged. The wolf on the car followed suit, and the fight was on.

Their howls still hung in the air as a new chorus rose up: a chorus of snarling, ripping flesh, hard fang against hard fang. Sarah climbed out of the Nissan, hoping that the two monsters were too busy with each other to bother with her. Ahead, there was a notch at the base of a large oak. She climbed inside, still clutching her breast. This seemed like a good place to die. Hopefully, they would find her before she started to melt back into the earth.

Outside, the monsters' fight raged on. The thing that was once Ray Logue took a giant swipe at the tender gut of its attacker. He missed, and the Jim-Wolf sunk its teeth into its neck. The Jim-Wolf snapped its head sideways with all its strength, forcing the Ray-Wolf to follow its lead. Ray tumbled to the ground, its deathly snarl abruptly turning into a high-pitched yelp of pain. It yielded, but still, Richmond clenched its teeth into it. The tendons in its neck snapped, its windpipe threatened to cave-in. The Ray-Wolf was beaten. Finally, mercifully, the victor let go.

The thing that was once Ray Logue floundered to its feet, shying away from the looming presence of its dominator. It sunk, slowly and painfully, back into the woods. Sarah watched as the wolf that had attacked her stood panting in the moonlight. It arched its back. Its spine protruded from the hair and muscles in a scoliotic wave, and it howled once more. *This time*, she thought, *it was a howl of triumph.*

With the interloper dispatched, it was time for the Jim-Monster to turn its attention back to its quarry. To the victor, go the spoils. It shoved its long snout into the air, and sniffed the wind, picking up the smell of cow shit, fresh meat, and…what's this? Another would-be attacker? The scent of the creature's urine burned the Jim-Wolf's nostrils. It was an affront, a dare. *Come and get me,* it said, *'cause I'm coming for you, and I won't stop until I rip your throat out.* The Jim-Wolf roared with hatred and anger. The thing it shared with its human counterpart was its ravenous territoriality. This was its world, and as the one it just subdued learned, woe to whatever got in its way. If it had any brains, it was licking its wounds far, far away from Maldus. The Jim-Wolf wouldn't be so forgiving to the other that dared spray its scent.

With one last growl, it lumbered up the embankment and back onto the highway. Sarah watched from her hole in the tree as it sniffed the air once more. It set its course towards Everly Ranch, towards Noah.

She had to warn them. Somehow, she had to will herself from her cozy, quiet, safe-haven and get back to tell them that there was a wolf—no—a monster, heading directly for them. She would wrap Noah up in her arms, carry him down to the storm shelter underneath the stairs, and lock themselves away until Ranse told them that the monster was either gone or dead. Her heart was racing now as adrenaline took hold. A fresh pool of warmth slowly crept into her lap. She was suddenly very, very tired.

She thought of her cell phone. She didn't chance letting go of the rip in her chest to check her pockets, and if her memory, as cloudy as it was, served her, then she distinctly remembered setting the phone in the center console as she always did. The trek to the crumpled remains of the Nissan was just too far, and she was too exhausted to even think of beginning it. She thought that this was what it felt like for those alpinists caught on Everest, or those castaways afloat in the middle of the Pacific after a shipwreck. There came a point where it was just easier to give up, give in, to close your eyes and hold out hope that there was, in fact, an afterlife.

Anyway, hadn't Ranse told her that they were sending a hunting team out tonight? Surely, they would protect Noah. They had to be hopped up on Mick's coffee, and most of them were crack shots. They would take care of everything. Sarah didn't have to worry. She closed her eyes and thought about the alternative. Cancer. Chemotherapy, a few months of pain and lingering only to die shriveled and shitty in a hospital bed.

She considered herself lucky.

***

The howl had shaken them to the core. Ricky sat wide-eyed in the deer blind, searching and listening to the night for any sign of its source. Diego had climbed down to take a piss, and Ricky Lee had to stifle a scream when his partner called up to inform him that he was making a run for the house for some more supplies, meaning beer. Ricky shushed him and gestured for him to get on with it then. Then thinking about it, he added,

"Whatever, ya pussy." Diego gestured back, telling Ricky Lee to go fuck himself, and headed back to the trailer park in the truck. The only truck. The only means of high-speed escape should the need arise. Ricky Lee watched as the taillights dimmed in the distance.

"Fuck," he grumbled.

That was a little over an hour ago, and Diego still hadn't returned. Ricky shivered and huddled inside the thin windbreaker he brought with him. It was chilly for a summer night, but not chilly enough to warrant a shiver of such force. He supposed he was frightened. No, that wasn't right at all. He *was* frightened. Plain and simple. The stories that he and Diego shared frightened him, the howl had frightened him and now the still, quiet calm that had settled over Maldus ever since Diego left was frightening him. He'd kill for that mouthy Mexican to talk some sort of shit right about now, if only to break the maddening silence.

He checked his pocket for his phone.

"Fuck!" He'd forgotten his phone in the truck. "Where the hell are you?" he said, hoping that the nonexistent echo of his whisper would somehow reach Diego back at the trailer. There was no answer. Of course, there was no answer. Ricky Lee settled back in, huddling closely against the heat of his own body, and waited.

Eventually, his mind wandered back to the tale of the Rougarou, as frightened minds tend to focus on the frightening when they are alone in the dark. What he hadn't told Diego, was that it was his grandma that first introduced him to the concept of the monster. "The Rougarou come fo de peoples dat gone and don' bad tings," she told a terrified six-year-old Ricky Lee in her hybrid of Creole and English. "Dey come, and dey sniff ya out. Got da head of a wolf, mindya. Head of a wolf, and de body of a man, only it stretch out really long. Dey claws as sharp as razor-wire, and dey rip right tru-ya. And while ya screamin' and a hollerin' dey rip da flesh from ya bone like it was warm butta." Ricky Lee remembered crying then, horrified and certain that any minute, the Rougarou would be pouncing through his door. But His grandma only chuckled and held him close. "No needin' to be getting' yoself in a tizzy, Ricky Lee," she said. "Dey only come for da bad men. The ones dat done horrible, terrible tings. And the only reason they eat at da flesh is to get to da bad men's souls. To clean da world like dey was sweepin a dirty floor."

And that was the end of it. Well, save for some nights spent wondering just how clean his soul really was. Not long after, Ricky Lee wasn't worrying about the Rougarou as much. He would have forgotten all about it if it weren't for Troy's disappearance.

The night of his birthday, instead of lying sleepily and lazily with a belly full of frog legs and his mama's chocolate cake with lard icing, he lay wide awake, jumping at every noise and bump in the night. Just like he was now. Of course, when he told his parents that it was the Rougarou that took Troy, they didn't believe him. Even his grandma didn't believe his ardent declaration that a monster took his big brother. Why would they? They were grown-ups, and somewhere along the shifty line that separates childhood and adulthood, monsters become invisible make-believe. His grandma reminded him that only bad people get visited by the Rougarou, and Troy wasn't a bad person, but what Ricky Lee hadn't told them was that Troy had in fact, done some rather naughty things. Things like taking money out of the church collection plate for comic books and candy. Things like peeking in the women's changing rooms at Theroux's Department Store. Things like torturing those little frogs and making them squeal before stuffing them in the burlap sack he took gigging with him.

The realization hit him hard in the gut: *Things like fucking around with the married neighbor lady.* The dread stuck in his throat like an overgrown sticker-bur. He wanted to scream but forced himself to swallow it down with the rest of the mess. Ricky Lee told himself he was just spooked. He was alone in the dark, and his and Diego's campfire tales were taking their hold on his mind as they would with anyone; a kid in bed replaying a recently watched horror movie, or a surfer finally stepping into the water after healing from a vicious shark attack. It was natural, it was expected, but it was silly. There was no Rougarou, Chappy-cabro, or werewolf. Worst-case scenario, *worst-case,* they were dealing with some gigantic rogue bear.

Just then he heard the distinctive rumble of the ranch's truck. He looked and saw headlights in the distance. Thankfully, finally, Diego returned. Ricky Lee straightened up, wishing for a mirror so he could check his face. He was sure that he looked spooked, and he worried that Diego would see it too. If it were discovered that Ricky Lee was scared, the ripping he would receive would go far past good-natured. He relaxed, let out a long sigh, and began to pantomime as if it had been business as usual in Diego's absence. He picked up the rifle just as the truck pulled up and scanned the distance.

Something caught his eye near the bend in the game trail. It was over a hundred yards away, but the thing in

Ricky Lee's sight was still massive. It stood on its hind legs, and in the night-vision, its eyes glowed like two sparkling pennies shining up from a dark wishing well. It was looking right at them.

"What the fuck is that?" Ricky Lee was barely able to say before the thing darted from his vision.

The truck door slammed below.

"You all right up there?" Diego asked. Ricky Lee heard him and heard his struggle with the paper sack full of supplies, but he didn't answer, didn't offer any assistance. He was too busy searching for the…

"Rougarou," he said with the same cold certainty as a man staring down an oncoming train. He caught sight of it once more. Now he could see its long snout full of razor-sharp teeth, its claws, and the fur that covered its stretched and contorted body. In the split second it disappeared, it had crossed the space between the game trail and the deer blind. It was coming right for them. "Diego, get up here, now!"

"What?" Diego called up, still struggling with the bulk in his arms. "I would if you'd come down and help me, you lazy pendejo!"

"Drop your shit and get up here!" Ricky Lee screamed. "It's here! The Rougarou! It's here!" The thing was so close now that Ricky could feel the rumble of its feet on the ground. Diego still had no idea that death was only several yards away, and it was tearing in his direction. Ricky Lee didn't have time to argue. He raised the rifle up and homed in on the monster. Slowly, he squeezed the trigger.

Diego finally gave up his fight with the supplies when the first shot ripped through the air. He let the sack fall to the ground. Sandwiches, cans of beer, and Ricky Lee's phone spilled to the ground. He covered his ears out of instinct, but the roar of the monster cut through.

The first shot went wide. Ricky Lee cursed and pushed another bullet into the breach. But before he could fire again, he watched in astonishment as the thing in his sight broke out of his field of vision and went airborne. "Diego! Watch out!" He looked down on his friend from above, seeing him for a split second before Diego disappeared in a blur of beer cans, denim, teeth, claws, and fur.

Diego screamed, his worst nightmare now real and sinking its teeth into his shoulder. The wolf ripped at him, shook him like a dog playing with a ragdoll. Ricky screamed right along with him, searching in vain for a clear shot. Diego punched at the thing with his free hand, hitting it in the chest, the arm, finally going for the snout and missing wide. His hand disappeared in a spray of crimson, caught in a thresher. He howled in panic. As it goaded on, the monster raised its head and joined him.

Ricky Lee didn't think and squeezed off a round the split second the wolf offered a preferable target. The top of the wolf's skull blew into the air, the bullet sparking as it made contact and illuminating little white pieces of bone, grey matter, and blood. As quickly as it had begun, it was over. The wolf collapsed on top of Diego and all was still.

A moment passed. It was silent and dead. Ricky Lee watched from his perch, willing for one of the two still bodies on the ground to move. He realized suddenly, that he was crying.

"Come on," he willed Diego, "Move!" But it wasn't his friend that moved.

The wolf got up with a grunt. It moved on shaky legs, stumbling around like a dizzy child fresh off a merry-go-round. Ricky Lee's sobs turned to screams of fury. He unloaded into the monster, ripping it to shreds until it was nothing more than a bloody, pulpy mass. Rougarou, Chupacabra, or werewolf, whatever it was, it was dead.

Ricky dropped the gun and scurried down the ladder. His eyes never leaving the mass of gnarled tissue close by. He ran over to Diego. He was bloody and mangled, his left hand missing, his right shoulder looked like it had been run through a car crusher. But he was alive. Deep in shock, unaware, but alive.

"Just…try not to move," Ricky told him. "You're gonna be fine. I'm gonna get you help!" He ran back to the truck and found his phone on the ground amidst the piles of sandwiches and beer.

Ricky Lee placed two calls. The first, to Maldus's modest emergency services, and the second was to his boss. Ranse arrived well before the ambulance with Mick in tow. They took turns attending to Diego and staring in awe at the bulk of whatever had attacked him. While they waited, Ranse called Grant Riddell.

"He'll want to see this," he explained.

The three men stood vigil over the creature long after the paramedics had come and gone. Diego would be taken care of, and so long as none of his wounds required major surgery, he'd be home in no time. Questions were exchanged, the most repeated of them were, "What happened here?" and "What is this thing?" Ricky Lee offered no explanation. He only shook his head.

Grant arrived a while later, looking sleepy, but excited. He forwent the usual happy greetings and went straight for the shredded corpse on the ground.

"Jesus," he whispered, looking over the thing like it were some prehistoric animal, long forgotten, that just appeared out of a hole in the ground. "This animal is crazy!"

Ranse joined him. "Any idea what it is?"

Grant shook his head, perplexed and ecstatic. The words exited his mouth like rapid-fire bullets. "I have no idea, a wolf of some kind, but I dunno what kind. God, this thing is big! I didn't know they could get this big!"

Tell them that it stood on two legs, Ricky Lee thought. *Tell them about the Rougarou, the Chupacabra.* Ricky licked his lips, forcing himself to speak. He was sweating in spite of the air's chill.

"Ricky?" Mick said, "You all right?" Ricky Lee tried to say something, anything. He stumbled on his feet, all the strength going out of his legs. Mick caught him just before he crumpled to the ground.

"Hey!" Mick called out.

Grant and Ranse turned.

"He's in shock," Grant said. "I don't blame him. I wouldn't have wanted to meet a thing this size while it was alive. He needs to get home. Get him wrapped up in a blanket and get some fluids in him, and not beer or coffee."

"I'll take him," Ranse said. "I gotta check on Noah, anyway."

Mick nodded. He helped Ranse take Ricky Lee to his truck. "I'll stick around here, and help the Doc," he said, once Rick was safely loaded up. "I'd like to find out just what the hell this thing is myself."

"Probably won't know that for a while," Grant said. "We'll take it back to my office, but I'm gonna have to send off some samples to get a definite answer...*maybe.*" He pointed to Ricky Lee. "Take him home and get him rested. Tomorrow take him to Doctor Engle's clinic. He'll have his hands full with

Diego tonight. Remember, no alcohol." He thought about it for a second then amended his orders. "Maybe a shot of whiskey, if his nerves don't calm down."

Ranse nodded. "Check back with me in the morning," he told Mick and drove off.

"There's a winch on the back of the work truck," Mick said, turning to Grant. "What do you say we load this fucker in the back and take it back to your office?"

Grant nodded. "Got any gloves?"

"Probably in the toolbox," Mick said. "Why?" The answer came without Grant even opening his mouth. They had no idea what this thing was. It could be crawling with all sorts of diseases, rabies chief among them. "I'll go grab a couple of pairs."

***

Ranse left his Dodge back at the trailer. He needed a walk. It had been a long day. In all, he lost three cows, been in a fight, had his license threatened, met up with his ex-wife, and had his son returned to him. And that had all been before the moon had come out. Now it seemed that it was turning out to be an even longer night.

Ricky was set up and seemed to be doing well enough. He told Ranse he'd be fine on his own. Ranse asked him if he could describe what it was that attacked him and Diego, give him some details on what it looked like before he turned it to scraps, but he let it go after seeing his ranch-hand's face. A description could wait. Whatever it was, had shaken Ricky Lee to his core. Now, he needed sleep.

Yeah, sleep sounded good. Right now, Ranse was working on nothing more than a microwaveable pizza and few cups of coffee that he had for a late lunch. He was suffering from sensory overload. He could get some sleep and start fresh on everything in the morning over a bowl of Cheerios with Noah.

But anxiety is a sneaky little thing, always rearing its head just when a solution is within reach. Ranse allowed himself to get drowsy, focusing on his bed as he made his way across the yard towards his house. *But wait! What about your problems with Maxxy and Richmond? What about your license? Sure, the problematic animal is taken care of, but do you think they're just gonna forget about kicking you out of Maldus? You're in their crosshairs, buddy. While you mull that over, why don't I give you a few more things to consider? You don't have a lot of food in the house. Certainly not enough for both you and your son. You'll have to buy some groceries. You gotta let Molly know about what happened last night. You need to check on Diego tomorrow when you take Ricky Lee in to get looked at. There's still the problem with the pond and those pesky snakes. And—*

"Goddamnit," Ranse sighed when he saw him. Noah was standing in the middle of the yard, staring up at the moon like he was studying a great piece of art from one of the Renaissance masters. Every so often, his son would dip or weave, like he was drunk. Sleepwalking, Sarah had told him. He's been sleepwalking. He started across the lawn in a slow jog, arguing with himself over the validity of the claim that one should never wake up a sleepwalker. He wasn't in the mood for tact. "Noah," he called. "Noah, buddy, wake up."

What he saw in his son's eyes when he reached him shook him almost as bad as the scene back at the deer blind. His eyes were glazed over, reminding him of a dead fish. Drool hung from his mouth in a long string.

For a moment, Ranse was certain that Noah wasn't sleepwalking at all but in a trance as if the moon itself had taken control of him and willed his feet to carry him out of the house and onto the lawn.

"Noah. Hey, Noah. You need to wake up!"

Noah's glazed eyes turned to his father. His lips pulled back in an eerie, haunting grin. Ranse saw that his son wasn't there. "The moon, daddy," he said. "Look at the moon."

"Yeah, it's big all right," Ranse said absently. "Noah, wake up." He put both hands on his son's shoulders and gave him a hard shake. "You're scaring daddy, son. You need to WAKE. UP!"

He gave Noah one more shake and his son's eyes cleared. He looked up at him like he didn't have any clue of how he'd gotten outside. "Where's bobba?" he asked.

Ranse sighed with relief. He wrapped his son up in his arms and picked him up. "Your mom had some things to do," he explained as he carried Noah back to the house. "For now, it's just you and me."

"Okay," Noah said, amazing his dad with how easily he accepted the explanation. Ranse wished he had that talent. It would certainly make falling asleep easier. He looked down and saw that Noah had done just that.

Chapter 9

Holes in the Ground

"Hey buddy, wanna go see some snakes?" The only words spoken over an otherwise silent bowl of Cheerios. By then, the monster wolf, Warren Maxxy and Jim Richmond, and even Sarah were all just a distant memory. This morning, Ranse felt downright chipper. The morning broke gorgeous and mild, much more befitting a morning in March rather than late May. The sky was blue and cloudless, and the air was filled with a potpourri of freshly cut grass, pine trees and of course, cow. Maldus seemed alive, much more alive than it had seemed recently.

Mick came in not long after the milk first splashed onto the cereal. He poured himself a cup of coffee, took a sip, and then promptly tossed it in the sink. He came over and sat beside Noah, tussling the kid's hair, and gave Ranse the morning report.

"Did you see Ricky?" Ranse asked.

Mick nodded. "A bit shaken up, but he seems to be doing just fine. I asked him if he wanted to come up here with me, that you were more than willing to take him to see the doctor. He told me he wanted to sleep a bit longer and promised he'd come by to check in with you."

"Good," Ranse said. "And you took…" he shot a glance at Noah who was happily munching away at his Cheerios, oblivious to much else. "*The thing,* to Grant's? Got it out of here?"

Mick nodded again. "Took some doing. That fuc…" He caught the curse before it was fully formed, glanced at Noah, and shot an apologetic look at Ranse. "That thing was heavy as you know what. Grant sliced his hand open on one of the thing's claws."

"He all right?" Ranse asked through a mouth full of Cheerios.

"Yeah," Mick shrugged. "Told me he was up to date on all his shots." They laughed, and it felt good. Ranse couldn't remember the last time it felt good to laugh. "Anyway," Mick continued, "He said he would get a tetanus shot from Doc Engle today."

"But he looked at it?"

"A little," Mick said, picking at a few stray O's that came loose from Noah's bowl. "Didn't find much, and after a while, he sent me away. Said he wasn't feeling that hot. Summer cold or something. So, if we got nothing better to do, I thought we'd go dredge up some snakes."

Ranse nodded. Business as usual around the Everly Ranch. He could live with that. He thought of Noah and second-guessed his invitation to Noah. He couldn't bring the kid out to the pond, not with potentially venomous snakes crawling around, and he and Mick with guns. Sarah hated guns, and a bit of her distaste rubbed off on Ranse as well. Especially after they had the kid. Noah could be unpredictable at times, and it wasn't beyond the scope of plausibility that he would reach into the water and grab one of the snakes or poke his head in front of them just as they cracked off a shot. The thought made Ranse shiver.

"We got any free hands this morning?"

Mick shook his head. "Fraid not. Well, Ricky Lee, but you know."

"Yeah," Ranse said. "What about Molly?"

"She's gone up to Missouri," Mick said, blushing a little.

Well, that settled it. Sarah would kill him if she ever found out, but he would make damn sure that nothing happened to their son. Ranse would make him sit still on the boat, and give him his iPhone to play with, maybe put some earbuds in to block out some of the loud noise. Besides, Noah liked watching the animals, even if they were blown to smithereens, and Ranse liked having his son around. He turned to Noah, tapping him on the shoulder. Noah's big, doe eyes looked up at his daddy like he was face-to-face with God.

"Are you ready to go see those snakes?"

Noah smiled and nodded ferociously. "Yeah!" he cried, jumping from his seat and running upstairs to get his shoes, his heavy footfalls tracing his course to his room.

Ranse watched him go, then turned back to see the disapproving look on Mick's face.

"What?" he asked. "There's nobody to watch him."

"If he gets hurt," Mick said as if Noah was his own child.

"He won't," Ranse ensured him, just as much as he ensured himself. "We'll both make sure of that."

"You know, I could go and do this myself," Mick offered.

"Don't even think about it," Ranse said. "I've let you pull too much weight as it is over the last few years. It's my ranch, and it's my responsibility. Just like Noah is my responsibility. Anyway, I like shooting snakes." Before the debate could get any further, Noah returned dressed in swim trunks and aqua-socks.

Mick looked the kid up and down then turned back to Ranse with a shit-eating grin. "You gonna tell him that there won't be any swimming?"

***

The house that Drake Best and Christina Marsh owned was a house in name only. To be perfectly honest, it was little more than a hole in the ground. There were two rooms in all. One, a multi-purpose kitchen, living room, and bedroom with the bathroom separated by a shower curtain, and the other was a garage converted into a cook-lab where Drake spent most of his days and the better part of his nights. Out in what they would consider to be the backyard, there were piles and piles of copper wiring. This, of course, was used to purchase the supplies needed to cook each batch of the yellowish crystal heaven that the two smoked more than they sold. There was so much copper wire in the back yard, that they had to resort to storing it underneath their little shanty, and it was what

Christina heard under there that brought her inside to wake Drake up.

She knew better than to wake her man unless it was an emergency. Drake's definition of emergency was very well defined. An emergency, in his mind, was one of two things: either the lab was on fire, or the cops had arrived. Anything else could wait until he woke up.

When he crashed, he crashed hard. Drake would stay up all night after getting good and iced down and would stay asleep for a good two, sometimes even three days, only waking up to shit piss or eat. If by some chance, Christina were to wake him up accidentally, a slam of the door perhaps, or dropping one of their commemorative *Garfield* drink glasses, then there would be hell to pay. Drake Best could beat the devil in doling out hell.

But whatever was under their house was a damn good reason, in her mind, to wake Drake up. She stood over him, staring into his sleeping but twitchy face, willing him to shake himself awake. He always woke up around this time to pee. Of course, today his bladder would hold. She reached out and gave his shoulder a little shove.

"Drake, baby?" she said, her voice a quivery and smoke addled drawl. "Drake, can you wake up for a second?"

Drake shot up with a snort. His sinuses, his throat, everything, had become a mucus-caked cesspit thanks to the meth. He wouldn't be singing in the church choir anytime soon.

"Goddamn, bitch, what I tell you about waking me up?" His yellow eyes were bloodshot from lack of sleep, but there was a redness in them that Christina only took as fury.

"There's something underneath the house," she said. "I went and got some wire from Maxxy's generator like you told me to, and, and when I was putting it up, something growled at me."

"It's probably a dog or skunk or something," Drake said, laying back down.

"I don't think it is," Christina said, just before his eyes closed completely. She could tell Drake was incensed, and she couldn't say what was scarier, the thing under the house or the thing in her bed. "Will you come and check it out? I promise I won't wake you up ever again if you just come and look."

Drake sighed, then ran his hands across his pock-marked face. He rubbed his eyes, then slammed his fists down on the bed several times as if to expel some of the rage.

"Fine!" he barked. He got up and crossed their little room in three steps, taking a shot at Christina on his way. His hand connected with her temple. "Hey!" she cried. "You don't have to be such an asshole!"

When he reached the door, he turned to her and jammed a finger in her face.

"You better hope that there's a bear underneath the house, bitch. Cause if I go out there, and all I find is a poodle, you won't be walking upright for a month!" He slammed the door as he left. Nursing her throbbing temple, Christina followed.

The crawlspace their house sat above had long since turned into something more akin to a burrow. The latch-access near the rear of the house had been left open a long time ago, and the space beyond had filled in with dirt, dead leaves, animal shit, and of course, copper wire. Perhaps a burrow wasn't the right term. It had turned into an overstuffed junk closet, where once Drake could crawl freely throughout, he could now only stick his arm halfway inside. He felt and listened, his caution screeching feverishly. Christina caught up with him, her arms folded around her chest like a worried housewife.

Drake looked up at her irritably. "Probably a cat," he grumbled, jerking his head in the direction of a pile of copper wire. "It dragged all that out so it could get inside."

Christina thought about it.

"I don't think so," she said. "Whatever I heard sounded much bigger than a cat."

"Well, it was a really big cat then," Drake said, rolling his eyes. Then, his hand brushed against something. "There you are," he said and jammed his arm a little further inside the crawlspace.

Ray Logue had been sleeping off the fight from last night in the crawlspace. He was beaten and hurt. His whole body, now naked and weak, ached and groaned with every passing second. This was the first place he stumbled across after the sun came up, after the change. The change back took a lot out of him. All he wanted to do was sleep.

But some pathetic creature had to come and disturb him. He gave her one of his best and most threatening growls and the girl scurried away like the scared little mouse she was. Ray thought that was the end of it, that he would sleep the day away and once the night came, he would head back home to his wife, or what was left of her. At least he wouldn't need to scrounge for food.

But wouldn't you know it? The little mouse returned, bringing another, bigger mouse with her. A bigger and braver mouse. This one was sticking his hand all the way into Ray's sanctuary. His hand brushed the hair on Ray's back. Ray turned with a snap, his eyes narrowing as it focused on the offending limb. He could make out the little fucker this hand belonged to. Recognized him. Drake Best's cracked and picked-at face was outlined in the shadow of the entrance. The little tweaker was a relentless sonofabitch. If he wanted to find Ray down here, he wouldn't stop until he did.

Ray let out another big growl, hoping to scare him off just as easily as he had the girl that he now realized was Christina Marsh. The growl accomplished one thing, at least. Drake pulled his hand back so quick it was like he touched a red hot flat-top griddle.

"Jeezus Pleezus, Chris, did you hear that?"

"That's what I was sayin'," Christina said. "It ain't no dog. Something big is under there."

"Do you think it's a lost tiger or something?" Drake asked. "Hey, maybe there's a reward!"

"Drake, I don't think—"

"Shut up and go get my gun," he said, and the hand came right back into the crawlspace. Ray continued to growl, as Drake pawed his way around in the dark. "The little prick just wouldn't give up! "It could be anything!" Drake continued, straining to get the whole length of his arm underneath the house. "It could be a bear, or a tiger, or one of those liger things!"

"Well, then don't you think you shouldn't be reaching inside where it's hiding?" Christina suggested.

With his free hand, Drake grabbed the gun from her. "Don't you worry about what I'm doing." Inside the crawlspace, the growling continued. "Once I grab whatever this is, I'll rip him out from under there and give him a good ol' double-tap—" His hand touched Ray's face just barely and Ray lashed out. In a split second, Drake pulled his arm from the crawlspace, screaming in agony. He dropped the gun, cradling the bloody mess of his right hand, now with only two digits instead of five.

Christina went into hysterics. She bent over to help Drake up, bobbled him, dropped him to the ground and ran off screaming into the woods. Drake went on screaming and bleeding out from the stump that was once his index finger. His head went swimmy, his skin taking on a much paler hue than normal. He passed out.

And Ray Logue went back to sleep.

***

While Christina Marsh ran screaming through the woods surrounding Maldus, Mick, Ranse, and Noah sat drifting peacefully on the pond near the game trail. It was quiet, broken only by the low drone of the trolling motor and the otherworldly grate of the dredge net as it pulled against the bottom of the watering hole.

"There we go," Mick said, pointing at a boiling mass of snakes as they swam for dry ground. Ranse and Mick opened fire, blowing the majority out of the water and watched as the shot dissolved them into a fine spray of blood and scales.

Noah, who was entranced with *The Wiggles* singing nonsense songs on Ranse's iPhone, barely noticed. He looked up and pointed. "Daddy, look! A snake!" A giant had popped up right beside the boat, its wet hide gleaming in the sunlight like a piece of wet glass. Its tail complete with a ten-chamber rattle, whipped wildly as it swam to get on the boat, playing its ominous electric symphony. Ranse pointed overboard and fired. The snake disappeared in an explosion of water.

"Did you see that?" he asked Mick.

"Yep," Mick said. "Rattler."

"Since when do rattlers hang out in the bottom of a pond?"

"They don't," Mick informed him. "And neither do copperheads." He pointed to another snake swimming furiously in the distance. "Ranse, is it just me, or has the animal life in Maldus been acting strange lately?"

"The understatement of the century," Ranse said. "Jesus, Mick, Ricky Lee just killed a monster wolf that belongs on Skull Island, not in the Ozarks. The cows are spooked. I have barely heard a bird chirp since April, the Cicadas started off strong but have since quit buzzing, and now we got a pond full of copperheads and rattlesnakes. So yeah, I think the wildlife's been acting funny. I wouldn't be surprised to find a nest of water snakes hanging out in a crack in one of the mountains."

Mick thought about it, his face growing dark. "What do you think is causing it?"

Ranse shrugged as he steered the boat around for another pass. "Global warming? Hell, I dunno. Maybe it's a La Niña year. Animals act funny sometimes."

Just then, the dredge net snagged onto something heavy. The boat jerked and almost went airborne as if they'd hit a rock. "What the fuck is that?" Mick asked.

Noah, alarmed by the sudden jolt, took his earbuds out. "Daddy?" he asked, "Did we hit something?"

"Not now," Ranse called to him. "Put your lifejacket on." Noah did as he asked, as Ranse struggled with the trolling motor. "We're stuck," he told them. "I'll try the outboard, but if that doesn't work, we're gonna lose a perfectly good dredger." Ranse flicked off the small trolling motor and started up the larger one. He gunned it and whatever was stuck on the bottom suddenly came loose. It looked like a log. A dozen or so snakes that had been using it for cover suddenly scrambled off. Mick went about dispatching them. One particularly large one took its time crawling off the log, and when it did, hitting the water with an enormous plop, the log shifted.

The dead, mangled face of Cole Vaughn stared back at them, bloated and pale. The three of them screamed.

"Jesus Christ!" Ranse said, reaching over and covering Noah's face. The boy shivered in his arms.

Cole was supposed to be in Oklahoma, gambling at the Indian Casino and scamming some of the local girls. Instead, here he was, bobbing in the middle of the watering hole. He was partially obscured by moss, but the parts of him that were exposed showed a purply-pale skin ripped in places that were now black and rotting.

Noah was crying now. Ranse picked him up and shushed him, rocking him this way and that.

"We gotta get him back home," Ranse said.

"What about the bod...what about Cole?" Mick asked.

"Drag him in too," Ranse answered. "Then call somebody to come and pick him up! Jesus Christ!"

Slowly, they motored their way back to shore, making sure that their macabre bounty hadn't come loose. Mick was on the phone with one of Ray Logue's underlings, telling him to get Doc Engle out there as soon as possible. Ranse took his time trying to calm Noah down. Here he thought today was going to be a good day.

On the other side of the pond, the surviving land snakes slowly slipped back into the water and disappeared.

***

Doc Engle was the only people doctor in Maldus, and the only pathologist, coroner, and medical examiner for that matter. His office was situated in a small concrete building aptly named with one word, like all the rest of the buildings in Maldus: Clinic. He'd just settled in for the morning, with a bagel and cream cheese, and hoped to follow it with a nice long nap on the couch in his office. He'd finished stitching up Diego Padilla not long ago, and after a series of rabies and tetanus shots sent him home. But then Grant Riddell came in with a gouged hand, which meant more stitches and another tetanus shot. God, he needed some help.

His dance card was full today. He had the autopsy of the drifter to deal with, a few general wellness visits, and he stared down a mound of paperwork he had to get through before he could even think of stepping foot out of this place. He'd get to it, but first…

He picked up the bagel and got close enough to his mouth to pick up a few tiny bits of cream cheese on his taste buds before a voice came over the PA. "Doctor Engel, you're needed at the ambulance bay. Doctor Engel, needed at the ambulance bay."

"Damn," Engel shrugged and let his bagel drop back to the plate with a heartbreaking thud.

Teague Childress stood by an idling ambulance using its bulk to conceal himself as he jammed a huge plug of snuff between his lower lip and gums. When he saw Doctor Engel arrive sullenly on the ambulance bay, he swiped his hands across the front of his pants and licked away the last bit of Copenhagen on his lips. The effort to conceal his use of tobacco was for not, however, as the plug gave him a distinct underbite. He smiled as Engel approached.

"How ya doin' today, Doc?" he asked.

"I'd be doing better if I could have my breakfast in peace," Engel grumbled. "What d'ya got for me?"

Teague hitched a thumb towards the closest ambulance and without thinking, spat a huge wad of snuff onto the ground. He looked up at Engel sheepishly.

"Sorry about that," he said, then straightening up, he added, "Got us another body. Found on the Everly Ranch. Real nasty."

"God," Engel sighed. Another body of course meant another autopsy, which of course meant another stack of paperwork to add to the already leaning tower he had on his desk. "I thought Sheriff Logue usually deals with this sort of thing."

Teague shrugged. "Yeah, we haven't heard from him today. Must be sick."

"Got any idea of who it is?" Engel asked.

"Actually, I do," Teague said. "Cole Vaughn. One of Everly's ranch hands. We used to hang out together back in the day." Teague shook his head and let another tobacco filled loogie fly. This time, he didn't apologize. "Really is a shame."

"Is he bagged up?"

"Of course, he is," Teague said.

"Well bring him inside. You know where the morgue is?" Teague nodded. "Good. Put him in one of the free lockers." Engel left and went back to his breakfast.

The deaths weren't what bothered him. Death in Maldus was as natural as snow in February. There were a little over fifteen-hundred people in town, and there were just as many free holes in the ground. Two, maybe three deaths in one day was not uncommon. What was uncommon was performing more than one autopsy.

Doc Engel was a multi-tasker and knocked out a bit of paperwork over breakfast. He did a few examinations shortly thereafter and got to the bodies sometime after noon. The morgue was a cold and quiet place, a place for the dead. Engel didn't like spending more time in there than he absolutely had to. On his list of jolly old times, autopsies were at the bottom. He became a doctor to preserve life, not to find a cause for why it ended. That's what he told everybody, anyways. The real reason he hated being in the morgue was because he hated the idea of death. Every time he performed one of these procedures it felt as if the dead were pulling him in close as if to be with them. By the time he was done, his mood was grim, to say the least, as if all the color had been sucked from the world.

To combat this, he played show tunes on the CD player he had stashed away upon first opening the clinic. Today's selection was from *Hamilton*. As Lin-Manuel Miranda waxed poetically about the life and times of Alexander Hamilton, Engel opened the cabinet containing the vagrant Ray Logue shot the day before. Autopsies on police-involved shootings were mandatory. Not by the powers of Maldus, but by the state attorney general. Engel rolled his eyes. If you asked him, Ray Logue did the world a favor by taking one more panhandler off the streets.

He turned the *Hamilton* soundtrack down, pulled out a small digital recorder, and began his recording.

"Subject is a male, white, approximately thirty-three years of age. Upon preliminary examination, the means of death seems to be three gunshot wounds. Two to the chest, and one more to the head. The cause, while blatantly obvious, is still unconfirmed. Making my first incisions now." He clicked off the recorder and turned up *Hamilton*.

With a shaky hand, he picked up the scalpel. He hated this part, show tunes or no show tunes. Cutting into a corpse, required by law or not, just seemed obscene. Not to mention the overwhelming feeling of the heebie-jeebies it gave him. Any minute, Engel thought that the corpse of the vagrant would open its eyes and ask just what he thought he was doing.

Engel made the first cut, slicing the man from groin to sternum. The man's blood had pooled near his stomach, and the slicing was a bit harder to do properly around this area. The scalpel stalled just near the man's navel. Engel pressed down with his free hand for leverage and began to pull the blade upwards again.

But the blade wouldn't move. The blood, it seemed, had hardened into a substance similar to frozen candle wax. Engel jerked it upwards. Still nothing. He tried it again, and again, each time moving no more than a centimeter. Finally, his frustration and eagerness to get out of the morgue got the better of him. With one great grunt of effort, Engel ripped the scalpel the rest of the way to the cadaver's chest. The noise it made was nauseating, like sutures being ripped from the skin. The congealed blood didn't spurt from the body so much as it lurched like a giant pustule being popped.

Engel's hands shook harder. There was a bright, brilliant, flash of pain.

"Oh, no," he said, realizing what he'd done. He looked down to confirm it. The combination of a shaky hand, his haste, and the tough belly of the cadaver had all led to this.

The cut was about two inches in length and had ripped through Engel's latex glove, and more importantly, through his skin. It cut almost all the way to the bone, slicing through muscle and tendon. And, Engel realized with a sudden rush of terror, it was intermingling with the cold, waxy blood of the vagrant.

With a cry of disgust, Engel pushed himself away from the examination table. He let the scalpel fall to the floor. He had no idea what the hell this man had in his system, and what could still be crawling around, albeit slowly, in his blood. Hepatitis? AIDS? The shake in his scalpel hand now wormed its way through his entire body. Whatever this man had, he now carried it.

"Jesus, God. Oh, fuck, oh, fuck!" Engel cried. In a purely reactionary response, he fell to his knees and puked all over the morgue's floor. "Oh please, don't let me have anything. Please, God, please!"

The paperwork could wait. As could the other autopsy, and the rest of his appointments. He called Sheila, his secretary, and told her he would be out indefinitely, and that all emergencies should be forwarded to Saint Vincent's in Fayetteville. Before she could probe him, the phone had hung up and he was out the door and running towards his car. There were fifteen-hundred holes in the ground in Maldus, and Henry Engel was certain he just took a step into one of them.

***

"Gentlemen," Warren regarded the group of Tyson executives with as much warmth as he could muster. There was a chill running through him. A piercing, brittle chill, and he knew at any minute one of Ray Logue's boys would come barging through the door to the AAA's conference room and ask him just why the missus was laid up in bed covered in piss and shit with a square-shaped dent in her noggin. That would end this little tête-à-tête pretty damn quick. That was if he didn't muck things up in the interim.

He was normally good at buttering up the people he wanted to come to Maldus, usually business-types or rich folks looking for a quiet mountain town to lay down roots, but he usually had Jim Richmond with him. Jim was the ice to his fire. Warren would talk the exciting stuff, then Jim would swoop in and talk beeswax. It was usually the beeswax that settled things, for good or for ill. Warren felt neutered without Jim there, like a bird with a bum wing. He was beginning to sweat, felt the cold, calculating eyes of the Tyson execs staring him down. He could hear the non-existent tick-tock coming from the digital clock mounted to the wall. God, he just wanted to go home, to slip into bed next to Geena. She was beginning to smell a bit sour, now, but that was okay. Just so long as she was with him and him with her.

"Gentlemen, I want to welcome y'all to Maldus." Ok, so far so good. "A town that is eager for your business and more than ready to welcome y'all in like family. Around each corner, in each store or on the porch of every single home, you will find a myriad of downhome, feel-good country life." Yeah, he was getting in the groove. It struck him how easily he could act like nothing was wrong.

"And that's what you would be investing in, should you choose to bring your business here: life. As you most assuredly saw on your way in, Maldus is set on acres upon acres of clean, unadulterated country, surrounded by the majestic Ozarks. Arkansas is called the Natural State, and we here in Maldus like to think we're a shining example of why we earned that moniker."

He took a pause for dramatic effect, to let the words sink in. He always sold Maldus as if it were a timeshare. Appeal to their senses and to their emotions. Let the big-bad businessmen feel like they were doing something good for the little folk. It worked like a charm. Now would usually be the time where Jim would thank him and get down to brass tacks. But Jim wasn't here, and Warren was finished with his spiel. Now it was time to do something he absolutely detested. He had to improvise, adapt. For someone so stuck in his ways, it was like losing a limb. Warren smiled a huge politician's smile.

"I'll tell you what," Warren nervously continued, "why don't we pile into my truck, and I'll take y'all on a little tour around town? That way, you can get the real feel of what a great place Maldus is."

"Cut the act, Warren," one of the execs, a big, burly black man who barely fit into his suit said while holding up his hand. He had a stern look about him, a no-nonsense, don't-try-to-sell me look. He was concerned with one thing only: bottom lines. Money. Mister Moneyman, Warren thought.

Warren quieted down immediately, cringing on the inside at cowering before a black man. It was supposed to be the other way around! He wasn't there when Warren visited their offices a few days ago, but moneymen rarely ever were on cold calls. *Jesus, Jim, where the hell are you?*

"You don't need to sell us on this place," Mmoneyman continued. "I drive through Maldus nearly every day. Three out of the four of us live damn near down the street! You know what I see when I drive through here?" Moneyman cocked his eyebrows, waiting for an answer.

"Well…" Warren began.

"I see another hole in the ground."

"Technically, a hole in the ground would be Pine Bluff," Warren corrected with a chuckle and snort. Nobody joined in.

Moneyman frowned back at him, unamused.

"Places like Maldus, are a dime a dozen," he said. "I came here under the impression that we would be discussing what you would want from us and what we want from you. I've been in this business for a long time, Warren. I've gone through my fair share of sales pitches."

"Well," Warren gulped. "I-I,"

Moneyman held out his hand and one of the other Tyson lackeys, this one a short balding man in a suit picked off the shelves of Wal-Mart, handed him a sheet of paper. Warren recognized it as a bid request.

"I thought we would be speaking to a…Jim Richmond? I was told he would have more information regarding things like licensing, tax incentives, pricing agreements…" he rolled his hand around as he continued blabbing about landholdings and equity and commercial zoning. Warren felt flushed. Moneyman was mansplaining money to him! He was basically telling Warren that his business acumen was for shit. That was something he just couldn't stomach. He owned the biggest ranch in Maldus. One of the biggest in the goddamn state! He'd rather this uppity bastard tell him he had a tiny dick!

No, don't go there.

Moneyman finished his lecture and reached into his pocket. He slipped a business card across the table, a small bone-white rectangle embossed with his important details. Uppity bastard.

"Here's my contact info," he said. "When you reach Mr. Richmond, tell him I'll be happy to discuss things further, though I have to say that his absence doesn't bode well for our decision." They got up and left Warren in the conference room to melt in his chair.

He checked his phone. Twenty-three calls to Jim in the hour leading up to the meeting, and not so much as a text message to tell him that his illness was worse than he thought. A thought occurred to him just then. Was it possible that Jim's absence was on purpose? Could it be that Jim had a change of heart, and no longer wanted a large conglomerate like Tyson Foods in Maldus after all?

Warren let out a small gasp as the thought evolved into something more sinister. Maybe Jim did want Tyson around, but he wanted them all to himself. Maybe he feigned sick, so he didn't have to show up today, throw Warren to the wolves to make an ass of himself and lose all credibility as a businessman and as a voice of Maldus. Could that be the case? The way the whole town seemed to be defying him lately, he thought it could.

The thought evolved yet again. Warren thought that Jim could be at his house right now, leading Ray Logue and his two Barney Fifes into his bedroom to show them Geena, what he'd done to her. Then he thought of what they would do to her. If he wasn't sitting down, he would have keeled over. His knees weak, his blood boiling, he forgot all about the Tyson executives and their uppity black leader, Mr. Moneyman. All he could think about was getting home.

****

"I just left him!" Christina sobbed as she ran full-tilt through the woods, certain that whatever bit Drake—no, whatever maimed Drake—was after her too, claws outstretched and teeth gnashing. She could feel its hot breath on the back of her neck, hear its heavy footfalls keeping pace with her, but Christina, despite her vices, was an inherently caring person. And despite his words and fists' best efforts to convince her otherwise, she loved Drake Best. She wanted to scream so loudly it would scare the monsters away, and she did scream, but what came out was, "I just left him!"

Eventually, she ran and screamed herself out, and she stopped her run dead in its tracks. She had cut a clear course straight through the woods, and though she knew them well, she was deeper than she or Drake had ever been before. She always thought the deepest part of the woods would be quiet, muffled by the thick branches and blankets of leaves, dark and still. What she found was a place teeming with life and making a symphony of sounds.

Things rustled in the brush, in nooks and crannies, they slithered, hooted, and brayed. For a moment, she thought she'd somehow slipped into Carrol's famed Wonderland.

A fox appeared in front of her, startled by her sudden appearance as much as she was startled by it. It froze, stared her down and then lifted its head ever so slightly. It sniffed the air. Whatever it was afraid of, Christina was not it, and it slowly slipped back into the brush.

The whole world came alive then. To her right, she saw sparrows, a flock of them, darting between branches. She couldn't remember the last time she saw a bird, let alone this many of them. At her feet, a colony of fire ants toiled away at building their new nest. They didn't bother with her and just kept on working. It was as if the human population was no longer a threat to any of the species of the world as if they were just one of many lower classes of the animal kingdom. Just to the left of her, a mother cat nursed her kitten. A pair of coyotes not far away left them alone. Snakes crossed from fallen limbs to the mucky wet leaves, curled up underneath them, and went to sleep. "What is this place?" she said, wondering if maybe she'd slipped into some upside-down world where predator and prey coexisted in peace, some haven where there was no need for food or drink. The Garden of Eden. She wondered if God allowed meth in the Garden. If he did, then she would be able to stay here forever.

But what good was Eden without her Adam? The last she saw of him he was clutching his mangled hand to his chest, making ungodly noises of anguish and pain. She couldn't leave him like that. She couldn't live here, in this paradise, without Drake. She wouldn't deserve it. Slowly she traced her steps back.

This was where it was quietest, closer to the town, to civilization. This was where fear lived and breathed in great shuddering gasps. Drake was where she'd left him. He was turned on his side facing their house, his hand still clutched meekly to his chest. She watched him for a moment, trying to pinpoint the moment where his chest would rise or fall with a subtle breath. He didn't move.

"Drake?" she said. "Baby, are you all right? Do I need to call an ambulance?"

Drake didn't answer.

"Drake, baby? Quit messing around. How bad are you hurt?"

The silence surrounding the house was broken as something underneath rustled around. The man she recognized as Ray Logue, the sheriff that had busted both her and Drake on numerous occasions, but it didn't quite look like the man she'd come to associate with buzzkills and overnight stints in the Maldus Jail.

Logue was naked, his penis a little lump in a bed of graying pubic hair. His crazed eyes searched hers as he relieved himself on Drake.

"Why are you here?" he heaved in a low, breathless grumble. "This is my place. You can't take it from me."

Christina searched for something to say, but her mind was addled by the vision in front of her. Never once, in all the time she'd spent either hiding from or unwillingly interacting with Logue, had she pictured him naked. His pale body was now paler than before, his farmer's tan now washed out. The only speck of color on his body was the dirt from the muck underneath the house, and the wide splotch of dark red that formed a sort of beard from his mouth to the top of his chest. His thinning hair stood up in tangles and strands. He looked like an escaped convict from the loony-bin on the Missouri border.

"But, Sheriff, I-I…"

"Why are you here?" he demanded again, his mind absent from his voice.

"I live here," Christina finally blurted out. She pointed a shaky finger at the body on the ground. "You know me, and you know Drake. Drake's my…well, he's my husband. I think you might have bit him or something. I came back to check on him and see if he was okay. I might need to take him to the 'mergency room. Do you need to go to the 'mergency room, Sheriff?"

"No," Logue grunted. "Go away. I'm tired."

"But what about Drake?" Christina said, a new panic rising in her throat. She wanted to be back at the haven then, back in Eden.

Logue regarded Drake coldly. With one barefoot, he flipped the body around to face her. Christina gasped. Drake had two mouths now. The one on his face upturned in an utter look of horror, and the other, the one just below the first, the one that used to be his throat, was smiling.

Christina was able to scream now. Ray didn't like screaming. He wanted to sleep, and this strung-out little creature wasn't going to let him do that. Christina went on screaming even as Ray stormed over to her. She kept screaming as his hands found her throat. She didn't stop until he pressed the front to the back, knotting the air off in her larynx like a pinched balloon. When he let go, he took the front with him, giving her a smile that matched Drake's.

***

"You sure you don't want a beer?" Mick asked as he took a seat next to Ranse on the back deck. "Been a long day, and as far as addiction goes, I don't think beer counts." The night was alien to them in its normalcy. Night birds were in the trees, hooting and chirping, and the electric buzz of the cicadas was announcing their presence.

The evening was warm too. Blessedly warm. Beer drinking weather.

Ranse sighed. "I'm good. Beer's not what got me into my earlier trouble, but why tempt the gods of sobriety?" Ranse held up a can of Coke, the drips of condensation matched the beads of sweat on his brow. "You know, with all the excitement, I forgot that today marks a whole year sober for me."

Mick raised his eyebrows. "Oh? Well, congratulations."

"Thanks. Don't really feel like celebrating though. You know what I was thinking while I drove Noah back? While you were dragging Cole's body out of the pond? I was thinking, Jesus, I could use a hit right now. A snoot or a bump or a shot." He laughed bitterly. "I guess that's my go-to for dealing with stress and all things nasty."

"But you didn't," Mick reminded him. "You got your son away from a traumatizing environment. You acted like a dad. That's a win in my book. How is Noah, by the way?"

"Sleeping, thank god." Ranse sipped at his Coke. It felt flat, coated his tongue like liquid aluminum. "I think he'll be all right. With any luck, he'll have forgotten all about it by tomorrow."

"Kids are resilient like that," Mick said.

"Yeah, I just hope some of it rubs off on me."

"You'd be surprised. You want me to stick around for a while? Keep you company?"

Ranse shook his head. "Na. I'm probably gonna pass out here in a little bit. What about you? Tomorrow's your day off, isn't it?"

"Supposed to be," Mick said. "But with Cole gone, and Diego out of commission for a while, I figured you could use some help."

Ranse waved the notion off. "Take your day. We don't have much to do. Me and Rick and a few other guys can take care of it all."

"You sure?" Ranse nodded, and Mick got up. He picked the six, now five, pack of beer from the deck and slung it over his shoulders. "Well, then I guess I'll leave you to it then."

"Where're you going?" Ranse asked.

"I dunno, but I don't wanna tempt you more than I have, and I hate drinking alone." Mick left Ranse on the deck. For a moment he considered taking his drinks back to the guest house with him and watching the Cardinals' game, but the thought of going back to a place still filled with the belongings of the recently deceased, frightened him a bit. There was a part of him that was certain he would open the door and Cole (bloated and rotting and leaking pond water from the mangled openings that crossed the whole of his body) would be waiting there for him.

He and Cole never saw eye to eye, but they did have a relationship that stretched further than being coworkers. Like a rambunctious son and a disapproving father. Mick realized that was the type of relationship he shared with everyone on the ranch. He realized that he had no one with whom to grieve. Halfway to the guesthouse, he took a sharp turn in the opposite direction.

"Hey," Molly said while sitting on her porch, drinking a mix of Earl Gray and Jack Daniels. She called this particular cocktail the "fishing trip." It didn't taste very good, but after one or two of them, she'd be out like a light and snoring with the same droning repetition as the cicadas. She had one more sip left to go and was contemplating making another when she spotted Mick coming up her drive, appearing from the darkness like a lost phantom. In his hand, he carried the remnants of a six-pack. One remained.

"Hey," Mick mumbled. Though it took much more to get him drunk, a few beers did wonders for Mick's sociability. He looked up at Molly, dressed in a flannel robe, and judging by its shape on her, not much else. Something deep inside told him to go to her, grab her and kiss her, but he remained in her yard. "Did you hear?"

"Yeah," Molly sighed. "Jesus, I'm sorry Mick. How are you holding up? How's Ranse?"

"I think…" Mick fumbled with his beer, trying to open it. He lost his grip and it tumbled to the ground, its bright metallic surface turning a muddy shade of brown. Mick tumbled right along after it and with a sudden shock, Molly realized he was sharing something with her that she suspected he hadn't shared with anybody else in his adult life: Mick was crying.

She ran to him, not minding the pebbles and sweetgum balls that dug into her bare feet. She'd just taken a bath, and knew by the time this was all settled, she would need another one. She wrapped Mick in her arms, feeling his body heave against hers as he wept. Molly suspected that deep down, Mick understood just how good it felt to let it all out. It felt good to remove a weight from his shoulders. It felt good to feel sane. It felt good to feel human, something that Mick, in his everyday no bullshit world, was very disinclined to feel.

Above them, the stars twinkled like a million luminescent moths drawn to the flame of the half-moon.

It was the first day of the lunar cycle.

Chapter 10

A Stable Pattern

In the days that followed, Maldus entered into what meteorologists would call, "a stable pattern." Ranse Everly was left alone, and his ranch was on the mend from the tragic loss of one of his foremen and the financial loss of a few heads of cattle. Fences were mended, calves were born, heads were sent to the auction block, business as normal.

Only a few things bothered him in that stretch between full moons. First, was the concerned call he received from Sarah's mother in Little Rock. It turned out that Sarah hadn't returned home the night she dropped Noah off.

"She never came home," Sarah's mom said. "She didn't stay there, did she? You two aren't…"

"Back together?" Ranse asked. "No. She made that clear enough last night. Sorry, I would have checked up on her when I realized that she never called to speak with Noah, but things have been a little crazy here, Tammy."

There was a long silence on the other end of the line.

"Ranse…you…didn't do anything, did you?" A stifled sob. "I know she broke your heart, but you have to realize she was only doing what was best for her and Noah, and you weren't in your right mind at the time."

"What? Jesus Christ, Tammy, no! I would never hurt Sarah if that's what you're implying. I swear on Noah's life, I wouldn't! The night she brought him here, I took him to bed and when I came back down, she was gone. That's it. I would have called, but like I said, things have been crazy here." He thought about it for a moment. "You don't think this has anything to do with her cancer, do you?"

"Cancer?" Tammy gasped. "What cancer?"

"Did Sarah tell you why she brought Noah up here?"

"She said that you wouldn't stop bothering her. That you were threatening legal action. Dick was planning on going up there and straightening you out, but she told him and me that it was your right after all and that you were clean."

That was it then. Ranse explained to a horrified and disbelieving mother that her daughter had come up here and told him that she had cancer. Though there were many explanations as to why she disappeared, the most believable one was that instead of facing the cancer head-on, she took her own life. The monster wolf they killed never once popped into Ranse's mind.

And besides the first and only outburst, murder didn't cross Tammy's mind. As much as it pained her, and as illogical as it was, suicide seemed the only logical answer. Sarah's demeanor had also changed in the last few weeks leading up to her trip to Maldus. And it all started after her trip to the doctor.

"We have to find her, Ranse."

Or maybe she just wanted to have one last fling before stepping into what was sure to be pure hell. Yeah, that seemed just as logical. Maybe Sarah just wanted a little fun.

"It is possible that she took a jaunt over to Oklahoma and is messing around at the Casino."

Another pause as Tammy contemplated it.

"Yes," she finally said. "It's not like Sarah to contemplate suicide. Her faith in God wouldn't let her dream of such a thing."

Are we thinking of the same Sarah? Ranse thought. "No, I'm sure she wouldn't."

"But we need to find her," Tammy said.

"Yes, ma'am, we do. Her son needs her, and if the cancer was as serious as she said, then she needs the doctor. You want me to call the local cops? Set up a search party?"

"I'll take care of it," Tammy said. "You know how perceptive your son is. If he senses something is wrong with his momma, he'll be inconsolable. Better to wait until we have answers. I'll call the state police."

"Ok," Ranse said. "Keep me updated. I'm sure everything will be fine."

That was several days ago, and there had been nothing sinse. No visit from the state police, no calls, no answers when he called. Yes, it was worrisome. Yes, he wanted to go out and look for her, and he was sure the guys would take care of the ranch if he did, but the husband in him just couldn't bring himself to do it. The husband in him, the dad in him, and the recovering addict in him. Answers could be a terrible thing sometimes. He could picture finding her shacked up with some random guy in a hotel somewhere, or hanging in its closet, stinking and putrid, or on a lonely stretch of Arkansas highway, obliterated by a hit and run. There was no coming back from those kinds of answers. Deep-down Ranse knew that it wasn't the husband in him, or the dad in him, or the addict in him that didn't want those answers, but the coward in him. He swallowed it down—no news, is good news—and went to work and cared for his son.

But his son was the other thing that bothered him. Noah had closed himself off a bit. Always a bit of a nature lover, he spent more time indoors, playing his Xbox. He didn't want to see the cows, he didn't smile or laugh as much, and their walks never stretched further than the edge of Ranse's front yard. Ranse was certain that it was still the vision he had of Cole Vaughn's dead body floating to the surface of the pond. That sort of thing would scar a child for life. He had to help him get over it.

The walks became an everyday occurrence. An inch past the yard, the walks became a carry, Noah never leaving his arms until they were safely back on their home turf. But it was something at least. He took him to Molly's and let him visit with the goats. He took him past the watering hole, as a sort of immersion therapy. That was always the worst part of their treks. Noah would hide his little face against Ranse's chest. Sometimes he would cry. Every time, he would shake. And as soon as they were back home, inside he would go, and he'd be back in front of the television for Xbox or the Wiggles.

It was a stable pattern.

Across the ranch, Warren Maxxy spent his days in bed with his wife. The bed had become a cesspit with pools of waste, old food, and sweat, but he didn't mind. He was safe here. He was home. He loved Geena more than life itself, and he thought that, now, she loved him too. They made love almost every day, and while a one-sided habit, he liked to think she had come to appreciate his prowess. Knocks on the door went unanswered, phone calls to the house went unanswered, his cell had not been charged since it died the day of the botched Tyson meeting, yet he wasn't worried. He could stay in bed forever with Geena, and he planned on doing just that even if the world outside burned all around them.

Under the house in the woods, surrounded by bones of small animals and the two humans unlucky enough to cross his path, Ray Logue slept.

In town, Doc Engel continued to see patients, though he'd been fighting an oncoming flu for what felt like weeks. His counterpart, Grant Riddell, did the same, under the same conditions.

Mick and Molly's relationship blossomed finally. At night, after work, they could be seen getting drinks at the Bar, or having dinner at the Diner. Afterward, they would retire to her house or his, mostly hers, and watch movies or baseball games. They talked, they cuddled. They made love for the first time the night after Cole Vaughn was found. It was nice, it was a special thing they shared, something all theirs, but it was never as special as the night Mick came to her and cried. He had shared something much more special than his body, then. Their relationship sprouted like a brilliant flower from that one act, and it was special. It was good.

Life went on. Business as usual. A stable pattern.

And it's in these stable patterns that chaos brews. A storm is an inevitability. This stable pattern lasted for fifteen days, the length between the new moon and its late phases. In these fifteen days, heat returned to Maldus. Pools reopened, fireworks were fired, barbeques were barbequed. People had come to see the events of last month's blue moon as nothing more than just "one of those things." That's how it always goes.

Consider the Florida Everglades. A small swath of land in the grand scheme of things, but rife with its own native flora and fauna. By the year that Maldus, Arkansas was ravaged by werewolves, it had become home to a vast and still growing population of giant snakes.

When the first Burmese Python was spotted in the Everglades, most likely the result of foolish pet owner releasing it upon discovering they could no longer take care of such a creature, it was shot and killed. Up to that point, pets went missing. Children and some adults arrived in the hospital with mysterious bites after fooling around in the wetlands, high grass, or brush. But the first snake, or what was believed to be the first, was killed and it went down in the annals of "just one of those things."

What they didn't know at the time was that the one reckless pet owner was instead, several reckless pet owners. Burmese pythons, red-tailed boas, an anaconda or two, and even a few exotic venomous snakes were released into the wild over a course of several years. And, of course, there were the hurricanes. They toppled ecological exhibits, zoos, aquariums, and herpetological tourist attractions. Hundreds of captive exotic snakes were now free to roam. Soon, a sole exotic animal that, by natural law, should have died away in this foreign habitat, happened upon another of its kind. They mated and made more exotic offspring. There was food, shelter, and as they were left unchecked, the species relegated to jungles and rice fields, lagoons on the other side of the world, were flourishing.

The spread came gradually, populations of native animals like marsh rabbits, foxes, and raccoons suddenly nosedived. More residents began to find large snakes in their pools, in their homes. They found them feasting on the family dog or cat. Three children went missing. Suddenly the question wasn't how did it spread, but how do we suppress it?

The werewolf problem spread with much more sickening rapidity. The virus, the curse, or whatever it was, was contagious, but not just spreadable by breaking of the skin. It was spread as easily as Grant Riddell sneezing while he waited in line at the Mercantile and the mother and daughter ahead of him breathing it in. The little girl went to day-camp the next day, subsequently biting a little boy who was picking on her. That little boy went home and during dinner, he talked with his mouth full. A wad of spit hit his father in the eye. Dad got pissed off and left his family to go have a drink in the bar. After a few too many beers, he got into a scrap with one of the local ranch hands and the two swapped blows, both breaking the other's skin. The ranch hand went home and fucked his girlfriend, a quite literal licking of the wounds. And on it spread.

Perhaps the host that did the most damage was Doc Engel. In the days leading to the full moon, he must have seen half of Maldus's population. That's a lot of open orifices. Humans, after all, are invasive by nature. All one has to do is look at war. The Europeans wiped out whole populations in the Americas with disease, slavery, and murder. Buffalo were wiped out in the Wild West by trappers. Big game in Africa, despite its protected status, is still sought after by poachers and rich, fat assholes. Humans are invasive. Vicious, unrelenting, and invasive.

Maldus was a small town, and sickness and gossip spread in small towns like a spark on dry grass. In the days before the full moon, if someone was out about town, chances were, they were infected. Those who were not, sat cloistered within their homes, sharing a bed with lovers. They tended to their cows or their goats or whatever else the first beast left for them to tend to. Others sat in their favorite easy chair, rubbing their temples and fighting off the ache of addiction as their little boy watched the mind-numbing Wiggles on television. All of them blissfully unaware that there were real monsters in the world.

All of them blissfully unaware that the stable pattern was just about to break.

Chapter 11

<u>New Moon</u>

The cold came back with such a ripping fierceness that Ranse had to put the heat on in the middle of June. The sudden change in barometric pressure, he assumed, was the cause of the monumental headache he was now suffering from, his temples at the epicenter. He rubbed and kneaded at them, every so often opening his bloodshot eyes to steal a glance at Noah, who was perfectly content with his own copy of the Lego Batman game. He thought it could have been that videogame (with its knocks, beeps, and whistles) that was causing the headache, not the temperature dip. Maybe it was both.

Maybe it was a combination of several things. The weather, sure, the videogame, undeniably, but the day had started with a phone call from Ricky Lee telling him that Diego was racked with some kind of nasty infection. The wounds, almost all healed now, were swollen and red. He had a fever and his stomach was, in his words, "all sorts of fucked-up." Doc Engel was out with a nasty case of the summer flu, so a trip to Rogers and a legitimate emergency room was in order. Ranse said he would take him tomorrow and charged Ricky with keeping an eye on him. Ricky said he would but had been cautious to keep his distance from Diego ever since he was attacked. Most everyone on the ranch did. It wasn't hard, seeing as how Diego pretty much kept to his bed over the last month. Ranse kept him on with worker's comp, hoping to get him back to full health.

But wait, friends and neighbors, there's more! Ranse got another call not long after that. It was Tammy, Sarah's mom. She called to inform him that Sarah's car had been found not far from Maldus, on the edge of Jim Richmond's ranch. It was completely totaled as if it had been hit by a meteor the size of the Ozarks, but there was no sign Sarah had been in it. The state police were now treating it as a recovery/missing person's case. Ranse felt his knees drop to the ground. The thrumming in his head intensified, nearly blinding him. He squeezed his eyes shut to fight the headache and tears. Tammy was going on about something. She was crying too, almost screaming. He wanted to ask her to keep it down but didn't have the strength to form the words. So, he listened. And listened. Words blended into others, but one thing did stick out.

"Sorry, Tammy," he said in a groan. "What did you say?"

"I said the state police will be over to talk to you in the morning. Will you be there?"

Other words she had spoken started to clear in his mind. "Foul play," were two of them. He wanted to protest, argue, and ask how she could possibly think he could hurt someone that he adored, but let it pass.

"Sure, I'll be here," he said and hung up the phone. He closed his eyes, settling back into his easy chair, and tried to relax.

Beep, bop, knock-knock, CRASH! All set to the theme song from Tim Burton's 1989 movie, *Batman.*

Ranse let out a miserable groan and shifted in his chair. "Noah, buddy, do you wanna turn off the game and maybe watch some TV?" He cracked open his eyes, and streaks of pain rushed through him. God, he hated Lego right now. He hated Batman, Robin, and the Swedish fuckers who thought a blending of their company with said intellectual property was a good idea.

Noah didn't turn to answer, his eyes fixed on the blocky visage of Batman as he constructed his Batmobile from a pile of pegged rubble. He sat on the rug, in the style that teachers nowadays called, "crisscross-applesauce,'" wiggling his ass to the cadence of the music. Ranse's suggestion not only threw him offbeat but seemed to fill him with an unspeakable anger that boiled just below his innocent features.

"No," he finally answered, emphatically.

Ranse sighed. It was a classic impasse with children. You wanted them to be happy, you didn't want to take from them, but you didn't want to suffer or worse, start a fight. And that was what he saw in his son's eyes, what every parent sees in their children's eyes from time to time. *Go ahead and make me stop. Better yet, turn the TV completely off and see what happens. Do it, old man, and I will come down on you with the weight of a million tons of bricks. I. Will. Crush. You.*

Every child had it in them, and in Noah's case, the result always seemed to teeter on the catastrophic. *Beep, boop, knock-knock. CRASH!*

"Noah, we really need to take a break," Ranse said, a little more forceful than before.

"No!" Noah yelled, his voice grating on Ranse's headache like one of those dental probes on an infected root. Outside, the sun was going down, sending beams through the blinds and right into Ranse's eyes. He realized then that he was losing his temper. God, he didn't want to lose his temper.

"Noah, I'm not asking. You turn that game off, or you won't be able to play it for a week. Do you understand me?" He thought that Sarah, wherever she was (please, let her be okay), would have approved of his parenting decision, just then.

"You can't tell me what to do," he retorted with such conviction that for a second, Ranse believed that was fact. "Bobba said I don't have to do anything I don't want to."

"Well, your mom… your mom isn't here right now, kiddo, and I am."

Noah finally turned to him. "Yeah-huh, she is. I saw heroutside my window last night!"

"Oh?" Ranse said, the last comment striking him as heartbreaking and odd, but nothing more than that. At least the game was paused, and the sounds were gone for the moment. He held on to the conversation like a drowning man would a life-preserver. "What was she doing outside your window?"

"She was dancing," Noah told him. "She said she was coming to get me soon and we would be together forever."

"Oh yeah?" Ranse grunted. "What else did she say?"

"That she loved me, and that I didn't have to listen to you."

That was it. Maybe it was invoking the memory of his mother, or the pure act of defiance, but Ranse lost his temper. He shot out from the chair and with his best bear growl announced, "You're grounded, buddy-boy. For the rest of the day. No TV and no Xbox. Now go to your room!"

"No!" Noah screamed once more, his shrill voice drilling holes into Ranse's eardrums. "No! No! No!" He threw the controller, the TV remote, a DVD box containing his favorite Wiggles video. All of them hit the wall, some shattering to bits.

Ranse stormed over and picked up the boy, tossing him over his shoulder. Noah kicked at him, pummeled his back with meaty fists, and god, did he scream. Ranse fought every urge to snap and silently marched him to his room. He put the boy down on his bed where Noah lay writhing in a fit of tears and shrieks of hatred. Ranse stormed out, slamming the door behind him. Halfway down the stairs, he heard Noah's voice. Thick with anger, it carried down to him.

"I hate you!"

Ranse rubbed his temples harder. He knew Noah didn't mean it, and he doubted the boy truly knew what hatred was, but those words hurt the soul of any parent unlucky enough to hear them. Ranse had said that to his mother once. Only once. Even with the years and chaos that passed, he never forgot uttering that ugly phrase to her. He never forgot the face she'd made. He never forgave himself for it either.

God, he needed a drink. Happy hour had come and gone, but as Alan Jackson once said, "It's five o'clock somewhere." Ranse hated that song, hated country music, but at the moment, truer words had never been spoken. *Preach on, brother Alan, preach the fuck on.*

There was a bottle of beer in the fridge that had been sitting there for well over a year. There was some Jim Beam under the sink that he hadn't touched in just as long. Maybe he'd take just the slightest nip in a cup of coffee, make it Irish. It couldn't make it taste any worse than it already did.

But before he could even consider licking his lips, another, more enticing thought occurred to him. It was amazing what sobriety could make you remember. In his workshop, there was the tiniest bit of meth he kept hidden away for a rainy day. After he'd gone sober, he left it there, too afraid of the temptation should he try to throw it out, and too ashamed to have anyone else do it for him. After the initial cravings abated, he supposed he kept it there as a reminder of the pain and trouble he had caused so many of his friends, his family. Maybe it was simply an endurance test, like seeing how long you could hold your hand over an open flame, or how long you could hold your breath underwater. Eventually, it faded away into the deepest, darkest shadows of his memory. Well, friends and neighbors, after the month he'd had, ol' Ransom Everly was about ready to come up for some air.

He went down to his workshop and unlocked his Craftsman toolbox. It looked more like a hospital crash cart, a vessel for electrodes and syringes and those little shock-paddle thingies rather than hammers and screwdrivers. On the bottom, underneath the last drawer, there was a hidden sleeve that could only be accessed by opening the bottom drawer far enough to relieve the pressure on a spring-latch. It was an inconspicuous little hidey-hole, one that most people would use to conceal loose cash or porno-mags (if those were even still a thing). Ranse reached inside and pulled out the one remaining vial of Drake Best's magic yellow crystal.

It couldn't have weighed more than an ounce at best, but Ranse felt like he pulled a boulder out of that little hidden sleeve. He stood up and bounced it in his hand a few times. He wanted it so bad he could just about eat it and not think twice. Sarah's disappearance, Cole Vaughn, Diego and the damage caused by that monster wolf. It was all too much. Then, there was Noah and his tantrum. And what did he say about seeing his mom at night? There was a flash of panic as he wondered, foolishly, if Sarah was hiding out somewhere on the ranch, keeping watch and waiting to see if pressures from the outside world would cause him to crack. If she was waiting for him to fuck up.

"Don't be stupid," he said. Sarah was missing, she needed help. And right now, the best way he could help her is by keeping their son safe and warm, not getting high. Gritting his teeth against the cravings, Ranse took the vial out of the workshop and tossed it to the ground. He stamped on it until the vial and the meth within, were nothing more than a fine yellow powder, and just when he was about to sweep it into the grass, a heavy gust came down from the peaks of the Ozarks and did the job for him. It was sharp, and Ranse, dressed only in jeans and t-shirt, couldn't help but shiver.

The cold was back. Funny, he thought as he stared up at the sky, the last time there was a cold snap, it was a full moon too.

Pleased with himself, he decided to head upstairs and see if he couldn't patch things up with Noah. It seemed like a good night for good decisions, and in that spirit, he decided that the best thing, for both he and his son, would be if he took a quick walk around the house to clear his mind of both stress and the dull pang of loss.

He first heard Noah's voice when he was halfway around the backside of the house. Sweet, almost ghostly, it rose and was quickly taken away by the gusty wind.

"Bobba?" he cried to the sky. "Bobba, are you dare?"

Ranse rolled his eyes.

"What the hell?" he said and trotted the rest of the way around the house.

Noah was standing in almost the exact spot he'd been standing the night he sleepwalked, but this time his eyes were wide and lucid. He knew where he was and what he was doing, and Ranse had to fight back a fresh rash of anger.

"Noah, bud, what are you doing out here?"

Noah broke his eye contact with the horizon long enough to give him a pitying glance.

"I'm looking for Bobba," he said. *As if you didn't know.* "She said she'd be here."

Ranse shrugged. He tried to think of a time when his parents had to break some bad news to him, and the only thing he could come up with was when his dog, Tanner, had to be put down at the vet. Heartbreaking, yes, but nowhere near this on the spectrum of completely shitty things the world has in store for a child.

"Buddy," Ranse said, taking a note from the Elsie and Richard Everly book of parenting, breaking it gently, in as comforting a manner as possible. Grimacing, he continued: "I don't think mom's gonna be around tonight."

Noah looked insulted as if Ranse slapped him across the face and called him a liar.

"Yeah-huh she is!" he protested. "She told me last night!"

Son, last night your mom was probably lying dead in the middle of the woods. It was a hard, bitter pill to swallow, but he swallowed it. Coming to terms with such a revelation was not an easy thing to do, but Ranse did it, so Noah wouldn't have to.

"Noah, son, your mom isn't here. You see, there was an accid—"

"Yes, she IS!" Noah screamed loud against the roar of the wind. "She promised! She came and gave me a kiss and said that we would be—" Something came over the boy and he paused. A sudden wave of nausea, or an upset tummy or like he just realized that he had to use the bathroom. It came and went quickly, and he shot his father a steely look. "She's coming."

Ranse was vaguely aware of the tears that were falling from his eyes. Tears of sorrow and frustration. He had no idea where his son's delusions were coming from, perhaps he was sleepwalking more than Ranse realized, but he couldn't in good conscience allow them to continue. He remembered what Tammy had told him, to keep Noah in the dark until there were answers, but what was crueler? Preparing a child for the eventuality of their parent's death, or to let them go on blissfully unaware, full of hope, only to dash it cold against the hard stone of reality? Ranse opened his mouth to speak, but no words could come out. Even if they did, they'd be swallowed up by the wind. Swallowed up by the whole world around them suddenly going crazy.

***

While Ranse stood debating whether to break his sobriety, a mile or so away, Warren Maxxy was having a "Come to Jesus" meeting of his own. He stood in the bedroom, looking down on his wife. Geena hadn't moved in over a month, still stuck in whatever limbo he'd sent her to with a simple swing of an arm. He spoke with her, loved her, held her, but still, she didn't wake up. He washed her, changed the linens, but she was putrid. The smell of her waste, his dried cum, her bed smell, was overbearing now. Warren now realized that it was time for denial to give way to acceptance of what he'd done.

Wait, what he had done? No, sir, not what *he'd* done, but what had been done *to him*. Yes, the action was all him. He swung the paperweight, he crushed the little bit of skull, sinking the weight ever so slightly into his wife's brain. He did those things, and that was the reason his wife lay in bed as still as a store mannequin. But was he not but just a vessel? Wasn't this just a culmination of hatred and misdeeds done unto him? Why he thought so! And though Geena still looked as pretty as she did on the day they were married—she hadn't started the clench that always came with a vegetative state, her muscles and tendons pulling in on themselves—Warren knew there was no coming back from where *they* had damned her to.

But who were *they?* Warren couldn't pinpoint one overall oppressor. All he knew was that he wanted, no, he demanded revenge.

Was it the faceless black men who had seduced his poor, weak-willed wife into adultery? Yes, but he didn't have time to launch a full-on assault on the black population of Maldus. Maybe in time he could, but not now. Was it Jim Richmond or Mister Tyson

Moneyman? Their slights had come after Geena's…accident, but still he held them just as liable.

The answer came to him in a flash, so simple that he felt stupid he didn't think of it sooner. In the time that passed, Warren nearly forgot all about the confrontation with the uber-liberal, bleeding heart, crackhead, Everly. He nearly forgot about the sucker punch, falling flat on his ass, and the look of pure enjoyment that he and his cronies had on their faces. The snide, contented look. He forgot all about the rage he'd felt driving on his way home. The same rage that simmered all the way to boiling when he lashed out at Geena. The very rage he was feeling now. It was all Everly. Every single bit of this was his fault. And Warren decided then, that Everly would pay in spades.

He looked down at Geena and smiled.

"Don't you worry, hon," he said to her gently. "I'm gonna make that boy suffer. I'm gonna make them all suffer. Every little beaner and jig that he has working for him. Those two asshole foremen. Hell, I might go visit the rug-munching sheep farmer next door and make her pay too."

He went over to the gun cabinet and pulled out a Thompson Center Compass. The last time he used the rifle was on a deer hunt down in Southeast Arkansas and it bucked so bad Warren was nursing a deep purple bruise that ran from his shoulder all the way to his right nipple for two weeks. He could remember the pain vividly, as well as the holes its bullets punched through the deer. On one side as big as a quarter, out the other the size of a grapefruit. The ammunition wasn't technically legal, but Warren had his ways of getting around such red tape. And he couldn't wait to see what kind of holes it would leave in Everly and his ilk.

Shoving handful after handful of cartridges into his pocket, he turned back to Geena.

"Once I'm done there, I'll come back for ya, baby. We'll have us one more nice night together and then I'll bury you in the azalea garden. You always l-loved those damned bushes." He had to stifle a sob, forcing it down into the mix with that anger and vitriol until the latter consumed it. He wiped at his eyes, loaded his weapon and headed out of the house. They would all pay. Every single cocksucking one of them.

Oh, dear God, how they would pay.

***

Ricky Lee poked his head into the bedroom that Diego Padilla now had to himself.

"Hey man, how are you feeling?" he asked. He was sure his concern was showing. For a while now, Diego seemed to be on the mend, but late this afternoon, he was beginning to display symptoms of a new infection: hot and cold flashes, torrential sweating, and so much puke come from one man. As the sun slowly set, the groaning began. Soft at first, then slowly turning into a chorus of agony that Ricky Lee did not envy. He brought Diego some water and Advil, tossing both bottles across the room to him. He felt awful for doing it, but he didn't want to catch whatever his pal was suffering from, lest it is contagious, and he thought it was. As he poked his head in, he saw that both the water and ibuprofen had not moved from where they landed.

"Diego, man, are you all right? Do you want me to call the ambulance? If you keep up with that moaning, I'll have to call Mick and knowing him, he'll come in here and put you out of your misery."

Diego answered with another painful groan.

"Get…out…" he panted, his voice the raspy growl of a chain smoker

"What are you talkin' about, man? I just wanted to check on you. Make sure there's nothing you needed."

There was a ripping sound as if Diego had torn his bedsheets. Ricky Lee took a step forward but thought better of it. Whatever he has, is just this side of Ebola, he thought. He called from the doorway, "You want me to make you some soup or something? I can run over to Ranse's and see if he has some Sprite."

Diego opened his mouth and the noise that came out was something Ricky Lee could only liken to the low squeal of a train's hydraulic brakes. The shift, though not complete, was noticeable enough. Diego whipped around and stared into Ricky's eyes, showing him there was no medicine that could cure his ailment. Fur, long and wiry, laced outward from his face like a wild beard. His hands were now slimy distorted claws with nails the size of a small tree limb. His mouth was still agape and filled to spilling with dozens of jagged razors. And his eyes, good God in heaven, his eyes were a jaundiced yellow with giant horizontal slits for irises.

Only one word came to Ricky Lee's mind and he spoke it aloud as if announcing it would somehow make it not real. "Rougarou." But there it was, lying in Diego's bed like the Big-Bad-Motherfucking-Wolf. Ricky Lee's bladder let go in a warm spurt. The thing that ate his big brother Troy was now ripping itself out of a small-statured Mexican man as if it had been waiting years to complete the set of Webster boys.

In a giant booming bellow, Diego said once more, "GET OUT!"

Ricky Lee obliged. The trip from the bedroom door to the front door of the mobile home couldn't have been more than ten steps, but it felt much longer. All the while, his ears perked to the violent sounds of the Rougarou ripping through his friend's skin like it was crepe paper. As he burst through the door, a deadly roar ripped through the trailer, making the tin siding shudder like a hundred loose teeth.

Ricky Lee didn't think but instead ran in a blind panic. His only instinct was to make for the only place he associated with safety. Ranse had told all of them every spring that in case of a tornado they were to come directly to his house. There was a shelter built under the stairs that could withstand the winds of an EF-5. Ricky Lee wasn't sure if the shelter could last a direct hit from a Rougarou, but right now, it didn't matter. Werewolf or tornado, a monster was still a monster.

He crossed the woods and into Ranse's yard. He chanced a glance backward and saw that for the moment, he wasn't being followed. But before he could breathe a sigh of relief, he saw something that drained all hope from his soul.

There, in the middle of the yard, was Ranse and his son. Not too far from them, coming down the trail that led out to pasture, was Warren Maxxy. He was armed.

And he was aiming right at them. "Ranse Everly!" Warren screamed. This was just too good! Not only was that sucker-punching bastard outside, but he had his little boy with him. Maybe, he'd plug that little retard first, just so his daddy could watch him suffer. Just like how he had to watch Geena suffer. He loaded a round into the breach and leveled the rifle. The plump, oversized body of Everly's son filled his sight. "I've got something for you!"

Ranse whipped around, but not in his direction. Something off to the side exploded in a roar of squealing metal. Something else was roaring too. Heavy footfalls were coming from that general direction and getting louder. Heading right for him. *Look at me,* his mind screamed. *Look at me while I kill you and your boy! Look at me while I take away what's most precious to you!* Slowly, he put pressure on the trigger.

Warren was lifted off his feet, the gun firing, but missing its intended targets by a mile. He looked over to see who was carrying him and his jaw went slack. The black man that worked for Everly, Ricky or Robbie or something like that, was carrying him. Carrying him! Who the hell did this dirty black bastard think he was? Nobody put their hands-on Warren Maxxy, especially not a nigger! Eyes wide with hatred, he fumbled with the rifle to take aim at his attacker.

Ricky Lee grabbed the barrel and pushed it out of the way, he dropped Warren, who hit the ground in a stumbling run. Ricky grabbed the man's collar and pulled him close.

"You need to run, Mr. Maxxy. You need to run for the house. Run for your life!"

Warren looked at him, stupefied.

"What the hell are you talking about, boy?" Warren asked, baffled. He wrestled the rifle clear and pointed it at Ricky Lee's chest. The two stopped cold. Ricky looked over at Ranse and Noah. Both were still looking off toward the trailer with awe. There was another great tearing sound, as what Ricky thought was the side of the mobile home, was torn away. The Rougarou was coming.

"Mr. Maxxy, you don't understand, you need to—"

"No, you don't understand! You all took my wife away from me! Deceived and contravened. This is all your fault. You are all defiant and you all need to be punished! Starting with him!" He took the rifle away from Ricky's chest and returned it to Ranse. Panting, sweating, a burning red fury in his eyes, Ricky Lee wondered who he should be more worried about; the wolf in the distance, or the man right next to him?

As if to answer, the monster broke free from the trailer, lumbering through the wreckage as though it were wading through ankle-high water. Ricky Lee chanced a glance in that direction. The wolf was livid. It tensed back on its haunches, and let out a great bellow, not so much a howl, but a war cry of fury and lethality, a final declaration that whatever got in its way would meet a gruesome and violent end.

"Jesus Christ," Warren mumbled to himself, gawking at the wolf in the distance like it were some awesome and terrible leviathan raised from the depths of Hell. Ricky Lee took this brief advantage. Turning on Warren, he grabbed the barrel of the rifle once more. He jerked it backward, and with his free hand punched Maxxy square in the jaw. The rifle came loose as Warren's hands instinctively went up to the point of assault. His eyes went from the wolf to the now armed black man. *Are you gonna shoot me, then?* they seemed to ask.

Without taking his eyes off the old man, Ricky called out to Ranse, "Run for the house! The storm shelter!" He addressed Warren now, "Look, you old fool, you can die out here, or you can try to survive with us. Choice is yours." And Ricky Lee ran for his life, taking the rifle and leaving Warren to weigh his options.

Maxxy watched the monster as it stretched and cleared the rubble from around its body with great, vicious swipes. He wondered if there was enough time and distance between it and him to make it back to his house, to crawl under the covers with Geena and wait the night out. Anything would be better than locking himself away with his enemies. He could start the retribution over in the morning.

The wolf sniffed the air and picked up on something. It snapped its head around, homing in on Warren's scent. The growl that emanated from it reached all the way to where he stood, low and rumbling, like a distant storm.

"Oh, Jesus," Warren gasped. "Oh, Jesus, oh God. This isn't real. This isn't real!" He turned on his heels, just glimpsing Everly cross the threshold of his house, and he ran, carrying his girth with all the strength he had left in his old knees, his old heart. He ran for his life.

And the wolf followed.

Chapter 12

The Winds of Change

Misty Robicheaux, five, a precious little girl and a favorite among the residents of Maldus, was sent to bed early, complaining of a tummy ache. Her parents and her big brother, Tommy, were all feeling a bit under the weather themselves, and skipped dinner as well, retiring to their respective rooms. By the time the full moon was in the sky, their home was in shambles.

Grant Riddell was sitting in his office, a cup of tea in front of him and a trash can half-full of his own vomit at his side. He didn't know what was worse; the overwhelming sick he was suffering from, or the report he received from the zoological department at the University of Arkansas. Upon reading it, shrieking electric buzzes of anxiety ran all through his body. The report was of the samples he took from that wolf killed on the Everly ranch. He was excited despite the dull ache in his guts, expecting to see that they discovered (and unfortunately, subsequently killed) a new species of wolf. Or maybe they found a species long thought extinct. Dire wolves came to mind, but he didn't think that animal ever got this large.

But it was not a new species, nor an extinct one. It wasn't a mutant dog or coyote. It wasn't even a fucking dinosaur!

The report stated it plainly. It was something so ordinary that its description at the very bottom of the report had no place being there at all. It was so normal, that it was abnormal:

Results of all tests show that tissue and hair samples belong to a male human.

A human. But how could this be? He was certain that the samples he took were from the wolf and not Diego Padilla or Mick. He drew the blood he sent from the wolf's veins, for Christ's sake! This all had to be some sort of big misunderstanding. Somewhere, something must have gotten mixed up. He would call the head of the zoological department in the morning. He had the carcass stored in the morgue, and he would have someone come by and see for themselves. See that it was not a human. Despite whatever accuracy their tests claimed to have, they were wrong. He would call them as soon as he got over whatever the hell bug had crept its way into his system.

He leaned over and let out a fresh stream of bile into the wastebasket, his shoulders arching and his body tensing in one giant clench of sick. He shivered as the wave passed, wiped at his frowning lips. He looked down at his hand and saw that the remnants of bile that had come with them were not white but now foamy and pink. *Blood,* he thought.

"Oh, fuck me."

A myriad of ailments ran through his brain. Cancer, the loudest of them all. Some rare form of stomach cancer. He reached for his phone to give Doc Engel a call but stopped short as a new pain overwhelmed him. His bones. His bones were on fire. They Stretched and distorted underneath his skin, cracking and popping as joints that were once single now became double and bent backward on themselves. He kicked off his shoes as his toes grew to three-times their size and ripped out of his socks. His pores opened letting in a quick puff of air before thick hair snaked its way from every single one of them. Grant screamed in agony. It felt like someone was pulling a thread made of barbed wire through his skin. He gagged, choked, moaned, and screamed.

"What's happening to me?" he called out, and in his final lucid moments, he was vaguely aware that his voice had dropped to a deep, dark baritone.

Several minutes later, the wall separating Grant Riddell's office from open air of Maldus exploded outward.

At the clinic, every single patient, nurse, janitor and even Doc Engel himself, experienced the change at once. When the last monster was free from the building, all that was left was the foundation on which it once stood.

Across town, further into the woods, Ray Logue crept from his hiding spot. He felt better. The wounds from the fight had healed, and he was rested. His strength had returned. Underneath his clawed feet, the bones of Drake Best and Christina Marsh popped and shattered like glass Christmas Ornaments. He could still smell them. He could still smell his wife. The scent of their meat still clung to him and reminded him that it was time.

Time to feed.

The monsters of Maldus traversed the town, hunting through the streets and the homes they came across. The front window of the Bar was now nothing more than a ramshackle opening. The Diner was on fire, its fryer grease left unattended, and its gas lines sheared open. The Maldus Mercantile, hosting a grocery store, clothing shop, book-swap as well as a number of smaller, more niche businesses, was reduced to an open-air flea market, its merchandise spread across the ground like a bazaar of the bizarre.

They roamed and hunted, snarled and screeched. They fought, ripping at each other, teeth gnashing against meat like living abattoirs. The streets were now a chaotic killing zone.

But for all the chaos, there was one thing that connected them all. Their species, whatever it could be called, was a species of violent and uncaring killing machines, but it was not a cannibalistic one. They all needed to feed, and there was one area their senses picked up on. A place where fresh meat with hot blood coursing through it was concentrated.

They converged upon Everly Ranch.

And as the winds of change howled, the monsters raised their heads and joined it.

Chapter 13

A Can of Sardines

Mick walked out to Molly's porch and buttoned his jeans. Molly was still in the kitchen, working on a pot of coffee that she insisted she make. He wished that she would move a little faster. The wind had picked up over the last few hours, and the odd cold returned. Mick hissed against it and wrapped his arms around his bare chest. It seemed that he'd be enjoying his coffee inside. He spotted Molly in the kitchen, holding two steaming mugs and his heart went out. Not only did he love her, but it looked warm in there.

He turned to go back in, but something caught his eye. Not so much something out of place, but something not there entirely. It was as if someone had taken an eraser to a beautifully painted landscape, jarring enough for someone to notice.

The goat pen was gone. Not destroyed, not broken into, but gone. The goats were just as phantom. Mick rapped on the window.

"Hey, Molly, you might want to see this."

Molly looked up and waved at him. Mick beckoned her to join him, and she held a finger up.

"Hold on, I'm coming," she called loud enough for Mick to hear through the glass and over the wind. "Or did you change your mind on the coffee?"

"Molly," Mick called back, opening the door. "You really need to come out here. NOW."

Noticing the look of alarm on his face, she set the cups on the counter and wiped her hands on the dishtowel hanging by the sink.

"What is it?" she asked.

"Not sure, but the goats are gone. Bring your gun."

Molly nodded and ran into the living room where she kept her gun safe. Mick took a step toward the location where the goat pen used to be, biting his lip against the cold. There was nothing. No blood, guts, chicken wire, or wood. Surely the wind couldn't have done something like that.

No, the thought came to him as suddenly as the wind had come. *No, the only thing that could have made a whole pen disappear, goats and all, would be one of those monsters,* "Wolves."

The porch underneath seemed to suck in as if it were taking a deep breath, then burst outward in a hail of nails and brackets and pristinely stained two by fours. Mick was launched backward, smacking his head hard against the roof. Somewhere, somebody was screaming. The monster came ripping upward. With one huge hand, it took part of Molly's front wall with it. It tossed the wall aside like someone chucking a wad of tin foil into the garbage. Its eyes set on Mick, whose injured head was clear enough to register what was about to happen. He thought of Cole, his late co-foreman. He thought of how his eyes had been gouged out, and his body had been ripped apart like it had been run through woodchipper.

"Please," he said, holding up his hand. "Please, God, I don't want to die."

The wolf clambered out from the hole in the porch. It had to duck under the ceiling, and Mick thought if it could stand at full height, it would have easily reached the second floor. He scrambled backward as the wolf took one lumbering step in his direction. It swiped at him in a great downward arc. It barely missed, but Mick could feel the hair on his head whoosh back as if a city bus just sped right past him. His head swam, and his vision, both from the bump and from his panic, had doubled. Still, he fought for escape.

"Molly!" he cried. "You need to run and hide! Don't worry about nothing else, just go find somewhere sa—"

His words were cut off as a loud blast shook the porch. Mick watched helplessly as the wolf's head split into three different parts. Brain and blood were carried away on the wind. The monster swayed on its feet, then crashed over the railing of the house to the ground below. Mick looked over at Molly, who held the rifle up as if waiting for another wolf to pop up like some sick game of Whack-a-Mole.

Mick got up and ran to her, but she wasn't done yet. She stuck the rifle over the side of the porch and unloaded into the wolf carcass. "Gotta make sure it's dead," she said when she was done.

"That's why God created double-tap."

"The *double-tap,* sure," Mick said. "You just gave that thing quadruple-tap."

"Shut up, Mick." She let the gun drop to the floor. Mick pulled her in just as series of ragged sobs shook her body. He joined her, and for the last time, they got to feel like humans together.

"Do you think there's more?" she asked with a final sniffle.

"If you asked me that yesterday, I would have said no way in hell," Mick told her. He looked down at the dead thing and shuddered. "But now?" He shook his head. "I suppose we better call Grant and let him know we found another one. And we probably need to let Ranse know so he can be on the lookout."

Molly went into the house and grabbed the phone. She listened for a moment.

"The phone's dead," she gasped. She tried it a few more times before slamming it down on the counter in frustration. "Do you think we should go over there and check on him?"

Before he could answer, a chorus of howls rose up to the night sky outside, piercing the thick shell of the wind. The two looked at each other with wide, frightened eyes. Yes, there were more of them. Many more.

"We need to go," Mick said.

Molly darted past him into the living room. She grabbed a few more rifles and box after box of ammo. She turned and saw him watching her.

"Well?" she asked. "What the hell are you waiting on? Go get some clothes on!"

***

Maxxy's heart felt as though it would cave in any second as he sprinted towards the house. The chuffing of the monster was close behind, the thing's whole body set firmly on kill mode. Before he knew it, he was bounding up the stairs to Everly's home. He charged through the door, looking around.

"Warren!" Ranse cried. Maxxy looked to see Everly's head popping out of a door underneath the stairs. He waved him over. His lungs were fighting a losing battle as they tried to suck in air, but Maxxy forced himself to sprint the rest of the way.

Suddenly, the front of Everly's house crashed down, the wolf announcing its arrival with brilliant ferocity. Maxxy darted inside the storm shelter, falling to the ground next to Noah who stared on in blank shock.

Ranse and Ricky Lee slammed the door shut behind him. Ranse fumbled with the latch, but the door burst backward, and a huge, lethal paw grasped onto the frame.

They pushed back with all their might.

"Jesus, Warren, get up and help us!" Noah began to cry.

"Don't let it touch you!" Ricky Lee screamed. "For God's sake, don't let it so much as touch you!"

The two men put their backs against the door and pushed. Something in the wolf's paw cracked, and it pulled it back. Ranse secured the shelter's locks and backed away.

A series of tiny explosions shook the house around them. The wolf was clearing away the drywall, the stairs. Ranse thought of a can of sardines, huddled together and protected by the thinnest layer of aluminum. As if to illustrate, the shelters side dented inward. They all screamed in unison. Then the whole house went silent except for Noah's sobs.

Ranse went over to his son, pulling him close for comfort. The boy's whole body was shaking violently from shock.

"Oh, buddy. It's all right," Ranse whispered. "You're all right. You didn't get hurt, did you?" He looked at Ricky Lee and Warren. "Nobody got hurt, right?" The two men shook their heads.

"That's a m-mean doggy," Noah blubbered. "He's mean, Daddy! Very mean!"

Ranse sighed, relieved that for the moment, he was okay. They all were okay.

"I know it is, pal, but we're safe in here. The mean doggy will go away and then we can come out. Okay?" Noah didn't answer but went on shaking and sobbing. Ranse held him and hushed him.

A metallic thud rang out in the storm shelter. Noah screamed, piercing Ranse's eardrum. Ranse let him go and turned to see the last of the vibrations shaking the shelter's door. There was another thud.

"It's trying to get in!" Warren screamed.

Ranse ran over and put all his weight on the door. Ricky Lee stood off to one side, aiming the rifle at the wolf's intended point of entry. Ranse nodded at him gratefully but wondered if his friend would be able to do enough damage to the wolf before it could get in. Once it was inside, it didn't matter how well armed they were. Once it was inside, they were sardines.

"Noah," Ranse said. He used his head to move to the far corner of the room. There was an old couch there. Dusty, unused, and perfect for a little boy to hide behind. "Go over there. Get behind the sofa. Don't come out until I tell you, understand?" Noah just looked at him with teary-eyed shock. There was another thud, and Ranse was knocked away from the door a few steps. He gained control and threw himself against it once more. "Warren, put Noah behind the couch!"

Warren blubbered something but did as he was asked. He picked the boy up and Noah went rigid in his arms. He walked him over to the couch and put him behind it. Noah disappeared. There was another thud. Ranse felt the door buckle a bit. The metal door, designed to protect against the strongest tornadoes, was buckling.

Ranse didn't know how long it would take the monster to break through. He didn't know if he could protect Noah, or if the thing would burst inside and rip him limb from limb, sniff the boy out, and do the same to him. He didn't know how much longer he could hold it off. But as another heavy thud shook the door in its frame, and the groan of giving metal could be unmistakably heard in that little shelter, he was certain of one thing:

Tonight was going to be a very long night.

THUNG! Ranse closed his eyes and held fast, listening to the fits of rage and wild on the other side of the door. Any minute now, that monster would burst through. He looked up and saw Ricky Lee and Maxxy both staring through him, through the door at what lay on the other side. "Warren, what are you doing? Come and help me!"

Warren stared. His eyes cleared and for a moment, he looked nothing like the hateful, racist, corrupt small-town bigwig that he was. Now, he was just like everyone else. Now, he was prey. He scurried over and put his weight against the door. It responded, sliding back to the jamb, though it groaned in protest.

Ranse looked at Ricky Lee, still standing vigilantly off to the side. The gun was raised and ready, but it shook violently in the air.

"If it gets through," Ranse said, "you unload on it. You understand? I'll make sure it comes for me first, you just make sure that everything you fire goes in one end of that thing and explodes out the other."

Ricky Lee nodded. "I-I'll try."

"No, you will. Do you understand me, Rick? Noah is behind that couch and—" As if calling out his name invoked some wicked curse, Noah cried out in pain quickly followed by the tell-tale splashing of vomit. It wasn't fair, Ranse thought. It wasn't fair for such a sweet little boy to be thrust into a world that was so wrong, into a world that had things that go bump in the night. No, that wasn't right. A bump implied sneakiness, stealth ruined only by a creak of a floorboard or an accidentally kicked toy. What this world had was a roaring, rabid monster unconcerned with surreptitiousness. It was here, it was loud, and it meant to devour whatever got in its way.

Like Sarah.

The pieces came together in his mind like metal shavings being pulled towards a magnet. The cops had found her car on Jim Richmond's land, shattered to pieces, but they hadn't found Sarah's remains. Jim Richmond hadn't been around since...

"The last full moon," Ranse said over the howl of the groans of giving metal. He looked at Ricky Lee again, who nodded. "This...no..."

"Werewolf," Rick said plainly. "That thing out there is Diego. I watched him change with my own two eyes."

"Oh, you have gotta be fucking kidding me!" Warren shouted. "That's a rabid dog is all it is. One of my boys said he spotted a skunk out in the day time foaming at the mouth!"

"A rabid dog that stands ten feet tall?" Ranse grunted. "One that can do this much damage?"

Noah wailed from behind the couch. Ranse couldn't tell if it was from fright or pain.

THUNG! THUNG! THUNG! The wolf let loose with another onslaught. The door was doing all the work now, barely holding onto its welded hinges. When it gave, both he and Maxxy would be crushed in the attack. The monster let out another sickening howl.

"What are you doing, Everly?" Maxxy asked as Ranse stepped back from the door. He couldn't be crushed. If He was, and if Ricky Lee failed, then Noah… He had to do whatever he could to take its attention away from the screaming hysterical child hiding behind the couch. The wolf would get him, rip his skin and muscle clean off his bones. The pain would be unspeakable, and Ranse would scream, cry, and pray to whatever deity lived up in the sky to make it stop. It would be slow. Excruciatingly so. Ranse would be alive as the monster, the werewolf, ate him.

And that would be okay.

That, he could live with. Just so long as Noah was safe. Just so long as the ten-foot-tall, hulking wolf thing spared his son's life in exchange for his. Yeah, that would suit Ranse just fine.

THUNG! There was a crack that Ranse was certain was the sound of his will breaking. All three men backed slowly away from the door. Two hairy paws pierced through, coated in metal and plaster. Its claws were prehistoric, menacing, and they tore away at the door. It howled in victory. It was through. The table was set, and dinner was served.

Noah squealed from his hiding spot. Ranse shushed him.

"I'm here, buddy. It's okay. Everything is just fine, but you have to stay quiet, okay? Whatever happens, you have to stay quiet!" His words were drowned out as the wolf tore away a chunk of the door. Its paws disappeared, and its snout came through, baring rows of gnashing, lethal teeth. Its growls shook the shelter, the snapping of its jaws the sound of a galloping horse. Noah screamed in response. Ranse couldn't let the wolf find him. "Noah!" he shouted with as much authority as his scared and now noticeably fragile body could muster. "Shut the fuck up!" Some things, like screaming daddies, were more shocking to a child than scary doggies. Noah fell silent.

The beast roared. This was it. Ranse stood firm, closed his eyes, and spread his arms in a futile protective gesture. *You'll have to get through me first, motherfucker. You might tear me to bits. You might tear these other two men to bits. But I promise that before you get to my son, I will tear each one of your teeth out.* He closed his eyes and waited for the inevitable.

A loud crack pierced the hull of the shelter. This one, more familiar. The wolf stopped its assault and focused its attention on the source. It roared in fury. A volley of gunshots rang out, pinging off the metal, bursting through the remaining plaster and drywall. The monster bellowed and howled, then something heavy thudded to the floor followed by a silence that seemed to last millennia.

"Ranse?" The unmistakable gruffness of Mick's voice was but a whisper. Ranse's heightened senses barely made it out, along with the clatter of boot heels crunching through the shattered remains of his home. "Ranse?" Mick whispered again. Why was he whispering? "You in here?"

Ranse didn't want to move, as if moving would somehow rouse the dead thing on the floor outside, but his willpower imploded. He ran to the shelter door, banging on it like a prison inmate pronouncing his innocence over and over again.

"Mick!" his voice cracked, but he didn't care. "Mick, we're in here! In the storm shelter!" He gained control of his faculties and flipped the lock, pulling the badly marred door back from the wall.

Mick was waiting for him, standing over the wolf like a triumphant hunter, but his face told another tale. It was pallid and fearful, his eyes wide and the wrinkles on his face more pronounced. His salt and pepper hair seemed to have gone stark white since earlier that morning.

He held a finger up to his mouth and whispered, "You need to see this." Mick looked over Ranse's shoulder at Maxxy and Ricky Lee. "Y'all come too if you want, but stay fucking quiet!"

Mick lead them to what used to be Ranse's front porch but was now a constricted cave made of housewares, shattered furniture, and old wood. Molly was at the mouth peering out. She turned.

"There's more of them," she said. "Guess the gunfire attracted them."

"The gunfire, or the smell of fresh meat," Mick said grimly.

Ranse peeked his head out of the opening and squinted into the dark. At the foot of his property were hundreds upon hundreds of werewolves.

"Jesus, that must be all of Maldus out there."

"They aren't moving," Mick said, "at least there's that."

Ricky Lee wasn't so sure.

"They know we're here," he said. "They're just waiting on us to move, to get out in the open. Easier that way."

Mick and Molly looked at them curiously.

"What are you talking about?" Mick asked. "How do you know what they're doing? We don't even know what these things are."

"Yeah, we do," Ranse said, still staring off into the distance, watching the lumbering shadows of hundreds of monsters holding vigil over his house. "Those things out there are people. People we know, I'm guessing." He jerked his head back to the shelter. "That thing you saved us from? Just a few hours ago, it was Diego."

"What?" Mick and Molly said in unison.

"It's true," Ricky Lee chimed in. "I watched him change."

"I still think it's a bunch of bullshit," Maxxy said, taking a look for himself. "This is just a wild pack of dogs or something. Fucking big dogs…"

"Oh yeah?" Ranse turned on him. "Well, where's your pal Richmond then, hmm? And what about Ray Logue? Weren't they supposed to come and bring me up on charges? Take my business license away? Now I might not be getting out much lately, but I have heard stories about some nasty bug going around. I have heard about people just up and disappearing." He jabbed his finger towards the wolf in his house. "And if Ricky Lee says that…thing is Diego, then I believe him, goddamnit."

An awful silence fell over them, broken only by the distant sounds of the congregation outside.

"So," Mick said finally, "Werewolves. What then?"

"Well, I suppose we all need to make sure nobody's been in contact," Ranse said. "Has anybody been bitten or scratched or anything?" They all glanced around, shaking their heads. "Well, assuming the myths are true—"

"They ain't myths," Ricky Lee interjected. "It's as plain as day. These things are *real!* Some of the things they say might not be accurate, changing back to human form after they've been killed, for one, but these are living breathing werewolves!" He slapped his hands to accentuate the point.

They all nodded, even Maxxy.

"Well…going by what we know," Ranse amended, "I suppose we need to find a place to hole up somewhere, ride out the night." He took in the devastation of his home. "One thing's for sure, though. It can't be here."

"What about my place?" Mick suggested.

"Too flimsy," Ranse said. "That thing nearly took apart a storm shelter. Imagine what a whole horde of them could do to drywall and stucco."

Warren straightened up.

"I have a fallout shelter," he said suddenly. "It's dug in deep. Got a kitchenette and food and some beds. Plenty of room to stretch our legs."

The others gave him a look. Of course, Maxxy had a fallout shelter. He was one of those Obama-hating, Trump-Loving, don't-tread-on-me survivalists. A part of the Alt-Right. And right now, they couldn't be more thankful for it.

"Is it hard to access?" Ranse asked.

"It's a basement within a basement," Warren told him. "Like I said, it's dug in deep. We'll all be safe there. Even your little boy."

Ranse snapped to attention. With all the excitement, he hadn't thought about Noah still hiding behind the couch. He darted past them and hurried back to the shelter, his feet coming down so softly he was like a stalking cat, traversing the crossbeam of a fence.

"Noah?" he called as he entered the shelter. He crossed the room and pulled the couch away.

The boy looked pitiful, curled up on his side like a baby in utero. His face was pale and drawn, his hair matted down with sweat. There was a sizeable pile of puke next to him. But he was alive. He was okay. Ranse let out a shudder of relief. "Noah, pal, what are you doing?"

Noah looked up at him. "You told me to shut up." His voice was so small and delicate that it broke Ranse's heart.

"I know I did, buddy, but it was only to protect you. You can come out now, but you still have to be quiet. Can you do that?"

Noah struggled to his feet, wobbly and woozy.

"Are you sure you're okay?" Ranse asked again.

"I'm okay, daddy. I have a tummy ache."

"We'll get you some medicine," he said as he picked Noah up. "If you feel like you're gonna be sick, though, tell me."

Noah said nothing but nodded his head against his father's chest. Ranse took him outside, glad the boy was hiding his eyes. Mick and Molly were examining the creature, pointing out the small scraps of clothing that still clung to it. Ricky Lee stood behind them, confirming that the pieces belonged to Diego. Warren Maxxy stood further back, antsy, shifting nervously on his feet.

"What do ya think?" Ranse asked, double-checking that Noah's face was firmly pressed against his chest.

"I think its Diego, alright." Mick shrugged. "What do you think about making a run at Maxxy's?"

"I think it's the only option we have. Any other shelters are in town and to get there, we'd have to go through those monsters."

"You don't think they'll follow us if we go towards Maxxy's?" Molly asked.

"Well, I dunno how fast they can run—"

"Pretty fucking fast," Warren offered.

"—But we've got your truck." Ranse fell silent. "And if we stay off the game trail, strictly go off-road, then we will have an advantage."

Mick thought about it and his eyes suddenly lit up.

"The propane tanks!" he asked.

Ranse smiled. "We shoot those babies, and we can probably take out a handful at a time, or at least keep them at a distance. We already saw that we don't need silver bullets."

Noah groaned in his arms.

"Hey, buddy, are you gonna be sick?" Ranse asked. Noah nodded, and Ranse let him down just in time for a fresh stream of upchuck to go flying back into the shelter.

Mick eyed the boy.

"Ranse," he said, "I don't like that."

"He's fine," Ranse said bluntly, eyeing his friend to drop the subject. Mick did. He motioned to their rifles. "How much ammo do we got?"

"Not enough for all those things," Molly said.

"Then we'll have to make every shot count," Ranse said. "Mick, you drive. You know where all the propane tanks are, better than anyone. Once we get close enough to the house, though, just head straight for it. Pedal to the metal."

Mick nodded and took the keys from Molly.

"Who's gonna be in the back doing the shooting?" she asked.

"I'm a good shot," Ricky Lee said, stepping forward. "And I know pretty much where the propane tanks are, too. I volunteer myself."

Ranse nodded. "I'll be back there as well," he said. "If you don't mind watching Noah."

Molly nodded and held out her arms.

"Of course," she said. Ranse made to give the boy to her, but Noah wouldn't budge. "I think he'd just as soon stay with his daddy."

"You wouldn't mind?" he asked her.

Molly shrugged and said, "I'm a better shot than you anyway, Kid."

They all turned to Warren, who was staring back at them with contemptuous disbelief.

"You really expect me to sit in the back of that truck?" he demanded. "We're going to *my* house, after all. I'm doing y'all a favor just by letting you in." He huffed and stammered. "Two guns can do the same as three!"

"What's the matter, Warren?" Ranse asked. "Not so trigger happy anymore?" He crossed over and jammed his hand into his pocket.

"Hey," Warren protested, "just wait one goddamn minute, Everly!" Ranse pulled out a set of keys and tossed them to Mick.

"There," Ranse said. "We got your keys. We no longer need your help, Warren. So, either you shoot in the back or you can hike your ass back to your house. What'll it be?"

Warren chuckled. "So, what? You got my keys! A lot of good that'll do you. Did you forget about the gate that surrounds my house? Those drugs rattle your memory too much, Everly? You need me to get into the gate!"

"No, we don't." They turned to see Ricky, who stared back at them with the look of a suspect copping to murder. "I know your code, Mr. Maxxy."

"What?" Maxxy spouted, his face awash with fresh blush. "How the hell—" Then it came to him. That rage, the hatred sparked up in him once more, little explosions of it popping in his eyes. His temples thrummed with the sounds of a tiny marching band playing the overture of Elmer Fudd's, *Kill Da Wabbit.* "Ohhh," he cooed. "It was you, then, wasn't it?"

"What are you talking about, Warren?" Ranse asked.

Warren ignored him and kept his gaze firmly planted on Ricky Lee as if he were trying to burn holes in him.

"You…sneaky, dirty little bastard. You dirty birdie. You know you left your socks at my house, don't ya?"

Ricky Lee shrugged and tried to explain, "Mr. Maxxy, I—"

Warren charged him, hands and teeth bared.

"I'll kill you!" Warren roared. "I'll kill you for what you did to her!" He grabbed Ricky Lee and rammed him up against the wall. The whole house shuddered. "Uppity dark-skinned invasive motherfuckers! You're all the same. Think you can come here and just take, take, take!" He slammed Ricky against the wall. The wolves outside seemed to hoot in return, as if they could sense what was going on inside and were grateful that they wouldn't have to expel their energy.

Ranse put Noah down and he and Mick ran over and tried to pull Warren away.

"What the hell are you doing, Warren?" Ranse cried. "What's going on? Get off him, you're gonna kill him! You'll bring the whole house down on us!"

"Just like Mr. Moneyman! Just like Jesse Jackson, Al Sharpton, and that Messican Bitch on CNN! You demand so much of us, want us to be nice, while behind closed doors you steal, kill, and fuck whatever you want! Isn't that right Lil' Black Sambo?"

Ricky got a hand free and stuck it right into Warren's face. Warren tumbled backward, bringing Mick and Ranse down with him.

"That's enough!" Mick growled in his ear. "If you don't remember, there's about a thousand werewolves out there ready to tear us to shreds! So, if you don't mind, why don't you put whatever petty bullshit beef you have aside for right now?"

"Guys," Molly said from her perch at the mouth of the opening. The only logical one in the bunch, she'd been keeping watch as the men let out their aggression. "The wolves are stirring. Getting restless. We need to go."

Tears, hot and foreign, spilled from Warren's eyes.

"You don't understand," he blubbered. "That son of a bitch fucked my wife!" He was just about to confess it all, telling them about the nasty bonk he'd given his unfaithful wife's head, sleeping with her, keeping her next to him while her brain turned to mush, but Ranse wasn't having any of it.

"I don't care if he fucked every woman in Maldus, Warren. Right now, we have to worry about one thing only: surviving. And as far as I'm—hey—where is Geena?"

Faced with the question so bluntly, the sudden urge of contrition left him. Warren straightened up. Took on a more distinguished air.

"She's at home," he said.

"Call her!" Molly said.

"She's…asleep. We don't keep a phone in the bedroom."

"I doubt my phone's working too well right now, either," Ranse said. The tension broke when the scope of what they were about to undertake settled over them. Ricky Lee stepped away from the wall. Ranse and Mick helped Warren to his feet.

"Now," Ranse said. "We got one hell of a trip ahead of us. Why don't we focus on that?"

Ricky Lee nodded and brought the gun up to his shoulder. He and Mick joined Molly at the opening. Ranse picked his son up and looked at Warren. "Are you ready?"

Warren mumbled something that Ranse took as an agreement.

Warren watched him walk away. That hate, that venom that had erupted only moments ago with Ricky Lee had settled back just underneath the surface. It was all he could do, to keep it covered with a blank expression. He would help them to his bunker. It would be easier that way, like a wolf in sheep's clothing. He would keep his cool for now, but he felt that hate pulsing just below the skin like an infected hair or a wasp sting. Soon, he'd have to let it out.

Kill them all. Kill them all.

Chapter 14

<u>Invasive Species</u>

The subdued, hateful look Warren gave them remained on his face until they were all loaded into the truck. Then, he took on an expression more appropriate to the situation. He looked out in the distance, never fully grasping the scope of what they faced until he was sitting on the cold, hard metal of the truck's bed. The gun in his hands felt like nothing more than a child's toy. He wanted to run. As fast as his old legs could take him, but it didn't matter where he went, just so long as he was far, far away from the sight before him.

The wolves stood together in the distance like a congregation of the faithful. The whole time they were in the house, they could hear a low, collective growl carrying through the air. It was steady and constant like cars whooshing by on a freeway, but when Warren and the others came out, the growl ceased. The wolves, that had been swaying and lurching suddenly tensed, stood stock-still like runners poised waiting for the starting gun. All their eyes locked on them.

"Jesus," Warren asked in a hushed whisper. "What the hell are they doing?"

"Readying themselves," Ricky Lee said. "You ever see a cat waiting in the bushes while birds peck at the ground a few feet away?" He nodded towards the gathered monsters. "They look exactly like that, 'cept these are much bigger and scarier than cats."

"Yeah," Warren said, though he felt like a mouse himself right then. "Everly, what's going on? Y'all ready to go or what?"

Ranse stuck his head out the passenger window.

"We're good in here," he whispered. "Remember, don't waste your ammo trying to pick them off one by one. Shoot for the propane tanks when they're close enough, and when we're far enough away. Mick will honk the horn when we're coming up on one." He stuck his hand out to show them that he had a pistol: the one Molly kept in her glove compartment. Molly didn't have the heart to tell him that there was only one bullet in the magazine. "All right. Hold on and good luck!"

Ranse disappeared into the cab of the truck just as Mick fired up the engine. It roared to life, and there was a collective twitch in the pack on the edge of the ranch as if they knew shit was only seconds from going down. Mick put the truck in gear and floored the gas. Gravel and dirt exploded in a cloud as they took off like wannabe competitors at the Indianapolis 500. It hung in the air, illuminated by the moon and the red taillights. The three in the bed looked at it, somewhat hypnotized, but whatever trance they might have fallen into was quickly broken as the wolves came ripping through it. They charged with fire and fury in their eyes, rumbling the ground like a freight train and making the truck bounce up and down like it was a lowrider.

"I don't think the shocks will put up with too much more of this," Mick said plainly, keeping his eyes straight ahead. He aimed at the white blimp-like structure in the distance.

"If they give, we can still keep off-road," Ranse said. "It just won't be very comfortable."

"We're liable to lose one of them in the back," Mick told him. Without shocks, the bed of the truck became unstable, wobbly, like a diving board or a catapult.

Ranse nodded and swallowed what felt like a charcoal briquette.

"One thing at a time, Mick," Ranse said. "Keep heading for the propane tank." He checked on Noah, who looked sicker than ever. He was dozing, stuck in a fever-induced trance. Ranse said a small prayer of thanks that he wasn't lucid enough to witness such horrors and stuck half his body out the window.

It was almost impossible to hear the horn over the high whine of the engine and the din of the ravenous monsters pursuing them. Ranse screamed from the window, but his words were drowned out and taken by the wind. It was Ricky Lee that got them to attention.

"There!" he screamed. "To the right! The wolves are on the right!" They snapped to two o'clock in unison like a military drill team. The white tank stood brightly in the dark.

"There's not enough of them," Molly shouted. "They're going wide. We need to pull them closer!"

As if hearing her, Mick pulled the wheel and made a wide banking turn, leaving serpentine tracks behind them. The wolves responded in kind, turning with pinpoint precision. It reminded Ricky of those old nature documentaries with Richard Kiley. He could have gone on watching them forever, but Ranse's screams somehow broke through.

"Now! NOW! Shoot NOW!"

They leveled their guns and let a volley of bullets go at the propane tank. Suddenly, the night sky was filled with a brilliant explosion. Blue and orange flames erupted upward and outward. Dozens of hairy carcasses flew up into the air, blown to bits and catching fire. The pack stopped all at once, watching as the truck sped off.

The cheer that escaped them was almost as deafening as the monsters' roars. They had escaped and were well on their way to Maxxy's house. Even Warren cheered. He was sure it was his bullet that pierced the metal hide of that tank. He pretended he was shooting Ricky Lee. He pretended he was shooting them all and watching them fall one by one.

The three of them relaxed in the bed, sitting back. A relative silence settled over them. Molly leaned back and closed her eyes. She took a few deep breaths. Warren and Ricky Lee, however, were locked in a staring contest for the ages.

"You know," Warren said, "I could shoot you right now. I'm well within my rights."

"Goddamnit, Warren," Molly sighed. "I was just starting to relax. You make a move, and I'll put you out of your fucking misery, understand?"

Warren settled back, but he wasn't done.

"You're lucky she's got your back, boy."

Ricky Lee grimaced. "Mr. Maxxy, I never said I was happy about what I did. I'm extremely sorry for it. If I could take it back, I would."

Warren scoffed, "It's just like you people, isn't it? All high and mighty and invincible until you get caught. Then it's 'oh, I'm so sorry!' And if someone does something about it, holds y'all to task, then you go on playing the victim!"

"That's enough, Warren," Molly warned once more.

"No, it's okay, Ms. Hyndman," Ricky Lee said. "Warren, do you know what entitlement is?"

Warren fumed. "Of course, I do!" he barked.

Ricky Lee smiled and answered for Warren, "Then you should have seen that your wife was entitled. She was entitled to flaunt her narrow ass all around town, picking up whatever random dick she wanted. She played you for a fool, Warren. She felt entitled. Just like you feel entitled enough to treat me, or anybody a shade darker than you, like complete shit. You feel entitled to call us things like 'boy,' or 'spic,' or 'nigger.' Well, I'm telling you right now, that that entitlement was stripped away as soon as that first fucking wolf showed up here. There's no more class. No more race, sex, gender, or anything. Now, it's just us and those things. Only the strong will survive, only the adaptable. Tell me something, Warren. In this new world of ours, how long do you think you'll last?"

Warren's eyes went wide like a gunslinger at high noon. He shot up from the bed of the truck and grabbed his rifle. Ricky Lee matched him. Soon they were both having a wobbly standoff as the truck navigated the bumpy ground of Maxxy's property. Ahead, the lights of Warren's house shone like a distant beacon.

"Hey!" Molly cried, getting up herself. "Put your guns down! If you want to point at something, why don't you scan out there for those—" A gunshot cut her off. It came from Ricky. Molly turned to see what he fired at just in time to see an airborne wolf come toppling to the ground, a hole the size of a golf ball sat in the center of its chest, its fur singed and burning.

"I forgot," Ricky said grimly, "that they can jump."

The attack came from the left. The horde had waited for them to get out of sight and had flanked the truck. The intelligence of it all was awe-inspiring, but what amazed them was the acrobatic way the things moved. They weren't the lumbering monsters that they originally believed. They darted, dodged, and flipped in and out of each other's way. And they could indeed jump.

The wolves took turns sailing through the air towards the truck. They each took their shots, some connecting, other missing wide only for the attacking monster to come crashing into the side of the truck. One hit so hard that the truck went up on two wheels, threatening to flip over, only to come back down with a jolting crash.

"The propane tanks!" Ranse yelled. "Where are the rest of them?"

Noah writhed on his lap, gripping his stomach.

"The last one is about a hundred yards in the opposite direction," Mick said. "We turn around, they'll overtake us."

Another wolf leaped, soaring through the air like a superhero. Molly aimed and squeezed the trigger. The click of an empty chamber answered.

"Oh no," she whispered.

The wolf came down hard on the gate, its claws sinking into the metal like it was softened butter. Molly scrambled back as its free paw took a large swipe at her chest, just missing it. Warren froze, realizing that his rifle was empty now, too. He reached into his pockets. His ammunition was spent. Ricky Lee put the barrel of his gun into the snapping jaws of the wolf. He pulled the trigger and the thing toppled from the truck missing its head. He looked at the others.

"That was my last round," Ricky Lee warned the others. He turned the rifle around, gripping the hot barrel like a baseball bat. Molly and Warren followed suit. They waited, watching as the horde quickly gained ground, all of them knowing that the next one that jumped would make it into the truck.

They were approaching the house too quickly now. Warren could see that. The wolves were much too close. Once they hit the gate, they would be surrounded, overtaken and swarmed. He supposed that they could circle the house a few times, maybe tire the things out, but the fact remained that they were just too close and so… so relentless. He looked at the people flanking him in the bed, seeing that their hope was dwindling from a flame to a simple snuffed puff of smoke. Something had to be done. What they needed was a distraction, a diversion. What they needed was a sacrifice. He knew just the person.

Just then, the truck hit a rivet in the ground. The bed went flying upward. Molly lost her balance and fell backward, smashing into the truck's rear window and leaving a giant spider web crack in her wake. Ricky Lee went flying upwards, his hands holding onto the gate and sinking into the holes made by the wolf. His grip was true, firm, and so long as it held, he would be okay. As long as it—

The butt of a rifle came down hard on his hands. Ricky cried out as the fingers on his right hand shattered into tiny pieces. He was coming down now, holding on to the gate with only his good hand. The rifle came down again. Ricky let go. His stomach hit the gate, knocking the air from him. His mind went black, but he could sense that he was slipping forward, hearing the crunch of the ground beneath the truck's tires, tasting the metal of the bumper. His mind cleared, and he opened his eyes. He was falling. Falling forward. Falling out of the truck. He twisted to try and find a free outstretched hand. There were none. Molly had fallen backward and disappeared from the edge of the truck. The only other source of help was glaring down at him like a lion over a fresh kill.

"Warren" he pleaded. "Please…" Ricky Lee slipped from the truck.

He hit the ground, skidded, and rolled. Ricky felt his knee give way, snapping into two sharp pieces. He screamed, but not out of pain, not out of agony or even betrayal. He screamed out of pure abject terror. The wolves were on him. They sank their teeth and their claws into flesh rough and leathered from years of working in the sun. The sun, how Ricky wished that the sun was out right now. In the sun, things didn't seem so scary. Things didn't seem so inarguably real. The teeth that clamped onto his limbs were, without a doubt, real.

They sunk into him and Ricky felt a cold, calloused paw wiping across his face. The whole world went black. He was alive but blind. He sucked in what air he could, taking with it clumps of hair and spittle, breathing in the rancid and rotten breath of the wolves, and he screamed.

He couldn't see, but his other senses were working perfectly well. He felt the teeth grab his thighs, sink into his chest, rip his genitals to shreds. He felt it all with such cruel acuteness, wondering if that's the way a seal might feel when it was ravaged by a shark. Yes. He was being ravaged.

In his final moments, he thought of his brother, Troy. The Rougarou was real. The Rougarou got Troy, and now it had gotten him as well. A set of hot, slimy jaws settled on Ricky Lee's throat. There was pressure, then a final, hissing pop.

Ricky Lee's screams fell silent.

Warren watched his oppressor, the man who defiled his wife, who caused his snap of madness, fall to the ground and land with a satisfying thump. The wolves were on him in an instant, the opportunity of a quick meal much more appealing than chasing a speeding truck. He fell backward onto the bed, feigning lost balance.

Molly shot up, rubbing her throbbing head.

"Is everyone okay?" she called. "Ricky? Warren? Y'all talk to me!"

"Yeah," Warren said, disguising his voice in a blurry, pained way. "Yeah, I'm okay. I'm alright. Are you okay?"

Molly didn't answer him. She'd opened her eyes and saw that the bed of the truck was now a bit more spacious.

"Oh, God, please no." She wheeled on Warren, grabbing his shirt collar. "Tell me you didn't do it," she demanded. "Tell me that you're less of an animal than I think you are!"

Warren put his hands up, giving her a shocked look.

"I swear!" he claimed. "I fell as soon as we hit that bump. Nearly fell out, myself!" *Yes*, he thought. *That's exactly what happened. Ol' Ricky Lee Wife-Fucker fell out of the truck. No need to think otherwise.* He forced his look of shock into more authentic territory.

Molly stared at him for a long time before finally letting go and sinking back into the bed. She put her face in her hands and cried.

Warren sat there looking at her. He frowned and murmured his condolences. He put a consoling hand on the woman's shoulder, thinking how easy it would be to toss her over the edge as well. That would give them a little more time, wouldn't it? And she was an oppressor as well. It's not like Everly or his butt-buddy in the truck's cab would see him. The rear window was shattered to bits. The side-view mirrors were ripped clean off. They would be none the wiser. His hand gripped onto Molly's shoulder tighter.

"You guys all right?" Ranse called out. His head appeared from the passenger's window. Warren's hand loosened. He turned in time to see Ranse's face grow grim with the revelation that their truck was down a passenger. "How?" Ranse asked.

"He fell when we hit the bump," Warren said, not abandoning any subterfuge. Pretending to be upset would be useless with Everly. He would see right through it. "I didn't see it, but it sounded ugly."

Ranse glowered at him, then retreated into the truck.

Warren frowned. He couldn't toss the rug-muncher from the truck now. No, he would have to wait. Get them all inside where he could pick them off one by one. They had weapons, but there was no ammunition in them. He could run upstairs and grab the remaining bullets from the gun safe. Then, when they were all cloistered inside, he could pick them off like fish in a barrel.

Kill them all.

God, they were so stupid. They were so trusting. They wouldn't know what hit them, escaping a horde of monsters only to find themselves deeply and inescapably…

Chapter 15

<u>In the Belly of the Beast</u>

They marched toward the house in a solemn single file: Ranse at the head, carrying Noah, Maxxy just behind them, and Molly and Mick bringing up the rear with their guns at the ready. They waited for the wolves to reach the gate, but the wolves weren't coming. Ranse wondered if Ricky Lee's sacrifice was enough to put an ample amount of distance between them and the monsters. If so, then maybe it wouldn't be so tragic. If so, then maybe Rick's death wouldn't be in vain. That was a good thought, albeit utilitarian. Ricky Lee died so that they, especially Noah, could live.

Sure.

He was no biologist. He wasn't Grant Riddell, though he was certain that Grant wasn't Grant anymore, but he did know that canines could smell for miles, and those things had to be in some way or another, canines. They were canines on every sort of steroid imaginable. No, the wolves knew exactly where they were. Their senses were homed in on them like hundreds of smart bombs. When they were done ravaging poor Ricky Lee, they'd come calling. Even if they stopped to pick the dozens of stables and barns clean of livestock, they'd come calling. The ravenous always do. Ranse quickened his pace to the front door.

He fumbled the keys out of his pocket and tossed them to Warren. Warren opened the door, and a putrid stench of rot hit them like a brick to the face. It was like walking into a port-o-potty that had been left out to bake in the sun. They all winced, all of them except Warren. "Christ, Maxxy," Mick said. "Do you have one of your heifers in there with you? I thought Mitsy Brennerman came and cleaned your house once a week!"

"Haven't seen her in the last month," Warren said grimly. He cast a glance to the second story. "Guess we know why."

"Where's Geena?" Molly asked, her voice buzzed and nasally from pinching her nose. She looked green. "How can she sleep with the smell, let alone live with it?"

"I told y'all, she's a heavy sleeper." Warren's voice cracked a bit. "I'll turn up the AC. That'll get the air circulating." Warren pointed to a narrow doorway at the end of the hall. "The shelter's that way, down the stairs. Y'all go on down and I'll run upstairs and grab some more guns and ammunition."

"And maybe wake up your wife?" Molly suggested.

Warren cringed but quickly recovered. "Of course," he said. He shrugged Molly's comment, and its implication, off easily. "Thought that was understood. She's in our bed, gun safe is in the bedroom." He waved them towards the shelter. "Go on, now, get comfortable. Looks like we're in for a long night."

"My son needs some stomach medicine," Ranse said, his face strained and worried. Noah had gone the color of bleached paper in the few minutes it took to get inside the house. He cradled the boy in his arms as though he were the most fragile, priceless piece of crystal. "Anything you got."

Warren nodded and turned to head up the stairs.

"I'll go with you," Mick said. It was something in Warren's actions ever since they crossed the threshold that made him suspicious. Something just wasn't sitting right with him. Werewolves notwithstanding. Either way, "Strengths in numbers, right?"

"No, no," Warren said casually, but adamantly. "I mean, I don't need help. I can collect what we need. Won't take me but a minute."

They split up, Warren heading upstairs, and the others going to the basement.

"I don't like this," Mick said. "Something ain't right."

"I don't like the idea of spending a night with that bastard any more than you do, Mick," Ranse said, "But this seems the best option."

Mick grumbled, "That's not it. It just doesn't feel right. He's acting funny. That motherfucker hadn't worked a day in his life, so why wouldn't he let me help him carry down some guns and supplies?"

Ranse nodded.

"Yeah, I can feel it too," he said, "and I've had a gut feeling that Ricky Lee didn't fall from the truck." He turned to Molly. "Are you sure you didn't see anything when we hit that bump? Anything at all?"

Molly frowned before replying, "Nothing. I hit that window so hard I lost my breath, and I guess I must have blacked out for a second."

Mick, who'd been morosely blaming himself ever since Ranse told him of Ricky's fate, registered a small glimmer of hope. "You really think he'd do that?"

"You do realize who we're talking about here, right?" Ranse said. "Just the way he looked sitting in the bed…It was quick, but I swear there was a flash of guilt in his eyes. And that smell…we've all smelled it before. Not but a month ago." Molly and Mick looked at him questioningly.

"The game trail," Ranse said. "The blood, the guts, the—"

"Death," Molly finished. "That's what it is. Jesus, Ranse, you don't think?"

"I don't think, I know," Ranse said, giving them both a grave smile. "Old, stale death. You don't forget that smell easily. It would certainly explain why he didn't want Mick's help."

A hot, blinding rage now built up inside of Mick, his face turning the same shade of red as the wolves' eyes.

"I ought to chuck his ass outside," he seethed. "Feed him to the wolves."

"There's been enough of that already," Molly said, placing a gentle hand on his shoulder. "One is too many as it is, and we still don't even know if Warren did anything at all. If he did, it's quite possible—in a sadistic, sick sort of way—that he thought he was doing good."

"That's absolutely no excuse," Ranse said.

"You're right, and when this is over, we'll get to the truth and deal with it then. But for now, as cliché as this sounds, we need to work together. Right now, we have no weapons and no shelter." She cocked a thumb upwards. "And he's coming down fully armed. So, let's try to be nice, shall we?"

Mick's blood went cold as Molly's words sunk in.

"Fully armed," he repeated, the red in his eyes turning over white as they widened to the size of saucers. "Jesus Christ…"

"What?" Molly asked as they all reached the foot of the stairs. The door, a stainless-steel block, loomed over them. "Mick, what is it?"

Mick didn't answer. He turned and bolted back up the stairs.

***

"Hi, honey-pie." Warren stood in his bedroom doorway, looking at the lump under the covers. Geena responded as she had the last month. She lay still and quiet in the bed, the moonlight illuminating her features, casting her in an almost spectral glow.

He didn't know what came over him just then, maybe the smell, perhaps the image of his slowly dying wife (had she moved while he was gone?), but Warren was suddenly overcome with a maddening queasiness. A heavy shudder racked his body. Tears of guilt, of hurt, and anger bloomed in his eyes. He felt nauseous. No, not nauseous, but plain sick to his stomach. He felt as though he could puke all over the floor, the bed, everywhere. *Yes, she did move.*

She was lying on her back when he left, as she'd done the whole month prior. Now, however, she was on her side, locks of her hair billowing up on the pillow and surrounding her like a halo. Warren watched her for a moment, willing her to move again. Had someone else moved her? Had Everly or one of his buddies come in here to play some sort of cruel joke on him? After all the kindness, all the hospitality he extended their way? He took a tentative step forward and his stomach caved in on itself. The feeling was alien to him. It had been what—at least a week—since he last vacated his bowels. The need to shit was as overwhelming as Geena's stench. He gave up on her and charged to the bathroom.

What came out of him was a rancid stew that felt like raw sewage pumped through the bowels of a volcano. He sat there for what seemed like hours, his stomach clenching, then releasing with every vile expulsion. Just when he thought the worst of it was over, it started to come out the other end. He painted the walls, mirror, and the bathtub with contents of his stomach. Warren wondered where he'd been storing all of it; he hadn't eaten much since he put Geena to bed. But as the heaves turned to bile, they dried out and he realized he must have caught what Jim Richmond had, or maybe what Everly's kid had. And it had come on him not only at the worst possible time but so violently and intense that he worried he wouldn't be able to carry out the promise he'd made to his dying wife.

No. No, that wouldn't do at all. They all had to pay for what happened to Geena, what happened to him. He had to see it done. Forget about the wolves, they had enough to worry about here. He would make them—

Another catastrophic volley of regurgitation and liquid shit racked his body. Warren was sweating profusely. He was shivering. Now was not the time to get sick. Frowning, he focused all his attention on quelling the beasts that were fighting within him. He had to get better. Had to get better.

Slowly, whatever fever he had, broke. His stomach unfurled, loosened, and then calmed. Warren couldn't believe it and chuckled at the sudden stroke of good fortune. He wiped the tears away from his eyes and the shit from his ass. The streams of vomit he expelled were so violent that they completely missed his clothing. Another stroke of luck. He got up and buckled his pants, went over to the sink, and rinsed his mouth. He took one good look at himself in the mirror. He wanted to look good while he took his retribution, and he wasn't ashamed to admit that he wanted to look good for *them.* Impressions were everything in this world. Even if the world was being ravaged by werewolves.

He sucked in a big breath of air, turned, and stepped out of the bathroom.

The cramps came back immediately.

Mick didn't notice him at first. Standing in the bedroom door, his eyes were fixed with appalled focus on Geena's motionless body in the bed. The sheets had been pulled back, revealing her grimy, unshaven legs. Warren stumbled over to her.

"What did you do?" Warren demanded. "Felt like getting yourself a look-see at my wife, pervert?"

Mick's mouth opened and closed, opened and closed, opened and closed. No words came out. He was stricken by the horror. He'd seen monsters, real ones, almost been mauled to death by one of them, but he realized then that the real monster was standing right in front of him.

"Warren," he finally spoke in a hoarse whisper. "What did *you* do?"

Warren busied himself with tucking his wife back under the covers, taking care not to disturb her too much. A low, muffled growl came from underneath, but he didn't have time to find out if it was coming from her mouth or stomach.

"Shh, baby girl, it's alright. I'm here. It's alright now." He turned to Mick, his face ablaze with white-hot fury. "What gives you the right to—"

"Warren," Mick said, gaining a bit more of his faculties back. "I didn't do anything. I haven't moved. I'll ask you again, what did you do?"

"I didn't do anything!" Warren hissed. "It was you! All of you! Everly and his trifling ways, you and that lesbo with the sheep ranch, and that dirty nigger I threw from the truck. All of you have been plotting against me for as long as I can remember!"

There was one confession Mick was looking for. Though he wanted nothing more than to charge Maxxy and beat him to a bloody pulp, Mick kept his anger at bay and calmly, silently held his hand out. "Warren, give me the keys to the gun safe."

Warren's hand instinctively went to the keyring clipped to one of his belt buckles. They jingled in the moonlight.

"What are you talking about?" he demanded. "You want this, so you can arm yourselves and leave me and my wife helpless? I don't think so!"

Mick shook his head. "Warren, your wife is dead."

"No, she's not!" His voice a shrill squawk. "I told you, she's just sleeping is all. Look at her! She's breathing!"

"Well she needs a doctor, then," Mick said. His hand still hovered in the air like the risen Messiah showing the doubter Thomas his wounds. "Warren, give me the keys. Now."

And for one brief shining moment, Warren saw reason. He came face to face with the gravity of his actions. He nodded solemnly and handed over the key ring.

Mick took them and hurried over to the gun safe, his mind running wildly. There was a dead woman in here with them. A dead woman he was sure Warren killed. Just as he admittedly killed Ricky Lee. And though she didn't look dead (Warren was right in that regard), she sure as hell smelled it. When Mick first arrived in the bedroom he nearly puked. Not out of horror or shock, but out of instinct, a natural synaptic reaction. He had to hurry and get the guns out of here, away from Warren. He had to get them to the people he could trust. Maxxy was willing to kill. The notion ran over and over in his mind like a great cultish chant. Maxxy was willing to kill. Did that mean Warren was willing to kill Everly and the others as well? Hell, they were his backup. There was strength in numbers, and numbers were what they needed if they were gonna survive the night. Would Maxxy really be willing to throw that all away?

The answer came to him as flat and blunt as a hammer to the head. Mick jolted upright and dropped the keys. He turned to see Warren standing behind him. No, not a hammer. A golf club. A Callaway Big Bertha, to be precise. Its steel head was tarnished with blood. Mick reached up and touched his scalp. His hand came away red, hot, and wet. Mick stumbled forward a few steps and Reached out for Maxxy. Warren stepped back. The world went a shade of purple. Dimming. Dimming. Dark.

***

The room they found themselves in was not so much a shelter to protect against severe storms as it was one to protect against a nuclear holocaust.

The shelter was divided into three smaller areas: a storage/pantry, a living room with an attached kitchenette, and a bedroom with two sets of bunks. Ranse put Noah down on one of the beds and set a garbage can next to him. He jogged over to the pantry and found a few bottles of chewable Pepto-Bismol. He brought them back and almost had to force Noah to chew them. Noah swallowed and managed to keep them down.

"There," Ranse said softly, stroking his son's hair, "that should make you feel better." Noah gave him one of the saddest, most painful looks he had ever seen. "How do you feel?"

"My…tummy really hurts," Noah moaned.

"I know, pal, but that's what the medicine is for. Now you can close your eyes and go to sleep and forget all about this crazy night…damnit." Ranse immediately regretted saying this, as his son's eyes grew two times their size. Noah remembered. Ranse shamefully wished he hadn't found that medicine. A stomach ache would have at least kept his little mind occupied, kept the scary parts at bay until morning.

"Is it coming back?" Noah asked.

"Is what coming back?"

"The scary-mean doggy." Ranse was holding out hope that Noah had missed most of the action. At least the horde that chased them all the way to Maxxy's. *Oh please, god, if you have a merciful bone in your body, please let it be that he missed that!*

"No," Ranse lied, smiling. He used to be so good at lying; to Sarah, to Mick, to everyone in town. It was always so easy to explain that he wasn't drunk, he just had a headache, nor was he stoned or wired but just had one too many cups of coffee. Those lies he told were for his benefit and left a trail of hurt and destruction in their wake. As hard as it was to lie now, it did feel good to do it for the good of someone else. It felt good to lie as parents do. *Don't make that face or it'll stick that way,* or *don't bite your nails or you'll get appendicitis,* or *no, son, the monster that I told you over and over again wasn't real is never coming back.* Ranse smiled once more. "It's far away from here by now. You're safe."

Noah looked like he didn't quite believe him—the boy was so intuitive—but he settled down anyway. The medicine was starting to kick in.

"Good," he said with a pained smile. "That doggy was really scary." His stomach let out a small *GLORP* and he winced.

Ranse stroked his son's hair some more, then leaned over and kissed the top of his son's head.

"Don't worry about that anymore, okay?" He reassured his son. "You're safe. I am right here. You need to sleep and think about fun stuff like The Wiggles and Lego Batman." Noah nodded. "I love you, buddy."

"I love you too, Daddy."

"I'm gonna go in the other room and talk with Mick and Ms. Hyndman, okay? If you need anything, just call out."

"Okay." Noah sounded dreamy, on the verge of a sleep that hopefully would not be interrupted, but Ranse couldn't help but fear that it would be. That was life, wasn't it? Life didn't care about what *should be,* only what *was.* It didn't care about what our interpretation of *fair* was. It wasn't fair to give such a sweet little boy a genetic disorder. It wasn't fair to give his mother cancer and stick him with his dad who, by his own admission, was a complete fuckup. And it sure wasn't fair to make him bear witness to what could very possibly be the end of the world via werewolf.

But that's fucking life, in all her bitchy glory.

Ranse got up and flicked off the light. As he closed the door, Noah was already softly snoring. He left it cracked a bit, torn between keeping an eye on his son and not wanting what was coming to wake him up.

"I love you, son," he whispered and left to join Mick and Molly.

It would be the last time he ever said that to him.

"How is he?" Molly asked when Ranse joined her by the door. He shrugged his shoulders, and Molly noticed just how old he looked. How stressed, tense, and worried. Worry would always do that to you. Ranse was only thirty-five, but at that moment, he looked like he could have been Mick's older brother. That was being nice.

"He seems to be feeling a little better. Dozed off just a minute ago."

"Is he scared?" Molly asked.

Ranse scoffed, "Aren't we all?" He stole a glance around the shelter. "Mick still isn't back yet?"

Molly shook her head. "I don't like the way he ran off like that, Ranse. And I hate that he's not back yet."

"You're worried," Ranse said.

Molly sighed, "God, yes." She closed her eyes and hid her face in her hand as if she were embarrassed to admit such a thing. "I can't stop thinking about Ricky. I know he killed him. I can feel it in my soul, Ranse."

"Yeah, I can too. And that smell. I can't help but think it's his wife up there rotting away. I should go check on them. See if they need help." A thumping came from above. Someone was moving. Ranse glanced in the direction of the footsteps. "And if he did? If he's come unhinged? What do you suggest we do with him?"

"Take his guns, for one," Molly said, "and we lock him out." Another round of thumps. It wasn't just footfalls, but something else. Like whoever it was up there was carrying something heavy. "We can give him one to protect himself with, but that's it."

The thumping reached the top of the stairs leading down to them.

"It sounds like maybe they have the guns in a duffel bag or something," Ranse said. "The way he was talking, it sounded like he had a full arsenal here. Even if he's carrying them by hand, it'll be too much to have one aimed at us. I say we grab the guns and Mick, throw them one way and send Maxxy in the opposite direction."

There was a clatter of thumps as whoever and whatever he carried came tumbling down the stairs. Warren cried out and cursed. Molly and Ranse stood on their side of the door, waiting for it to swing open, their muscles tensed and aching as they readied themselves for action.

Then it opened, and the sight before them took any strength the two of them had left.

Warren stood in the doorway baring stained teeth that looked like he'd binged on a bunch of red licorice. His breathing was rapid and heavy and wheezing. He seemed to be on the verge of a heart attack or a laughing fit. Ranse recognized it immediately. One of his first attempts to get clean was a voluntary stint in a mental hospital in Rogers. Though mainly relegated to the narcotics wing, he was able to roam around every so often, taking in the sights of the other patients. It was one of these other patients that came to mind when he saw Warren's face. A lunatic laughing madly, always smiling. Hysteria.

In Warren's left hand was the source of the thumping. It gripped around faded denim, squeezing it so hard it looked like it might tear. Mick had lost his boot and his sock foot jabbed the side of Warren's ample stomach. He was badly hurt, his hair matted with blood, but his chest rose and fell, and his lips moved the slightest bit. Molly cried out in shock and tried to run to him.

But then Warren showed him what he had in his right hand.

"I guess I owe you an explanation," he said coolly, "but I've always been of the mind that actions speak louder than words." With that, he leveled the gun and fired.

Ranse was blinded by a bright orange burst from the end of the pistol's barrel. A deafening crack rang out in the close quarters of the shelter. He couldn't hear. Deaf, blind, and trapped. An intense searing pain ripped through his shoulder, and he fell backward onto the floor.

From somewhere deep in the dark of unconsciousness, Mick stirred. He couldn't remember how he fell asleep, except that he didn't want to be disturbed. He twisted to his side. And as memories always do, especially the bad ones, it all came flooding back to him just as he reached the precipice of deep sleep. Warren, Geena, the wolves—he stiffened—the guns! Another shot rang out and Mick was awake.

The twisting behind him sent Warren's second shot wide. It sprang off the steel shelving in the pantry. Growling, he dropped Mick's leg and took a more appropriate, cop-like stance and leveled his weapon at Ranse.

"No, goddamnit!" Molly cried. "Warren, stop!"

"Nobody hits me!" he screamed at her. In his lunacy, his voice had gone up three octaves. "Nobody disrespects me in my fucking town, Everly! Not you! Not my wife, not Mr. Moneyman, not Jim Richmond, not that dirty Bayou-Nigger you had working for you!"

Molly charged blindly. She had to stop Maxxy or they would all be dead. Warren squeezed the trigger.

The attack came just as the gun blurted out another harsh, but shorter, blast. Mick tackled Warren from behind, slamming his face into the ground. Warren could feel teeth shatter in his mouth, his nose giving way, but Warren fought back. He had them all right here where he wanted them. He had to finish this. Had to keep his promise to Geena. Two calloused mitts gripped Warren's and lifted him until he had a vertical panorama of the shelter.

Ranse was on his side, gripping his wounded shoulder. A pool of blood formed on the front of his shirt, mixing in and warping the plaid. Molly was on her knees right in front of him, looking with wild wide eyes, her mouth agape as though she were holding a long note in a choir. Then the panorama went blurry, and his head smacked against the cold, hard concrete floor once more. The gun skittered out of his hand. He heard Mick, Everly's butt-buddy yell for someone to pick it up. Slowly, Warren's eyes seemed to melt into the darkness. A thought, fleeting, came to him right before everything went black. Where did that third bullet go?

When Warren woke, his mouth was full of concrete. His lips, dry and parched, were parted and his tongue lolled out on the floor. He breathed in sharply, inhaling a wad of his own spit and choking on it. He tried to move, but his hands and feet were tied together like a pig awaiting slaughter.

"He's awake," a voice, hoarse and pained, called out. Warren knew it was Everly, although he couldn't see him, nor could he see the boot that was aimed right at his side. The contact it made with him was all the more painful.

"Good," Mick growled, as he kicked Warren over so that he could see them.

The world was upside down, but familiar. Ranse and Mick stood over him, looking like two angry gods about to exact their vengeance. Everly's shoulder was tied off with a bit of bedsheet. The Egyptian cotton had once been a stark white but had muddled into a faded shade of pink. Mick's blood-clotted hair stood at attention, giving him a pair of dark red devil horns. Warren couldn't help but laugh.

"Shut up," Mick ordered, giving him another hard boot to the side. Warren shut up, the air was forced out of him. The same pair of hands that rammed his head into oblivion grabbed him again. Warren's head was forced up, and aimed at a lump on the floor, covered by a blue tarp. "Look at what you did, you sick piece of shit!"

Ranse went over to the tarp and whipped it away. Molly Hyndman stared at Warren with wide, lifeless eyes. Her mouth still hung open, and Warren knew why. She was gasping for air, drowning in the blood that filled her trachea from the bullet he'd sent through it. She reminded him of Geena.

On the other side of her, was a pile of his rifles and handguns.

"Y-you're not supposed to have those," Warren said through a wrecked mouth. "Those aren't yours."

"They are now," Mick said, whipping Warren into a sitting position against the wall.

"What should we do with him?" Ranse asked, carefully and respectfully covering the body of his friend with the tarp.

Mick pulled out his Gerber and flicked it open. The freshly sharpened steel of the blade gleamed in the fluorescent light. He didn't answer Ranse but spoke directly to Warren.

"Everything tells me I'd be well within my rights to give you a hole to match hers or to keep you tied up and throw you over the fence to those monsters out there." He let Warren think on that for a moment, watched with glee as the man's eyes went wide as he pondered his own death. "But I'm not going to," he finally said. "First of all, I'm not like you. Even though you killed my friend, and the only woman I've ever loved, I just can't stoop so low as to take your life." He took a step back, let the knife fall to his side. Warren let out a sigh of relief. "I've been ranching all my life, Warren," Mick continued, "and I know a stubborn, mean bull when I see one. Jumping and bucking and charging. Making all the other, more peaceful livestock antsy and irritated." He stuck the knife out at him. "That's exactly what you are. You're a mean, racist, evil little man. You know that, don't you?"

Warren nodded. He didn't know anything, except that he had to get out of here and back to Geena. Back to his safe space next to her.

"You know what we did to those bulls? You call yourself a rancher, so you should. Hell, what am I thinking? Of course, you don't! The most ranching you've ever done was step in a pile of cow shit. Well, let me enlighten you a bit, Warren. When a bull gets too rowdy, when the livestock and the rancher can't take anymore, we look at the root cause of its orneriness and take it away. And do you know what the root cause ninety-nine-point-nine-nine percent of the time is?" The point of the knife dropped from Warren's face and pointed at his crotch.

"Y-you can't do that," Warren said. "You can't castrate me! I'm a man! You can't take that away! I swear, once this is over, I'll sue you! See you put in jail!"

Mick smiled and turned to Ranse. "You mind holding his legs for me?"

"Everly! Don't you even think of it!"

Ranse looked down at Warren hogtied against the wall. How pitiful, how sick and deranged the man looked. For a moment he thought he felt a pang of sympathy, but then Ricky Lee and Molly, even Geena came to mind. Their deaths at the hand of this man, not by some accident, not by some freak of nature, this man, was unforgivable.

"You were supposed to be human," Ranse said. "One of us." He had never heard Mick say the word love before, regarding a woman. He knew how he felt about her, had known for a very long time. Mick got her, only to have her taken away by a lunatic with a god-complex and a gun. He looked at Mick.

"It would be my pleasure," Mick said.

Warren struggled in his binds as the two men went about prepping him for a DIY neutering. His shoes were torn off, then came the pants, the underwear. Ranse pressed down on his legs with as much strength as he could muster. His shoulder ached and throbbed and bled, but still, he held fast.

Warren's tiny penis poked out like a worm through a bush. Fearful urine trickled out. Mick readied the knife.

"Please, don't do this!" Warren begged, switching his voice from threatening to bargaining. "I'll sell my land to you! I'll give it to you dirt cheap and leave town. Y'all will never hear from me again! Just let me go. Let me get my wife and go!"

"Your wife's dead, Warren," Mick said bluntly. "Cold-as-the-earth dead."

"No, she's not!" Warren cried out once more with such conviction that Mick paused.

He really believed that she was alive, didn't he? Mick thought. He had to admit that other than the grime that had grown on her, and the massive head wound, she didn't look all that dead.

"Hold him tight," Mick told Ranse after clearing his mind. "Don't wanna nick a vein." He brought the knife closer. Closer. Warren was screaming, pleading with them to release him. Gritting his cracked and shattered teeth together, he waited for the cold of the knife and the burn that would follow.

But nothing ever came. He realized suddenly that he wasn't screaming anymore. He hadn't been screaming for a while now, but someone was.

"Daaaaddddiiieeee!" Mick and Ranse stiffened and looked at each other. All of a sudden, Warren Maxxy and the justice he had coming to him, didn't matter anymore. The knife fell from Mick's hand.

"Noah," Ranse moaned. They got up and rushed to the other room.

Warren lay there, naked and humiliated, his eyes glazed and wandering off to space. It was his typical reaction to harm, his only defense mechanism. The night he caught Geena with that black man, the night he first realized her adulterous ways, he sat in his office staring at the wall for hours. The day of Everly's trespass which in turn led to the night of Geena's mishap, he sat in that same office chair staring at the same wall, his meditation finally interrupted when his wife opened the door. It didn't take much to lose his concentration; the opening of a door, a bang against a wall, a scream, or the glint of a fluorescent off the broad side of a blade.

Warren's eyes flicked to it sitting there harmlessly on the floor. The tool that only moments ago was so threatening was now his only source of salvation.

***

They slammed against the door, almost knocking it off its hinges. Noah was on the ground on all fours, a pile of pinkish vomit in front of him. Ranse rushed over to him, avoiding Mick's grasping hands.

"Ranse," Mick cried out, "we still don't know if—"

"Don't!" Ranse shouted, shooting a furious look at his friend's way. "Don't even think of it." He looked down at his son. "Noah? What's wrong? What hurts?"

"My tummy," the boy said. Ranse had to dodge as another stream of vomit came splattering down.

"Ranse, Ricky Lee said Diego was sick to his stomach too."

"Don't you fucking dare, Mick! Diego was bitten. We saw it. Noah hasn't so much as left the house..." His mind wandered to the sleepwalking. To Noah telling him that he'd been talking to his mom. *Jesus, could it be?* Ranse's face went hot. He pushed the thought away. "Noah, you need to calm down. Okay? I'll give you some more medicine and that will make you feel better. Just calm down for a minute."

"I don't think medicine's gonna help," Mick said desperately. "Not if he's turning into one of them."

"Fuck you!" Ranse hollered.

"No. If that's the case, then we're both fucked. Ranse, if he so much as sprouts one hair where it shouldn't be, you gotta be prepared to—"

"He's my son, goddamnit!" Hot desperate tears streamed down his face.

"He won't be if he changes! You saw those things out there! Those were people we knew! They turned into bloodthirsty killing machines and they didn't recognize us!"

"Mick," Ranse began, his voice a low ominous monotone.

"Are you prepared to do what's necessary?" he asked again.

"You can't make me think about something like that," Ranse said between volleys of shushes. He was patting Noah's back, not realizing that in his anger, he was patting a bit too hard.

"You're going to have to. Because if, or when, he changes, it'll be too late.

"He. Won't. Change!"

And as if on cue, Noah began to change.

Noah opened his mouth as if to puke, but no vomit came this time. His mouth widened and widened, like a snake eating an egg. Strands of pink spittle hung from his lips like vines in a grotesque hanging garden. Tendons in his jaw creaked and moaned, popped in and out of socket. Noah shut his eyes tight against the pain, and when he opened them again, Ranse and Mick were horrified to see that they turned from his normal bright hazel to a deep, unearthly black.

His hands were splayed in front of him, spread apart like he was trying to make them as big as his dad's. Now, they were. The tendons in his hands twisted and contorted, growing a brand-new set of knuckles. The tips sprouted needlelike protuberances that thickened and thickened to the size of twigs. *Claws,* Ranse thought. *Jesus Christ Almighty, my son is growing claws!*

"Ranse, we gotta do something!"

But Ranse didn't hear Mick's cries. He was hovering over his son, wishing there was something more he could do other than wishing.

"Daddy!" Noah moaned, his black eyes crying tears of pain and confusion. What was happening? His little boy's brain couldn't fathom, couldn't come to terms with what kind of hell his body was going through. Noah's back arched, his spine protruding through his pajamas and snapping into a weird dinosaurian shape. "It huuurrrts!" His high-pitched voice turned into a demonic growl.

It was that growl that snapped Mick into action. He broke from the room and went to the guns on the floor. He didn't see the pile of shredded bed linens in the corner, or that Warren Maxxy was gone. With one hand, he snatched a pistol from the floor. His other located a magazine and with cougar-like fluidity, he smashed it in place. He cocked it, saying a quick prayer that he could live with himself after this, and ran back into the bedroom.

"Noah?" Ranse said, his voice panicked and shrill. "Noah, can you hear me?"

Noah answered with a series of short barks and growls. Ranse pulled him in close. He didn't care if Noah bit him. He wasn't ready for this, wasn't ready to confront the meaning of the tears that streaked down his face.

"Hush now, buddy. It's okay. Daddy's here. Do you wanna sing a song?"

"Ranse," Mick said breathlessly, the gun in his hand shook like a violent earthquake. Ranse ignored him.

"I know, how about The Wiggles? The wheels on the bus go 'round and 'round, 'round and 'round, 'round and 'round. The wheels on the bus..." Ranse cradled his son as he writhed and twisted into some strange golem, holding onto the very last bit of him and willing it to stay there. The last of Noah's cries turned into snarls which turned into growls. The boy's body quivered and quaked, contorted into inhuman proportions. "The wheels on the bus go 'round and 'round..."

Noah howled.

"Ranse," Mick said with a little more authority in his voice. He lifted the pistol. "Get out of the way! You have to get out of the way!"

"All through the town..." He couldn't leave his son. Let the boy rip him to shreds. Let Mick shoot him in the head. It would be so much easier than having to cope with a life without Noah. "The wipers on the bus go swish, swish, swish..." Noah's ears shot to a point and pressed into Ranse's chest.

Though he didn't know why, and he had time to ponder it later, it was the ears that did it for him. As Mick watched them turn lupine, something inside of him broke. There would be a fight, oh yes. Ranse would come at him with everything a bereaved parent had. There was a possibility, though Mick didn't want to consider it, that Ranse would come with intent to kill. That would be okay. At least he'd be human when he did it.

"Ranse, please," Mick begged, "you've got to let him go. You've got to back away." He brought the gun up and leveled it at Noah.

Ranse's eyes were shut tight as he wept for his son. He opened them and saw Mick next to him, his gun raised. "Just kill us both," he said with a low, pitiful sob.

"Can't do that," Mick apologized, and he pushed the gun against Noah's head. "Please, Ranse." Ranse squeezed the boy tighter than before and shook his head. "Okay then. Don't look, and please forgive me." He pulled the trigger.

The whole world boomed and shook. As soon as the shot was fired, Mick dropped the gun in disgust, hating himself for what he'd just done. He thought if he ever got out of this alive, he would go on hating himself forever, but it had to be done. He tried to think of it like putting down a lame horse or a rabid dog, but it did little to quell the hurt and guilt in his heart. Mick's soul died in that bunker right along with Noah.

Ranse's screams racked the small bunker worse than any gunshot could. He held the boy close to him, rocking him back and forth. The room was awash with the siren song of the plaintive and sorrowful. Mick let him scream. It was as though he was the one dying, and Mick supposed that in a way, it was. What's a son if not an extension of the father? And Mick had taken it away from him with one pull of the trigger. He wanted to call out to Ranse. He wanted to run over to him, and comfort him, tell him how sorry he was, and try to get him to see reason. Instead, he just let Ranse go on screaming.

Scream, Ranse. You don't have to stop if you don't want to. Scream for your son. Scream for the monsters out there. Scream for your soul and if you can find it in your soul, scream for mine as well. The world's a horrible, bitey-grabby thing. Scream at it and maybe make it make sense again.

But the screaming stopped. Ranse looked up at Mick, his tear-streaked face red and puffy, hot and shocked with disbelief and hatred. Mick's heart broke again.

"I'm sorry," he said. The words held no weight.

"Get out," Ranse said. "Leave me alone."

Mick hung his head and nodded. He turned and left to mourn in his own way in the front room. He tried closing the door behind him to give Ranse some privacy. It moved about halfway before coming to a stop. Mick huffed in frustration. He couldn't even give his friend that courtesy.

"Goddamnit," Mick said. "Goddamn me…"

He plopped down on a small couch that was far enough away from the bunkroom that he couldn't hear Ranse's cries. He was exhausted. His brain hurt, his heart hurt, his whole body hurt. He never felt so old in his life. He looked at the lumpy tarp on the floor. *Molly*. He thought of her, Rick, and the little boy in the other room with his dad sobbing over his lifeless, wolf body. A loud sob escaped him.

Sleep, something that eluded him this evening, never sounded better. At least when he was sleeping, the world made sense. At least when he was sleeping, he lived in a world where there weren't monsters, where he hadn't just killed a little boy. But he knew that if he closed his eyes, he would be damned to see Noah's innocent face in his dreams. Damned. That's what Mick was, and he knew he deserved to be.

Ranse screamed something loud enough for Mick to hear, but he couldn't make out the words. For a split second, he thought about checking in on him, but he let it pass without moving from the couch. Ranse said to get out. He would let the man grieve in peace, if there was any peace, to be had.

His eyes flicked to the spot where Warren had been. He's Gone. Mick chuckled. The Little worm got away again. That sounded just about right. As right as sleep sounded. His wet eyes fluttered.

Sleep sounded amazing right now.

Mick closed his eyes.

Ranse's screams continued.

Chapter 16

<u>Reckoning</u>

Warren made it to the bedroom window, punched out the screen, and unleashed another stream of sick onto the roof. When he was emptied out, when he had control of his functions, he looked toward the edge of the property.

The wolves had arrived.

They stood in an almost militaristic fashion, lining the fence that surrounded his home, studying it and waiting to get their hands on anything foolish enough to come close. Their eyes trained on him. He knew they could see him, but why weren't they attacking? His stomach cramped again. As he fought it, he heard a loud pop come from downstairs. The shelter. That was a gun.

Had one of the wolves cleared the gate? Had they made it into the house? Did Everly and the old man have a falling out severe enough to warrant gunfire? No, it was the boy. It was his screaming that had saved him, distracting them long enough for Warren to get free, grab a couple of guns and get up here to this room, his safe space. The place where he would make his final stand, either against the werewolves or his oppressors. And he would be victorious.

He always was.

Warren lost nearly everything twenty years ago after a failed deal with Costco left him cash poor and in some very deep water with debtors. His first wife, Diana, left him for some bigwig Mexican lawyer in Texas and took everything that wasn't nailed down. He lost his first house, he went bankrupt, and he ended up working as a hired hand for Jim Richmond.

But during that troubled time, he saved, scrimped, lived off the land, and led a frugal life. Mick Ashley was dead wrong about him not working a day in his life. For those few years in the poorhouse, he worked his fingers to the fucking bone.

Soon, he was able to rent out a few stalls from Richmond and he purchased a few heads of cattle at the Mercantile's annual auction. He nurtured the animals in his free time, cared for them, fed them, and raised them to turn a very nice profit when a high-end meat company purchased them. Small-stock breeding is what they called it, a nice little name that just meant they could sell the same type of cow only at a hundred percent markup. And Warren took to it like a fly to shit. Soon, he didn't need Jim Richmond's help. With small-stock breeding, he was able to reap very large rewards for very little risk. His assets grew and grew, and his costs never did. Soon, he was the richest man in Maldus. Soon, he met Geena and the two of them got married.

He was victorious.

He spat to clear the mucus from his mouth and quickly took inventory. He had two rifles, both loaded, and three boxes of ammunition. It was not enough to take on the entire horde on the doorstep alone. But if he barricaded himself in this room, blocked the door, and the window, then maybe he and Geena would make it through the night.

First, though, he thought that he'd let a little steam off on those animals outside. The war with Everly and his ilk was over. Though he suffered no casualties, Warren had lost, and he was still angry. He grabbed a rifle and put it on the windowsill, clamping down to keep it from falling as his stomach clenched again. A wave of nausea came but produced nothing. Whatever he had, he feared it was serious. If it was what the little boy had, if that gunshot was meant for him, then it was very serious.

He opened the box of bullets and set two aside. One for Geena and one for him should the need arise. Then he picked up the rifle and took aim.

"My son!" Ranse screamed. "My son has no face! Oh my god, he has no face! Where's his face! Where's his fucking face!"

He knew where it went. The change had taken most of Noah's face, turning it into an oblong, canine mask. The bullet did the rest of the work. Ranse looked down at his son's body, but it wasn't Noah at all. He would have nothing of his son to bury, only the creature. Ranse felt whatever grip he had on his sanity slowly start to slip away.

A new emotion took over. Hate. Anger.

He flashed to Noah being born. It came in blurry, like an out of focus picture, and for good reason, too. Ranse was so fucked up that night in the hospital he was bordering on obliterated. He watched Sarah moan and cry as she pushed the boy out. Ranse remembered crying himself, proud and so taken with the small child that he and Sarah created. But as soon as Noah was out and safe, he flopped onto the hospital room's couch and was instantly unconscious. He stayed that way for the rest of the night and the better part of the following day. He missed Sarah nurse him for the first time. He missed holding him and the initial awe and wonder that came with holding your child for the first time, something they should have done together. The hate inside him swelled.

Those weren't the only firsts he missed. Noah's first steps came and went while he was out drinking with a random college girl passing through town on her way to Missouri. His first laugh, Ranse was high on crystal with Christina Marsh and Drake Best. His first words, goddamnit, his first words! Ranse missed them too, while he was in the bathroom stall of some honky-tonk in Harrison, getting coked out of his skull. To add insult to injury, not to Ranse but Noah, his first word was, "Daddy." He missed so many firsts both before and after getting clean. So many breakthroughs, so many heartaches and tears and laughs, all missed, like blinking just before a shooting star.

But he was there for the end. As he held his son's misshapen, lifeless body in his arms, he was there for the end. He supposed that death was a first as well. Noah's first and only.

Ranse let out one last plaintive moan and let the hate completely take over him, hate for himself but hate for Mick as well. The man who took Noah's life. He could justify it all he wanted, he could say he showed Noah mercy, putting him out of his misery and keeping him from turning into one of those…things, but he still killed Ranse's baby boy. Justification was for shit when you took the coward's way out and shooting a child in cold blood was the ultimate act of cowardice. Ranse couldn't let that pass. He couldn't go on living and breathing knowing that the man who killed Noah, the man he once thought of as his best friend, was doing the same thing.

Ranse went into the living area. The pile of guns was still there. He picked up a pistol, checked to make sure it was loaded. He felt its weight, heavy and lethal, packed with little life-takers, and his mind was made up. First Mick, then himself, and he would be off to a world where he and Noah could be together forever. Perhaps Sarah would join them too. They would live there, forever, in a world where there were no such things as werewolves, no such things as sickness or hard decisions. A world where the right answer came instantly for everyone and never at anyone's expense.

Yeah, that seemed nice.

"Get up," Ranse said, kicking Mick in the ankle. Mick, who was dozing on the couch, snorted and came to, instantly. Mick's eyes cleared, and he saw Ranse standing over him like the angel of death. He saw the gun in his hand pointing right at him. Mick put his hands up.

"Ranse," he choked, "I know what I did was unforgivable, and I would act the same way in your position, but—"

"Shut your fucking mouth," Ranse interrupted. "You have no idea what it's like to be in my position! No idea! All you know is your own selfish will to survive. We could have locked Noah away, put him up until we found a cure or something, but you took him from me!" His voice cracked with sorrow.

"Locked him away?" Mick asked, his voice registering anger now. "You know who you sound like? Warren Maxxy! That would have been cruel, Ranse! The boy was in pain!"

"We could have saved him! We could have made him comfortable and found a way to..." His voice broke off as a loud report echoed through the Maxxy household. Warren was upstairs and shooting at something. Ranse looked up then back at Mick, but his friend had moved. The gun he used to kill Noah was still in the waistband of his jeans. It came out with blinding speed as Mick hopped from the couch. He brought it down on Ranse's head. There was a thick crack, and Ranse crumpled to the floor.

***

Pheromones, hunger, and the promise of sweet, fresh meat brought them to this place. For now, any territorial disputes could wait. There was food in this place, and it was so much easier to scrounge than it was to hunt. It was less exhausting, especially if they worked together. Some had found easier meals in the places with cows, goats, and chickens, but those were lesser meals, less savory, less filling. First, they would get to the prey inside, tucked away like little rabbits in a burrow, and then they would fight.

Slowly, the town of Maldus gathered at the gate of Warren Maxxy's home, sniffing out their quarry, listening for the soft thumps of blood being pumped through rapidly beating hearts.

Ray Logue paced at the gate. He huffed and growled while growing impatient. His fur, as white as a drift of snow, rippled in the heavy frontal winds. Betty Ashford, a woman whom most men in Maldus had a slight infatuation with, though none of them were ever as lucky with her as they were with Geena Maxxy, stood in a clearing nearby, turning in circles. The smell of meat was faint here, but she could sense it right beneath her feet.

Once a very pretty woman by small-town standards, her hair had turned coarse and quill-like and had spread across her whole body. Blood from the freshly slaughtered Ricky Lee matted it down, turning it muddy and clumpy. She had her share of the man, but she was still hungry.

The meat, the prey, was close by but very well concealed. While the others waited at the fence, watching for the sign that would signal their attack, Betsy began to dig. This was the right place to be, and she knew it. Her wolfen head lowered and stared intently at the earth. Below her. The meat was below her. She let out a hoot of satisfaction and continued her excavation.

Others joined her. She let them. They would make the job easier. Get her to the meat faster. Let them waste all their energy. She would save hers for the hunt to follow.

Grant Riddell shot back and forth from the gate to the dig. Remnants of his lab coat billowed behind him like a superhero's cape. On his way here, he came across a dog and made a quick meal of it. Its collar still hung from its teeth like a scrap of meat. He dug for a moment, then ran back to Ray Logue waiting at the gate. It was staring at something. Cocking its ears, Grant Riddell followed the alpha's gaze.

Back at the dig, the smell was stronger now. A pungent mix of perspiration, blood, and fear. All the wolves began to drool in hunger, and the digging quickened. Dirt and rock flew into the air, flinging away in violent, hungry anticipation. PVC was launched from the hole, sending a geyser of water shooting upwards. And then they were there. Growls and snarls lolled from their snouts; they were angered by what they found.

Grant Riddell watched the old man in the window. There was something in his hands. A dangerous something. It was pointing right at them.

A box. A big, concrete and steel box. This wasn't good at all. The smell was as close as it could be. The wolves were ravenous. Betsy's ears pricked up when she heard something inside. Voices, a scream. Something was wrong inside. Something that meant she wouldn't be fed. She snarled and snapped her way through the pack. She circled the box, traced its perimeter, listening, smelling, focusing all her senses on the meat. And then she found it. Just on the other side of this thick, concrete wall. Two heartbeats now, both excited and rapid, beating in perfect succession as though it were only one. This was perfect. Excited hearts meant excited minds, and excited minds meant mistakes were bound to be made.

Betsy swung a claw across the wall. Large chunks of concrete came loose and tumbled to the ground. She crouched. Sniffed it, and then repeated the process. More concrete, this time mixed with steel, rebar, earth, and some of her blood fell to the ground. She snarled in pain but kept slashing.

***

Half the pack broke away from the fence and went to investigate the hole in the ground. Grant wanted to join them, but it was too taken with the little figure in the window. It could sense Ray Logue tense beside him. *Was the charge about to happen?* Grant thought. They could clear the gate in a matter of seconds and be up in the window in the same amount of time. They could make quick work of whatever was inside. The little man with his little popgun would be first. He was plump, well-fed. He would be delicious. Grant hooted, antsy to get on with the attack while the majority of their kind were busy with the hole in the ground, but Ray Logue waited. He was the biggest of them, the alpha, and Grant didn't want to expend his energy in a fight for supremacy right now, not with food so close. He watched Ray closely, waiting for any sign of a charge.

Then, the night sky exploded.

A crack of thunder followed, but the damage was already done. Grant watched as Ray Logue's snout imploded and came out of the back of its skull. The wolf swayed for a moment, then fell backward with a great thunderous crash. Dust and blood particles flew up into the air. Grant whipped around and howled at the thing in the window.

The charge was on.

***

"Take that, you cocksucker!" Warren cried out in victory.

For a moment, he wondered if his aim would be true until his stomach suddenly constricted. He was sweating again, and his body was aching all over as though he were going through another pubescent growth spurt, but as he watched the wolf's head explode in the distance, he was delighted to find that it his aim had not failed him. The wolves didn't react right away. He took that as an opportunity to push another bullet in the breach and take aim, but before he could bring the sight up to his eyes, another vicious cramp took hold of his stomach.

A loud, grotesque noise escaped his wife's body, accompanied by a foul odor. He was sure another bodily function had slimed its way from her. While the prospect of investigating it was alluring, like watching one of those cyst-popping videos on YouTube, he didn't think his stomach could take it. Besides, the wolves outside were finally whipped into a frenzy. The gate was down, and they were coming for him. Warren brought the rifle up and took aim once more.

"Come on, you bastards. Come and get me!" he shouted as he fired.

A wolf who was perched on a leaning bit of gate, wearing the remnants of a nightgown, was thrown backward, a gaping hole in its chest. Two more were crossing his lawn, taking time to sniff out the truck in the driveway. He took the two of them out as well.

"You see, honey?" he called out, turning to Geena and not noticing that her hair had grown a little longer, a little coarser in the last few minutes. "You coulda been one of those things. I saved you from it like I always have. Like I always will." He turned quickly and fired another volley. Four more wolves fell to the ground. Warren wailed in triumph and pain. His fingers felt like they were ripping through the skin.

Geena Maxxy opened her eyes.

"This is my house! This is my town!" He fired again. A wolf with patchy grey hair that looked vaguely like Doc Engel fell to the ground, its claws clutching at a stump where its left leg should have been. The pack split apart, flanking the house. Warren could hear glass shattering, feeling the whole structure rumble. He thought of hopping out to the roof, maybe take a few more of the wolves out before they tore his home to shreds. He made to grab for his rifle but paused.

The fingers on his left hand were discolored and disjointed. His fingernails were peeling back exposing something much sharper underneath.

"Oh no," he whispered, ignoring the ravaging of his home's first floor. "Oh, Jesus, please, no." This couldn't be true. He didn't have any contact with those things. In the last month, he hadn't so much as stepped a foot out of his house.

But as he watched his fingers bend and stretch, he realized that he was changing. He was becoming one of them. He dropped the gun in disgust, watching it clatter to the roof and slide into the rain gutter where it hung like a stuck kite. He brought his hands to his face, studied them with dawning horror like a life-long smoker finding a patch of bloody phlegm on his pillow. He screamed, and just when he was about to call out to a God who'd long since abandoned him, he was cut off.

The growl came from beside him, low and guttural. He felt hot breath on his neck, smelled the stink of shit and piss and puke mixed with the long dimmed flowery scent of Chanel No. 5.

"G-Geena?" Warren blubbered. "Is that you, honey?" Another growl, more vicious, answered him.

Warren let his bowels go in his pants as he turned to see the wolf beside him. The wolf that only moments ago was his wife. Then it all came crashing into place. Jim Richmond was gone. He thought the man deserted Maldus, making some backroom deal with the Tyson Co. he took the cash and retired to the Keys or somewhere in Mexico. Later, he thought him eaten alive by one of those things outside. But that can't be.

The last he saw Richmond, he was sick, just as Warren was now. He was bleeding too, and Warren clearly remembered scolding him for bleeding all over Geena, remembered cleaning the flecks of crimson from his wife's face.

And then you went and fucked her too, didn't ya, Warren thought. *Oh, Warren, you dirty birdie.*

Geena's face, so peaceful only moments ago as it teetered on the border between the living and the dead, was pulled back into a vicious sneer. Her eyes, once a deep, seductive green were now blazing red and fixed on him. Warren felt the hot shit seep down his legs, which burned as they stretched into long tree trunks. Geena smelled it and blew a loud shuddery breath through her dripping snout.

"Is that you in there?" Warren asked again. "Can you hear me?" Blindly, he reached for the rifle. The wolf stared at him for what seemed like forever, growling and breathing, rotating its noises between a motorboat engine and the distant crash of waves. "Run along, now. I'm not feeling too well. Leave me alone."

The wolf didn't move. It was confused. Its tongue whipped out and licked the foam dripping from its razor-sharp teeth. The man was changing, and it went against the law of its species to eat its own kind, but it was so… so hungry. It was left unfed for a month.

Warren brought the rifle up, ignoring the long hair sprouting from his hand, the grip of his stomach, and the sharp searing pain ripping through his bones.

"I already taught you your lesson once," he said, trying to disguise his shaky voice in an authoritarian timbre. It used to be so easy. "You broke my law once and look what happened. Don't go doing it again. I don't wanna punish you again. This time it'll be permanent. You hear me, Geena? Go away! Now! Don't make me…"

His threats turned into a yelp as one clawed hand reached out and grabbed him. The wolf sunk its teeth into Warren's outstretched arm, the gun clattered to the floor as his hand disappeared, torn away and lying limply in the monster's mouth. Warren had time enough to see how deformed it had become before Geena swallowed it whole.

He fell to his knees. Cradling the bloody stump of his right hand with his left. He looked up at the wolf, its snout dripping blood onto his face like some twisted baptism. His gums burned as new teeth replaced the ones smashed from his head earlier. *I'm one of them,* he realized. *I'm one of those things!* The thought of being one of the others, one of the many nameless and faceless tormentors that infiltrated the country, his home, frightened him more than the prospect of being eaten by his wife. Warren began to scream. Hot, sticky tears rolled down his cheeks. He wiped at them with his stump, leaving a streak of blood across his face like war paint.

The wolf towered over him, curiously watching as he sobbed, prayed, and changed. It let out a hungry, ear-splitting howl. Warren howled along with it. His fight was over. The wolf lunged and knocked him backward. Two heavy feet dug into his stomach, rupturing every internal organ inside. Warren's guts splashed into his pants, pushed out of him like a smashed cockroach. It seemed like God answered his prayers. He wouldn't turn into one of those creatures after all.

Mercy. God was good. Warren smiled. It was the second time this evening that he'd escaped. Death was a small price to pay. As the wolf's mouth closed around his face, Warren began to laugh.

***

When Ranse came to, Noah, the wolves, Warren's attack, and the chaos of it all, they were nothing more than part of a terrible dream, but when he saw where he was, saw Mick sitting on the couch with a more morose look on his face than usual, it all came crashing down.

Noah was gone. He turned into one of the monsters that were lurking outside. Mick put him down.

Jesus, Molly was dead too. Warren had shot her in the throat just after—he looked down at his shoulder. The bleeding had stopped, but it was ugly, he would need to get it looked at, maybe get the slug removed.

"It was a through and through," Mick said as if reading his mind. His voice was terrible, as though he'd wailed all day at a funeral after smoking a carton of Pall Malls. "I looked at it while you were out. You'll need stitches, but I don't think much else." He gave Ranse a sick smile.

"How…" Ranse swallowed an obstruction, something that felt like a billiard ball. "How long was I out?"

Mick sighed and shifted on the couch.

"Couple minutes," he said. "Guess fifteen or so."

"That's all?"

Mick nodded. He glanced toward the bedroom. "Listen, Ranse, I—"

Ranse held up a hand and interrupted him with, "Don't. Just, don't. I know why you did what you did. I want to hate you, but I can't. I should say thank you, but I can't. I think the best thing would be to not mention it for a while. Maybe when this is all over… I want to say I'm sorry for holding a gun at you—"

"But you don't have to," Mick finished for him, smiling that sick smile one more time, like two estranged friends reuniting at the gates of hell.

Ranse flicked his head in appreciation.

"I didn't even think about Molly," he said. "I'm sorry."

Mick frowned. "Fucking Maxxy," he spat. "The motherfucker got away, too. I dropped the knife when we went to…" he shrugged his shoulders. "He got it and cut himself loose."

"It doesn't matter," Ranse said. "He'll get his. They always—" He looked up at the ceiling, listened for a minute. "What's that noise?"

Mick smirked. "I think Maxxy was shooting. Whoever it was must have thrown those things into a tizzy. That sound you're hearing is them tearing up the house above our heads."

"Jesus Christ," Ranse said. "Do you think it's like that all over the world? Did werewolves just sprout up out of nowhere? Like the zombie apocalypse or something?"

"Hell, I dunno," Mick said. "Knowing our luck, it's like one of those rain clouds in the cartoons that just follows that one, miserable fella around. That would be for the best, I suppose. At least it would be contained. For all we know, the White House, Hollywood Boulevard, shit, even the Kremlin could be crawling with those things. I guess the better question is, do you really want to know?"

Ranse shook his head slowly. "I suppose not," he murmured, still eyeing the ceiling and listening to the destruction above. "But I suppose we'll find out eventually, won't we?"

"I reckon we will," Mick said, his bushy mustache curling up at the sides. "I covered him, you know…and your son. I just couldn't bear to have him sitting there out in the open like that. He deserves much, much better."

"Yeah, he does." Ranse was speaking more about himself than his son's burial arrangements. There was a loud parade of feet on hardwood upstairs. Mick and Ranse listened. It sounded like the wolves were leaving. The house stood still, quiet enough for a new sound to emerge: a grating noise on all sides of them, like nails being drug across a chalkboard. No, not a chalkboard, concrete. "What the hell is that?" Mick asked. But Ranse knew. By God, did he know? And he saw. The tiniest ripple in a sea of hard concrete.

Though part of him screamed to not say anything, to let Mick suffer the way he made him suffer, Ranse jumped to his feet and hollered, "Move! Mick, you have to move!"

Mick twitched just slightly, the message reaching his brain fast, but not fast enough. By the time he sensed the danger as well, it was far too late. Now he looked like a deer just hearing the click of a gun's hammer, a sea lion watching a dorsal fin part the waters ahead. He was too slow. He was dead.

The claws ripped through the concrete, shredded down to bloody nubs but still filled with the same fire and fury. Their strength hadn't faltered. Dozens of hands covered in the same thick, coarse fur as the wolf from a month ago—as Diego and as Noah—wrapped around Mick's heaving chest. Though he wanted to, he didn't scream. Mick was like that. He could face a million lions with nothing more than a hickory switch and his fortitude wouldn't waver.

Ranse jerked toward him, but Mick held out his hand. Better to be eaten alive than to change into one of those things.

"I'll be okay," he mouthed. Ranse wanted to argue, he wanted to run screaming to his friend and rip him away from those things with all his might. Then he saw what Mick was feeling.

His shirt was ripped at the chest where the wolves were pulling at him. Blood, his blood, was running down the front of his shirt in small rivulets. Ranse understood then. He understood that Mick was doing to himself what he had done with Noah; sparing him the pain of being a part of the legion of damned.

Ranse watched in utter terror as Mick was lifted from the couch. He slid up the wall as if attached to some magnet that was attracted to flesh and bone, stopping at the hole. Ranse could hear the wolves feasting on the exposed parts of his body. He could hear flesh ripping, bones crunching, but still Mick did not so much as flinch. *Let them eat,* his eyes said. *Let them eat.*

And all at once, Mick was doubled over like a man possessed, his eyes bulging as his back broke in half. There was a sickening crunching noise as he was pulled through the hole in the wall.

Then Mick was gone.

And Ranse was alone.

Chapter 17

<u>Ranse Everly vs the World</u>

anse watched them through the hole as they made quick work of it, tearing off chunks of concrete like they were pieces of white bread. The wolves on the other side were furious, mad with food so close, but Mick was only an appetizer. Ranse was the main course. He still had time, but he needed to make good use of it. Although part of him didn't care if he was in this box when they broke through, he set his mind on survival. For now.

As he kept his eyes on the wolves through the hole, he backed toward the storage room and blindly felt for the supplies he needed.

The hole in the wall grew.

He dragged Molly's body into the bedroom and put it next to Noah's. He covered their bodies with the same tarp and doused it with the lighter fluid he found in the pantry. He wasn't much of a praying man, and his belief in a higher power was sketchy at best. But as he doused the two bodies with lighter fluid, he prayed. He prayed harder than he ever prayed in his life. He asked God for forgiveness, for not being a good father, for wasting what time he had with Noah and his ex-wife. He prayed for forgiveness for what he was about to do, thinking of anything in the Bible that forgave killers in the event of a sudden outbreak of a werewolf plague. Like it or not, believe it or don't, the things outside were people he knew. Some he knew better than others, but he knew them all, as folks in small towns do. They were people. And he was going to try and kill them all. Either way, he thought it warranted forgiveness.

That brought up one final issue, something more befitting an interrogation than a prayer.

"Why?" he said aloud. "Why, out of everything the people in this world have done to slight you, would you take him? Are you just that sick in the fucking head? Are you some bad comedian? Do dead baby jokes give you a hard-on or something? Why, God? You tell me why!" He waited for a moment, for an answer that never came. "Fine then," he said in a voice dripping with spiteful finality. "If that's how you want it, fine. Then you can burn too, motherfucker." Ranse flicked a match and flung it in the air. The tarps, and the lumps underneath them, went up in an audible *whoomph* of flames. Ranse took one final look at what would be the final resting place of his son and his neighbor, leaving the fire burning in his wake.

The wolves were waiting on him when he returned to the living area, their snouts jammed into the opening, taking long whiffs of Ranse's scent and still steadily scratching away at the concrete. Every bit that came away was bigger than the last. He went over and gathered a few guns with some ammo, never breaking his gaze. The wolves went about their work. Ranse wondered if this was how folks on either side of a demilitarized zone might feel. On one side a farmer toiling away, on the other a small child playing. They go on with their lives, but a wary eye is kept on the person on the opposite end of no man's land.

A bigger block of concrete tumbled from the hole, hit the couch, and clattered along the shelter's floor. The wolves' upper bodies could fit through easily now. Ranse screamed at them with a fury that raged like the funeral pyre in the other room. His whole world burned like that fire. Everything he knew turned to ash. All that was left was him and these goddamn werewolves. The monsters howled in return, shaking the whole basement shelter like a dirty martini. They broke the hole wider, their heads so close he could hear their jaws snapping like drooling, vicious little castanets.

The smoke poured out from the other room and billowed for the hole in its search for higher pressure. The wolves disappeared, and when they reappeared, Ranse saw that two or three of them had wormed almost all the way into the basement. This place was done. Either die of smoke inhalation or mauling. Time to choose, Ranse ol' buddy.

But there was a third option, wasn't there? Ranse's eyes flickered to the small collection of weapons in his hands. Yes, there was another option. He could go out on his own terms. He could take his own life. Maybe feel a little bit of the pain his son had felt. It seemed only fair, and it sounded a hell-of-a-lot better than the slow burn or the way Mick went out. Ranse counted himself lucky in that regard. Not too many people got to choose how they kicked the bucket.

No, those weren't the only options. *Death* wasn't the only option. His son's voice, distant, ethereal, filled his mind. *You can fight, Daddy. You can live.*

Ranse doubted *living* was the correct word. Survive, perhaps. He supposed he could survive but would surviving really be something he was up for in a world without his son? Without Sarah? Could he go on surviving knowing there was absolutely no way to make things right by them and be a family again?

Not to mention the Hell that waited for him outside.

Make no mistake about it, Hell was real. It had fur, gnashing teeth, and howled at the fucking moon, but it was real, and it was on this earth. It was an "invasive species," to quote Warren Maxxy. Ranse Everly was part of the old ecosystem, and his time in this environment was limited.

Before he could mull it over much longer, there was a loud crack and a sizeable portion of the wall fell inward. A wolf, one in tattered white lab coat, fell belly first onto the floor. Ranse let the guns in his hands fall to the floor. All except for one. He whipped it up and leveled it at the thing's head as it tried to gain footing on the new concrete terrain. Just before he fired, blasting the wolf's skull into oblivion, his eye caught something curious. Pinned to the lapel of the tattered coat was a gold-plated nametag. "Grant Riddell, Doctor of Veterinary Medicine," it read.

"Sorry, buddy," Ranse said over the blast of the rifle. He didn't have time to feel sorry for himself, nor did he have time to feel sorry for Grant. As soon as the carcass fell to the ground, two more wolves took its place. Ranse laid them out just as quick. He got to his feet and closed the gap between him and the hole. He kept firing, and one by one, the wolves fell backward without eyes, faces, and bits of head or chest. What they lost didn't matter, just so long as they lost their lives with it. Soon, the gap in the wall was covered in a baptismal font of gore and loose bits of bodies, and it was clear. Ranse reloaded his weapon and investigated.

He could only remember a very few profound moments in his life. Though it was blurry, Ranse could swear to God that the birth of Noah was one of them. The carnage of September Eleventh was another. Watching the super moon rise over the Ozarks on a fall night long ago. But this…even if he survived to be a hundred years old, he surmised that nothing would ever take his breath away as much as seeing the whole town of Maldus, Arkansas swarm into the gulch they had dug around that basement. There were hundreds of them, snarling and growling and drooling. They were on the attack and hungry for Ranse's meat.

They were coming for him. Dear God, they were coming for him!

Ranse scrambled away from the hole. He grabbed what weapons he could, stuffing some in his jeans and hoisting the rest over his shoulders. He felt something give inside of him, knew that it was going to hurt like hell tomorrow… if there was a tomorrow. He had just enough time to ponder that. He'd heard the thought echoed in a million horror and sci-fi movies: if there was a tomorrow. Now, he realized just how powerful that statement really was.

Ranse hit the basement door in a full sprint, crossing to the stairs just as the basement wall caved in and the horde on the outside suddenly found itself inside. Their roars were brutal, ear-splitting cries of insatiable hunger that were dampened as he slammed the door shut.

The door would be down in a second. A few well-placed hits and the thing would crumble like a stale cookie. Ranse knew this, and he knew the only chance to survive even a little while longer would be to go up. But as soon as his foot hit the first riser, he froze.

The thing at the top of the stairs had to be Geena Maxxy. The mane that covered it was the same color as her hair. The stench of her (the one he first smelled when he came in with the group) was now so pungent, Ranse felt as though he'd entered a gas chamber. It was a fitting feeling. Her snout was pulled back in a grimace so lethal it was practically a death sentence.

Geena stood at the top of the stairs, chuffing and hooting. Her nose rose to the air as it homed in on Ranse's scent. It didn't take her long to sense him there. Her head snapped down, eyes narrowed. He had her full attention. The soft hooting noises she was making turned into something more insidious: a rumble deep in her chest and gut. Her claws clenched and relaxed, clenched and relaxed, and she took a step down.

Geena Maxxy was once a slight, slender woman. She could be picked up and tossed around on a whim. It served her well on the dance floor. She moved with such weightless grace. Ranse remembered watching her dance one night at the Bar. The way she moved was seductive, lithe. He felt almost hypnotized before Sarah popped him on the shoulder.

"Sorry," he remembered telling her. "Just daydreaming." Sarah had laughed then.

"Daydreaming," she had said with a nod as sarcastic as her tone, "sure you were. Ranse had turned his attention back to his wife, but every so often stole a glance at Geena on the dancefloor. The way she moved. She flew. She was beautiful.

But there was no grace with the thing she turned into. It thudded, lumbered, its footsteps shaking the stairs. She raised her head to howl, no doubt, but Ranse cut her off with the blast from his rifle.

Geena Maxxy flew one final time.

Up, Daddy. You have to go up!

Noah's cries from beyond the pyre urged him on. Ranse would go up, but then what? Outside? Out to meet those things head-on in a clash of fur and blood, bones, and sinew? Ranse thought not. *Up, Daddy.* The answer presented itself as a flash of bright, brilliant light. He would go up. Up from the basement to the house, up the stairs, and then up again. It was like one of those stupid Wiggles songs. Up, up, up! Right up the stairs and onto the roof!

As soon as he hit the second story landing, the first floor exploded. The horde flooded in. Ranse fired off another volley, managing to kill one while pissing off the rest. The element of surprise was gone. No hiding anymore.

He went for the only open door he could see. Crossing the threshold, he slammed the door behind him. The stench greeted him in here. He could hear the wolves' heavy footfalls pounding up the stairs. Ahead, Maxxy's bedroom window sat open like a gaping maw. Moonlight flooded in, illuminating two rifles that had been discarded on the floor. He could see the slant of the roof outside. It looked climbable. Ranse made for it like a drowning man spying a life raft, but he paused just before taking the first step outside.

Maxxy's body was deflated and elongated like one of those balloons clowns used to make animals. His head was gone, leaving behind only a gape at the top of a thickly furred neck. *He was changing.* His clothes sat lifelessly on the floor, spattered with gore and guts, like a butcher's dirty laundry. Ranse spat at it and climbed onto the roof.

There was dew, one of the very odd byproducts of this very odd summer. Ranse slipped and slid on his way up. He grabbed for purchase with one hand while holding onto the arsenal like it was the Holy Grail with the other. The bedroom door flew off its hinges and sailed through the open window. It landed on the ground some thirty feet down and was quickly surrounded by the rogues that decided to wait outside. The ones that had followed him were close behind. Ranse heard them clambering over each other, trying to find where their would-be meal ran off to. Though the futility of it all tried to convince him to just wait for them to catch up, he kept climbing.

Some followed him to the roof, but their claws couldn't find traction. Their weight and their clumsiness sent them falling to the hard ground below. Ranse himself fell and stumbled, scraped his hands, tore his pants, and scraped his knee caps, he almost lost the pile of guns several times, but he eventually made it to the highest point.

The condensation that had settled there soaked through his pants and underwear. His crotch was a wet muggy mess of dew and sweat. The roof came to a sharp point, the shingles jammed into his thighs and balls as he straddled it. He put the guns in a teetering pile in front of him. He pulled out a rifle and took in the sight before him.

The wolves dug all around the basement shelter, all the way down to it. A trench circled it on all sides, and it looked like a recently unearthed coffin. Ranse could see a soft, faint glow coming from the now-abandoned hole in the side. Things were moving inside, and puffs of smoke billowed out.

His heart broke for Noah again, shattering into a million pieces. Those pieces turned to sand when he thought of everyone else he lost; Ricky Lee, Molly, Mick. But it was so much more than that, wasn't it? This was how it felt to lose everything. His town was gone, his home. Even if he made it out of this alive, it's not like he could live in Maldus anymore. There were too many bad memories. Too many ghosts. Too many wolves. He was the sole witness of the destruction of a whole population of people. A whole way of life.

The wolves stalked and skittered across the lawn. Some fought with each other, others darted in and out of the house. All of them searched for Ranse. In the distance, over the din of the chaotic animals below, Ranse thought he heard the braying of the animals native to Maldus. Cows, horses, goats, and even llamas screeched and hollered a collective wailing.

They had known all along, hadn't they? Now that Ranse had a little time to think about it; now that—for the time being—he was safe, he realized that all the animals around town, not just the ones locked away in stables and pens, were acting funny.

Well, funny wasn't the right word. A few weeks ago, before all of this, Ranse found himself wondering if one of his heifers might be suffering from the dreaded Mad Cow Disease. Back in the Nineties, Oprah Winfrey had come to Maldus and interviewed his father about that same disease. Ranse's dad always ran a clean, safe ranch, and though he repeated this over and over again to the talk show host turned wannabe journalist, his business and many others like it suffered. Things looked grim, but thanks to a few studies and a nice fat class-action lawsuit, Mad Cow Disease became a distant nightmare. None of his dad's cows had the disease, and none of Ranse's cows had the disease either. They were acting funny because they were frightened.

He tried to remember the last time he had seen a coyote, a cougar, or the rare black bear. This year had been relatively quiet as far as predators go. *Well,* he thought as he looked out to the horde of werewolves, *relatively speaking.* Then there were the snakes. It wasn't far-fetched for snakes to congregate in dens in broken tree trunks, caves, or old abandoned wells, but in a pond? They weren't water snakes, either. Come to think of it, Ranse could barely remember hearing the caw of a bird in the last few months.

There was a loud screech of twisting metal, and it tore Ranse away from his thoughts. Aluminum siding was being torn away by sharp claws. The wolves were climbing up the side of the house. Ranse could hear them pulling bits of it away, digging into it and hoisting their large, hulking bodies toward him. He pulled the rifle up to his shoulder and waited.

The first wolf popped its head over the edge of the roof like a Hollywood jump scare. Its lips pulled back into a starved grimace, and a low, fatal rumble flowed from its open mouth. Ranse fired, sending a bullet through the thing's glowing green eye. It fell from the roof and hit the ground with a final sickening thud.

The next two wolves, drawn by the report of the rifle and the death of one of their own, came quicker. With a running start, they scaled the house in seconds, ripping down the sidings and shingles, breaking glass and pieces of frame in the process. The whole home shook. The two charged at Ranse. He made quick work of them, but they didn't fall off the roof. Instead, they crumpled into a mass of fur and teeth. Ranse screamed and fired into the crowd below.

More wolves came for him, snarling and grabbing, wanting to pull him into their giant open maws. Ranse put them down one by one, and he never stopped screaming.

The rifle ran out of bullets, he tossed it aside where it clattered down the roof and into the waiting pack of nightmares below. He pulled out a fresh, loaded weapon and continued.

The wolves began to crawl on top of each other in their pursuit of fresh meat. Soon, Ranse would be overcome, but he knew that it would only take one of them to get through. He considered it, weighed the options. If he just let it happen, then the nightmare would be over. Sure, there would be pain, but the pain would be fleeting. *Maybe,* he thought, *just maybe, there is a heaven, and along with Noah, the rest of who I killed will be there. Maybe they'll even thank me.* He thought of one of his son's favorite movies, *All Dogs Go to Heaven,* and began to laugh hysterically.

And he cried.

And he screamed.

And he fired his gun.

The wolves below began to flank the house on all sides. Ranse noticed, but he kept his attention to the front. The next gun clicked empty. He tossed it aside and pulled a new one. It would be easier if he didn't see it coming, like how victims of a hit and run died quickly and unknowing of what was about to happen. He was okay with that, but he'd be damned if he didn't take as many as he could with him on the way out.

The house rumbled as the creatures pulled their way up. Berserk howls of hunger and rage ripped the night air. Their prey was at hand. Ranse hoped it would be quick. He fired a few more rounds as three of them came charging over the edge.

The whole world screamed around him. It screamed with howls. It screamed for him to give up, to get to safety, to fight! Ranse screamed back, his mind slipping away and gone to a more feral place. He didn't notice the beam of light break through two distant peaks, didn't feel it warm his skin. Creatures caught up in the fight of their life rarely notice such things.

Then, the whole world fell silent.

Chapter 18

A Tomorrow, After All

The wolves tumbled from the house like dead flies falling from the walls. They hit the ground like a distant, drawn-out crack of thunder. Ranse sat there, unsure of what was going on. The silence that hung in the air unnerved him. He got up slowly, making sure to find his footing, and scooted down the side of the roof. He peered over.

The wolves, their fur, sharp claws, and toxic teeth were all gone. Ranse watched the things melt away, shedding their dreadful husks and revealing the fragile human skin underneath. Whatever spell the moon had over them, was broken. No longer were they snarling, drooling, lethal hunters. They were human again. Flesh and bone. Easily recognizable, easily harmed.

And they were all sleeping.

Ranse watched them for a while, waiting to see if they would wake up or go lupine once more. He stuck the rifle into the air and fired. The gun cracked what little peace there was, but the people below didn't stir. Instead, they slept like they hadn't slept in days as Ranse would sleep after a week-long coke binge. He chuckled, thinking back on those days. This wasn't too far off to be perfectly honest. After the first day or so of pure chemical sustenance, he would begin to have visions from lack of sleep, the whole world would feel like one giant nightmare. He wondered, briefly, if he hadn't ditched that meth after all. Soon, would come the sleep, then the hangover. Then the comfort in knowing that all the horrible rest was just one bad dream.

But this wasn't a bad dream. This wasn't a hallucination. Sorry, bucko, but this was absolutely, one-hundred and ten percent, genuine. Werewolves had come to Maldus. His friends, his neighbors…his son had gone with them. They were dead now, and the rest were dozing in the soft sunlight of a dawn Ranse never thought would come. The only thing left for him to do was to escape.

There were four waiting for him in the bedroom; Ben Smith, the local hardware dealer; Dean Estes; Hunter Boone; and Edna Gray. Edna, a grandmother of six, always had candies in her purse and she was indiscriminate on who she gave them to. Ranse always bumped into her at the Mercantile and always walked away one or two Hershey Kisses richer afterward. Ranse made her death quick, as well as the others'.

He stood there in the bedroom for a moment, his eyes going from the smashed remains of the late cattle baron Warren Maxxy to the four fresher corpses, wondering how things could have happened so quickly. How could a town so steeped in both good and bad reality, just up and go topsy-turvy and turn into a slobbering, snarling mess? Ranse pushed the thought away. It didn't matter how it started anymore. It only mattered how it ended. And it needed to end. As far as he knew, or rather he hoped, this was an isolated incident. He had left the majority of the guns back on the roof but picked out a few choice tools; a couple pistols, for the closer work, which he stashed in the waistband of his jeans; a rifle should any of them wake up and make a run for it; and a whole shit-ton of bullets. As Ranse made his way out of the bedroom and began to search the rest of the house, he hoped this would be easy. He hoped it would be quick.

There were two more in the kitchen, Rachel and Lisa Hardy. They were sisters only a couple of years older than Noah. Ranse put a bullet in each of their brains then ran over to the sink where he lost what little he had left in his stomach. He would kill a slew of people in the next few hours, but those two were the worst. It was like watching Noah being killed all over again. Ranse sobbed as he wiped the remaining vomit away from his mouth, then grabbed his pistol.

The basement was filled to bursting with heavy black smoke. Ranse opened the door all the way and let some of it drift out. There were ten of them in there. Folks he recognized as the only real churchgoers in Maldus. He supposed they recognized each other's smells. In the center was Reverend Thomas Peck, obviously the alpha of this little clique. Ranse killed him first, then went around to the others, dispatching them in quick succession, pausing only to reload his weapon. They didn't stir. They just kept on sleeping until the bullets put them out permanently. Ranse looked in the pantry and found it empty. He didn't look in the bunkroom. He couldn't look in there. There was another can of lighter fluid in the pantry, another box of matches too. He grabbed those and took them with him, soaking the stairs in the flammable liquid on his way back up. He emptied the rest of the fluid in the front room's curtains and carpet. He lit a match. The curtains went up with a soft *fwoomp*. The carpet went up in flames too. His stomach lurched as he thought about the sound that Noah's body had made when it caught fire and how very similar it was to the curtains, like old dry paper. He watched as the flame trailed down the stairs to the basement, waited for it to flicker like a strobe light in a Halloween haunted house, and went outside.

The population of Maldus lowered with each crack of the gun. By the time he was finished, the grass of Warren Maxxy's lawn had turned a muddy crimson. A red moat of blood surrounded the house on all sides, and it filled in the trench that the wolves had dug around the basement, making it look like some sick remnant of a World War I battle. The town of Maldus was done, its sole resident standing over the carnage, panting and sobbing like a repentant mass murderer being strapped into the electric chair.

"Ranse?"

But he wasn't the sole resident, was he? Ranse turned and saw her.

Sarah was making the face she used to make when he disturbed her sleep, clambering into their room drunk or high in the wee hours of the morning. She was a ghost now, her naked body pale, her hair disheveled and matted down with the blood of a previous kill. *The hair*, he thought. It *shrunk* back into them. As appalled as he was by the sight of his ex-wife, by the knowledge of what she was, he couldn't help but still be amazed by her beauty.

"Sarah," he croaked.

"I missed you, Ranse," she said. "I've missed you for a long time."

Ranse stared at her, a myriad of questions running back and forth through his brain. He clung to the first one he could. "What are you?" Simple, but apt.

"I'm hungry," she answered, flashing him a sly grin, "and I'm sleepy. More sleepy than I am hungry."

"That's not what I meant."

Sarah's smile faded.

"I'm…well, I *was* one of them." She waved a hand at the bodies that surrounded them. "When you turn, you can still think a little, and all I could think about was why *you* were running? I wasn't going to kill you, Ranse. The rest of them weren't going to either. We could communicate, and they knew that you were off-limits. "I only wanted to give you a little nip, or maybe a little scratch. That's what happened to me. I don't remember much, but I do remember that. And I remember how sleepy I got. I slept forever, it seemed." Then Sarah started to jump up and down like a hyperactive child. "And when I woke up, guess what?"

Ranse stared at her, a realization dawning somewhere in the back of his mind. Something Noah had said just last night though it seemed a lifetime ago.

"What, Sarah?" he asked, the answer already hanging in the air like a bad note played on the world's loudest tuba.

"My cancer was gone!" Her voice echoed in the silent morning air, carrying down into the lower Arkansas valleys. "I could feel it, Ranse. My body was stronger. I felt like I did when we were in college, like before Noah was born!"

"You did it, didn't you?" Ranse asked, his face pulling back in a hurt and angry sneer. "He told me you came to visit him at night. I thought he was pretending, but you did come, didn't you?"

Sarah said nothing but stared at him with sleepy eyes.

Ranse nodded, gripping the gun tightly. "What did you do? Bite his finger? Give him a little scratch on the back?"

"I kissed him," she said.

Ranse let out a sob.

"But now we can be a family again," she continued. "We don't have to worry about anything at all. No cancer, no drugs, no jobs or money. Just be a family. Doesn't that sound nice? All you have to do is give me a kiss." She took a small step forward but paused and looked around. "Where is Noah?"

"Dead," Ranse spat. "He started to change, and Mick put a bullet in him. Kept him from turning into…into one of you. I guess that makes him a better parent than either of us, huh?"

There was a moment that Sarah's blank face registered something along the lines of heartbreak, but it was fleeting. Her eyes, her soft, pale blue eyes, looked up at Ranse hopefully.

"Well that doesn't mean you and I can't be together, right?"

"You left," Ranse said. "The night you dropped him off. You just left. We could have been a family, then. I was gonna beg you. I already had. But you just left."

Sarah's lips quivered. "I don't think I was ready, then."

"So, it took you turning into a monster to forgive me? To want me back?"

"I loved you, Ranse. I loved you so much, and I forgave you too many times to count. And remember, you were the monster first."

Ranse's legs wobbled, his head swam from the verbal blow his ex-wife just dealt with him.

"I…I wanted to ask you something else," he said. "Before you left that night. How do you make your coffee taste so good?"

Sarah smiled, her lips pulling back to reveal teeth stained pink like she'd missed with her lipstick or drank too much fruit punch.

"I add a pinch of salt," she said. "You never could make a decent cup of coffee, could you?"

The blast of the shotgun answered. Sarah and Ranse hit the ground simultaneously. Sarah was dead, and Ranse was crying out in agony. The wind, so fierce and savagely cold the night before, was now soft and warm. It carried the shot and Ranse's wails of loss across the valley where they disappeared to whatever realm noises go to. Where the howls, the screams, and all the other violent, chaotic noises from last night were.

Ranse sat on his knees and cried. In a flash of hot desperation, he brought the shotgun around on himself and pulled the trigger. He knew it was empty before he even heard the click of the empty chamber. He tossed it aside in disgust.

Eventually, he went home, walking as aimless and disoriented as someone walking away from a car crash.

He climbed through the wreckage of his living room and went upstairs. Without looking, he shut the door to Noah's bedroom and went into his. He took a shower, making sure to scald his bare skin, to wash away the sins of the morning. He wanted nothing more than to fall into a deep sleep, like the one the wolf-people had fallen into. His bed, even messy and rumpled as it was, looked so inviting, but Ranse knew that if he allowed himself to sleep, he would most likely sleep the whole day away. When and if he woke up, the moon would be high in the sky. It would be full and so close to the earth that you would think you could reach out and pluck it out. He couldn't be sure that he killed every last one of the monsters, just like he couldn't be sure that some hadn't found their way outside of Maldus. He supposed the savvier of them possibly stowed themselves away in a barn, feasting on cows and horses.

There was a flash of thought. *Maybe he should stay one more night and finish them off?* He thought better of it and decided no. His job was done, and if there were more of them, well, that was the nature of an invasive species, wasn't it? Survival of the fittest.

Ranse got dressed, went downstairs and out to the stable. He opened each chute, and the cows rambled out to the field. They seemed fine. A bird cawed from above him and there was a rustle in the air filled with life. He suspected that maybe the job was done after all.

By the time he was driving out of Maldus, the temperature had reached the highest it had been all summer: 96 degrees. He turned on the AC in his truck and kept on driving, pausing on the outskirts to take one last look at the town that he was leaving behind.

In the distance, a flock of buzzards soared on thermals. One by one, they dove to the ground to greet the feast of carrion left for them. All seemed as well as it could be.

Ranse sighed and got back in his truck.

Chapter 19

A New Hunt

The Arkansas State Police showed up at Ranse's house later that day as promised. They planned on keeping things informal. Despite all Tammy Patterson's nagging and accusations (which is any grieving, worrying mother's right), they didn't believe that Everly was connected with the disappearance of his estranged wife. This was supposed to be a quick and easy thing. A few questions regarding the missing person, a few about his whereabouts, a quick check on his son, and they were out of there.

But when they got a good look at Everly's house, or what was left of it, they quickly realized that this would be anything but an easy day.

Lead detective Bronson Diaz went to the car and radioed the National Weather Service. He asked if there were any freak weather occurrences the night before. Something like a massive windstorm or freak tornado. The person at the NWS reported no radar anomalies.

"That's what I thought," Diaz said. "Thanks anyway." He hung up the radio and saw that his partner, Gal Hubert, was already starting to climb the rubble. "Hey!" Diaz cried. "Be careful. You wanna fall through and get impaled on a loose clapboard or something? Wait for me!"

Hubert wasn't paying much attention but called back to him.

"I see something," she said. "Looks like it could be a body."

Diaz hurried over. Hubert waited for him to cross the lawn. When he arrived, she grabbed her flashlight and pointed to the farthest point in the house.

"What the fuck is that?" she asked. "A dog?"

"If it is, it's a goddamn big one." Diaz cupped his hands over his mouth and hollered, "Hello? Is anyone in there? Mr. Everly, can you hear me? Does anyone need assistance?" He started to sweat then, the sun had grown angry today. Diaz lived in Little Rock, where it was a sweltering 102 degrees. He thought the trip up to the mountains would be a nice reprieve of such high temperatures. But the heat, just like the law and death, always finds its man. He pulled out a handkerchief and dabbed absently at his forehead.

"Mr. Everly? Are you here?" he called out.

Total silence.

"Maybe he went to the hardware store," Hubert suggested, "or to go talk to his insurance agent or something."

"I guess," Diaz said, "but I figured that by this time of day, that would already be done, and the rebuilding would be underway. At least put a tarp and some plywood up to cover the holes. I guess he went and put himself up in a hotel, or maybe he's staying at a friend's place."

As they walked across the property to the guesthouse, Hubert referenced the town's manifest.

"Says that there are two ranches bordering this one," she said. "One belonging to Molly Hyndman and the other to a…Warren Maxxy."

"I know that name," Diaz said. "Some sort of bigshot around here. Works with the folks at Wal-Mart and Tyson." They arrived at the guesthouse and Diaz knocked on the door. When no one answered, he knocked again, harder this time. Still, nothing. Nobody stirred on the other side of the beveled glass. They didn't hear footsteps or the grumpy call of some tired rancher saying they'd be down in a minute. The place was still.

"What the hell?" Hubert said. "Is this the town that dreaded sundown?"

"I'm sure there's a reasonable explanation," Diaz said. There most always was. In most cases that at first appeared odd, when looked at from a different angle, or when a new, subtle detail was added, the thought of anything out of the ordinary seemed laughable. Alien abductions were more often than not a case of self-hypnosis or self-harm when the victims reported being experimented on. There was the time Diaz responded to a frantic call from a woman in Little Rock who claimed her home was haunted. She swore to every god in the sky that there was an evil presence lurking somewhere between the veils of this world and the next. As it turned out, her home was haunted, but not by any ghost or goblin. Diaz had found a drifter in her attic. Rummaging around, sleeping on a bed made of old clothing and surrounded by bottles of every cheap beer, wine and liquor you could imagine. The man was arrested and found to be an escaped mental patient. Weren't they always? Somehow, he would have preferred the ghosts. Either way, it was a simple explanation. "Maybe they're pulling a long day out in the fields," he said. "I saw a cart trail closer to the main house. Why don't we take the car and go exploring?"

Hubert agreed, and a few minutes later they were driving down the bumpy path into the further stretches of the ranch.

Cows littered the valley on either side of them. A large group of them congregated near a small pond, drinking and lazing in the hot, late afternoon sun.

"Nobody's watching them," Hubert remarked.

They were just about to turn around when Diaz saw something in the distance. A large plume of deep black smoke in the distance. Its source obscured by a large rise a half-mile away.

"Look at that," he said. "I'll bet they're doing some sort of controlled burn. It's nearly wildfire season. How much you wanna bet we'll find some folks there?"

Hubert glanced at her watch.

"It's getting late," she said. "And what are the odds one of those people is Everly?"

Diaz shrugged. "It's worth a shot. Let's just go see real quick and then I'll take you back to town and get you some dinner."

"Think they have a hotel here?" Hubert yawned. "I don't think I could make the six-hour trip back to Little Rock."

As they cleared the rise, a few things happened all at once. First, they noticed the Maxxy estate. It had long-since caved in on itself, resembling a large bonfire rather than a home.

"Oh my god," Diaz said in a low, frightened whisper.

The radio squawked to life, making both of them yelp surprise.

"Detective Diaz?" It was the voice of Casey Dupont, the trooper tasked with searching the town for any sign of Sarah Patterson, formerly Sarah Everly. Missing since last month and presumed dead.

Diaz reached for the radio without taking his eyes off the fire. "Go ahead," he said.

"I just reached Maldus," Dupont reported, "but Maldus isn't here!"

"What's all that scattered around the house?" Hubert asked, as though she hadn't heard Dupont at all.

Diaz cast her an irritated glance.

"What are you talking about?" he asked the radio.

Dupont clicked back on and responded, "I'm saying that there *is no* Maldus, detective. No stores, no buildings. Practically everything in town is destroyed. Fires are burning on every street. Looks more like Fallujah than it does Bumfuck, Arkansas."

"Wait…" Hubert said.

"Are there any witnesses?" then thinking better of it, "Any survivors?"

Hubert rolled down her window and hung herself out. If what she saw was indeed what she thought it was, she was wary of putting one foot outside the relative safety of the car. She squinted, trying with all her might to focus on the little dots in the distance. "No witnesses, sir. None that I've come across. It's like I just walked into the rapture a minute past the deadline."

"Call rescue crews," Diaz ordered. "Fire Department. Ambulances. Get me a whole forensics team out here." He let go of the radio and let it clatter on the center console. It dinged off the mounted shotgun with a plastic *thwap*. Diaz took stock of the situation. Fires in town, fire at this residence. Destroyed building in town, Everly's home was destroyed. If this wasn't an act of nature, he didn't know what was. How could a whole town seemingly be wiped off the map overnight? If there was a crisis, why weren't the authorities contacted? And— "What the hell are you looking at Hubert?"

"Bronson," she said, still staring off into the distance. "I think we found the missing residents."

***

As weeks passed by, the circus around Maldus, Arkansas slowly wound down. The bodies surrounding what used to be the Maxxy Estate were identified, autopsied, and sent back to their families to be interred or cremated. Those who didn't have an immediate family, and Diaz was surprised to find that it was a good number of them, were tagged, bagged, and rolled into the massive cold storage at the state police headquarters.

Though a massive manhunt was launched, they never found hide nor hair of Ranse Everly, either among the living or the dead. Diaz was sure they'd find him holed up in some cottage in the Ozarks or burning ass through Texas on his way to Mexico. There were checkpoints put up in every major metropolitan airport, but those dwindled down to nothing more than the TSA and local police they always had there. The last holdout was in Little Rock, and that was ending today. Suddenly, Diaz found that his career had taken that giant step into the absurd. How could a man just drop from the face of the earth? It was just so odd.

The whole afternoon and the evening that followed would be tattooed into his brain, his soul, forever. Diaz was sure of that. But the thing that struck him most, the thing that still woke him up a couple weeks removed from the incident, were the animals they found littered amongst the human carnage.

It wasn't because he didn't feel for the people he found blasted to bits around that ranch. He did, but in his career, he'd come across more bodies than he cared to count. It never got any easier, but it did desensitize him after a while. The violence, though it turned his stomach, didn't keep him up either. Neither was it the hundreds of Maldus residents still missing.

No, it was none of those things. It was those goddamn dogs.

Diaz had never seen anything like them. The biggest they found measured twelve feet in length. The things looked rabid, with bloodshot eyes, mangy hair and…what would he call them? Not claws. Cats had claws. Not talons either. These things had railroad spikes for fingernails, and just by looking at them, he could tell they had been busy. They sat there roasting in the sun, big purple tongues lolled out of their death masks. Flies and all sorts of scavengers circled them. The smell was excruciating. Two forensic techs lost their lunch trying to take a sample. Finally, one of them came in a facemask and was able to retrieve something to send off to the American Zoological Society. Diaz waited for days for their response, and he was sure that until it came, he wouldn't have a decent night's sleep.

As if by the grace of God, Hubert came rushing into his office a few minutes later. Her face was flushed, excited, and her hands were waving for him to pick up the phone.

"It's the zoological society," she said hurriedly. "They got the results. They're on line three!"

Diaz looked at her dubiously, then snatched up the phone and hit the call button.

"This is Detective Diaz," he said, trying to mask the excitement in his voice. He listened to the voice on the other end, nodding every so often, jotting down notes on the yellow legal pad on his desk. Hubert tried to get him to put the call on speaker, but he waved her away. "I see," he said. "And you're sure there could be no other explanation? Mm-hmm. Mm-hmm…" He wrote something in the legal pad in big block letters and circled it four or five times, each time digging the pen into the paper harder and harder. "Thank you," he said through gritted teeth. He flung the pen onto his desk and began to rub his temples. "I'll need a copy of your report for my files if that's alright. Email or fax. Thanks again. Have a good day." Diaz slammed the phone down. He wouldn't be getting any sleep after all.

"Well?" Hubert said. "What did they say?" She was practically jumping up and down.

Diaz shot her a look that said it was a little more than just bad news.

"I need a drink," he said. He looked up at the clock. "It's quittin' time. Wanna come with?" He got up and grabbed his sports coat and flung it over his shoulder.

Hubert nodded, the wind taken from her sails.

"Yeah," she said. "I'll meet you downstairs."

Diaz flashed her something she thought was an attempt at a smile, opened the door to his office, and left. Hubert waited for him to hit the stairs before crossing over to his desk. She picked up the legal pad and stared at the notes he had taken.

There was a list of the tests the zoological society had run on the samples sent to them. Hair, blood, and tissue diagnostics were run. DNA analysis turned up as a 100 percent match. This was all good news, so why was Diaz so upset? She scanned down the page, picking up a few more things he jotted down. Apparently, there was a similar sample sent from the same location to the zoological department at the University of Arkansas. Grant Riddell, the local veterinarian and one of the missing, had sent it in a little over a month ago. U of A in turn sent it to the AZS for further testing. The results were the same. Hubert went to the bottom of the page, the paper still hot from Diaz's scribbling. When she saw the word he'd written there, her blood went cold. It couldn't be. She saw the things with her own eyes. She would never forget them. But the word was as clear as crystal, circled a dozen times as if Diaz was trying to convince himself that it was true.

HUMAN.

Epilogue

They reopened Maldus the next summer. Tyson Chicken purchased the majority of the town, and the new population consisted of younger executives, blue-collar workers, and their families. Warren Maxxy's land was parceled out and a new subdivision was built over most of it. The Everly Ranch became the site of Tyson's processing plant. Molly Hyndman's ranch was the parking lot.

A new Wal-Mart stood on the grounds of the Mercantile, and businesses were bought up and given proper names. The Bar had become Pokey's Lounge, the Grille was now The Purple Cow Family Restaurant and served old-time burgers and milkshakes. A new shopping center sprung up as they do, boasting a Home Depot, a GameStop, and a Guitar Center.

It was five o'clock when a strange face, bearded and aged too early, walked into Pokey's Lounge and sat at the bar. The man ordered a beer and sat quietly sipping it, then another, then another, until the bartender (a recent implant from Eureka Springs) wondered aloud if the man was alright.

"It's just beer," the man said. "Beer doesn't count."

The bartender shot him a leery glance, aware of something called the Dram Shop Law, but served him one more when he asked for it.

"What brings you to Maldus, mister?" The bartender asked. It was still a few minutes until the happy hour crowd poured in, and the Cardinals' game on TV was nothing short of abysmal. A good conversation was his only choice. That, and the AC/DC coming from the jukebox. The bartender, a younger man named Rick Pendleton, was more of a hip-hop guy himself, so a conversation it was.

The bearded man looked up at him slowly, with eyes glazed and weary. He reminded Rick of a beaten basset hound, no matter what, they always looked sad.

"What's your name?" the man asked.

"Rick," the bartender told him. Without thinking or weighing the consequences, he reached down and produced another beer. He slid it over to the man who caught it without looking.

The man laughed, "I knew a Rick once."

"I suppose most people do," Rick said. He rolled his eyes. "It's not, like, a very uncommon name or anything."

The bearded man continued, "He was a good guy. Lived pretty close to these parts."

Rick's eyes went wide.

"Oh, shit. You knew somebody that lived here? One of the…you know…"

The bearded man smirked and replied, "Sure did."

"I heard it was one of those cult things," Rick said, "or that one of the ranchers went batshit and slaughtered the whole town. They say he's still around these parts."

The man shook his head.

"Na," he said. "Just one of those, whatdoyacallit, natural phenomena. From what I heard, it was just one seriously fucked up event. You know?"

Baffled, Rick said, "I have no idea what you're talking about."

"Maybe that's a good thing," the bearded man said.

"Did you know anybody else from around here?"

The man took a chug of beer and set the bottle down. He wiped his mouth, sighed, and said, "Damn near all of 'em."

"Jesus, I'm sorry," Rick said. "Is that what you're doing in town? Coming to pay your respects or something? See what we've done with the place?"

The man shook his head and motioned for his tab.

"No," he said as Rick turned around to the computer to print the check out. "I'm just passing through. I'm not a big fan of mountains, especially these mountains. The weather is funny up here. Animals are funny too."

"What?" Ricky said, slipping the paper face down on the bar. "What do you mean? I've been here all summer and it seems the same as my hometown. And there are plenty of animals, and they seem to act exactly as animals would. Dogs bark, cats meow, yadda-yadda-yadda."

The bearded man nodded and put a twenty on the table.

"That's good to know," he said. "Keep the change."

Rick looked at the twenty and at the tab. The change was four bucks. Shitty tip, but by the look of him, maybe it was all the guy had. Rick shook his head and held the twenty out.

"Sir, I really can't take this. Beers were on the house. Why don't—"

A hand shot out and gripped Rick around the wrist. Rick cried out and tried to pull it away, but the man was strong. He looked up and saw that for the first time, the man's basset hound eyes were as clear and knowing as any sober man's.

"You listen to me," the man said. "If the weather changes, if the animals start acting funny. You run. Understand? You run, and you never come back, cause all that follows is hurt and horror. If you don't run, then you lock yourself up at night, nice and tight. Hide in a basement, a storm shelter, something."

"What the fuck are you talking about?" Rick demanded. "What the hell is wrong with you?" He pulled and pulled but the man's grip and his gaze remained locked on him. "Let go of me!"

"You listen to me!" the man hollered. "This is good advice, man. Trust me. You lock yourself up or you run!"

Rick pulled his hand free and backed up to the neon-lit back-bar. Glass bottles, highballs and jiggers chattered and chimed behind him.

"You need to leave," Rick said again, his voice more assertive. "Leave now or I'm calling the cops. And I suggest that wherever it is you're passing through to, you just keep on your way. Leave town."

The man laughed a sad, twisted laugh. "You read my mind. That's what I did before, and that's just what I'm planning on doing now."

"Yeah? Good!" Rick said, flinging the twenty back at him. "And take your goddamn money back. I don't want it."

Ranse Everly watched as the bill floated down to the floor.

He warned the bartender one last time, "Just remember what I said. If the weather changes, if the animals change…run far, far away from here." He opened the door and let in the sunlight. He closed his eyes and breathed it in, let the light sink into his skin. "This is the good stuff," he said.

He stepped outside and was gone.

About Your Author

Karle Johnson is the author of *Mishaps, Monsters, and Madmen: A Collection of Unique Conversations, Survivor's Guilt,* and *Messiah Complex.*

He plays guitar and sings in Arkansas punk rock band, Narrow Dinero. He lives in Little Rock, Arkansas with his wife, May Johnson.

Other HellBound Books Titles
Available at: www.hellboundbookspublishing.com

Mother Legs

A giant, telepathic spider befriends a small boy, seeing the world through his eyes, with murderous intent... When Blake Turner's addict mother disappears in rural Canada, he assumes she's simply relapsed. But, when his search for her uncovers evidence of a terrifying monster and the sinister conspiracy to hide its existence, he must decide just how far he is willing to go to protect his loved ones. With only a depressed park ranger and a local reporter to aid him, Blake delves deeper into the mystery to discover what the creature is, and why it wants to start a family.

The Devil's Hour

A new and altogether awesome anthology of all things horror!

Seventeen spine-chilling tales of the darkest terror, most unpleasant people, and slithering monsters that lurk beneath the bed and in the blackest of shadows…

Satanic Panic

An incredible homage to 1980's horror!

Satanic Panic, a mass hysteria created in the nineteen eighties, has returned to a small college town in the Midwest.

Ritualistic murders and the presence of the occult have bled below the surface of the town in the form of icy accidents and other coincidences.

And when three lifelong friends find themselves on the radar of a killer—and leader of a satanic cult—they must fight for what's good without being seduced by the evil that possesses their campus.

Deadly Nightshade

Thirteen years ago: summer's end. A final night of vacation at New Mexico's Gila Cliff Dwellings. A picnic under the moonlight for high school sweethearts meets a deadly end...
Things will never be quite the same again.
After eloping, newlywed Virginia Campbell's bright future grows dim. Eerie night visions begin to haunt her. Are they real or imagined? Her husband's sudden aloofness raises suspicions of an affair. Unable to sleep, doubts torment her—doubts about her marriage, her unborn child, her sanity. Then, there is blood. She awakens to blood-soaked sheets.
Is it too late to save her unborn child? Her only hope is her charming doctor for whom she is falling. Can he save her from this living nightmare?
Ten-year-old Kyle also suffers from insomnia and eerie night visions. Something, or someone, sinister has brought them together... waiting for the moment to strike.
Three years later: Mother's Day.
The nightmare is not over.

A surprise visitor greets Virginia with a gift one morning. What begins as a day of celebration is twisted into a violent, bloody confrontation as festering wounds reopen.

Them

Ray Sanders returns home from Florida to bury his mother.

Soon, the supernatural evidence behind his mother's demise begins to surface in the form of dreams and mysterious happenings.

During all of the madness, Sanders must face his destiny and vanquish the generations-old evil that has plagued his family since the 1800's…

In 1854, Louis Sanders, with the help of Elias Atkins, dug a well to provide water to the family farm. What they did not anticipate was the water to be infested with Odomulites - ancient sins. These malevolent beings - were trapped in our world on their way to the spirit world - formed a pact of protection with both Sanders and Atkins; the families would serve as guardians of the Odomulite nests and in return, a blind eye would be cast when the Odomulites took host bodies to inhabit and feed upon. It was this pact, which in 2016 would propel Sanders and Julie Fontaine - a young woman with a special connection to the Spirit World - into the heart of the last active nest to rid the town of its insidious Odomulite population.

**A HellBound Books LLC
Publication**

http://www.hellboundbookspublishing.com

Printed in the United States of America